A Hayley Powell
Food & Cocktails Mystery

DEATH of a COUPON CLIPPER

LEE HOLLIS

KENSINGTON PUBLISHING CORP.
http://www.kensingtonbooks.com

KENSINGTON BOOKS are published by

Kensington Publishing Corp.
119 West 40th Street
New York, NY 10018

All Kensington Titles, Imprints, and Distributed Lines are available at special quantity discounts for bulk purchases for sales promotions, premiums, fund-raising, and educational or institutional use. Special book excerpts or customized printings can also be created to fit specific needs. For details, write or phone the office of the Kensington special sales manager: Kensington Publishing Corp., 119 West 40th Street, New York, NY 10018, attn: Special Sales Department, Phone: 1-800-221-2647.

Kensington and the K logo Reg. U.S. Pat & TM Off.

ISBN-13: 978-0-7582-6739-9
ISBN-10: 0-7582-6739-8
First Kensington Mass Market Printing: July 2013

eISBN-13: 978-0-7582-8911-7
eISBN-10: 0-7582-8911-1
First Kensington Electronic Edition: July 2013

10 9 8 7 6 5 4 3 2 1

Printed in the United States of America

Chapter 1

It would be a cold day in hell before Sal Moretti allowed his employees at the *Island Times* newspaper to go home early. The picturesque little hamlet of Bar Harbor, Maine, certainly wasn't hell. In fact, to all the hikers and mountain bikers and cruise ship passengers and lobster lovers and vacationing families from all over the world who flocked to Mount Desert Island for the breathtaking scenery of Acadia National Park, it was a nature lover's paradise.

But that was during the summer and fall months. Today, on this midafternoon during a particularly brutal February, the temperature was hovering just below ten degrees. Outside the picture window of the newspaper's main office, where Hayley Powell sat at her desk, all she could see was a white blanket of snow. She couldn't remember the last time she had seen it come down so hard.

Hayley stood up and poured herself a cup of hot

coffee from the pot she had just brewed and took a big gulp to warm herself up. Sal had allowed her to turn the thermostat up a few degrees earlier that morning, but he kept a watchful eye to make sure she didn't crank it too high and send his heating bill soaring.

She had dressed appropriately for the workday. Long underwear. Flannel shirt. Bulky wool sweater. Fleece snow pants over jeans. Big, clunky boots. However, as she looked outside at the nasty weather, it still chilled her bones.

Bruce Linney, the paper's handsome crime reporter, with whom Hayley maintained a love-hate relationship, ambled out to the front office, from the back, to get some coffee. He was dressed in an expensive black cashmere sweater and khaki pants.

"Hayley, would you mind running out and picking up some of those delicious warm blueberry muffins from the Morning Glory Bakery?" he asked. "I'm sure the reporters would appreciate it."

"Of course, Bruce. Let me just get my dogsled team ready and I'll be on my merry way," Hayley said, shaking her head.

She couldn't believe he was serious.

Maybe their relationship was more tolerate-hate.

"Is that you being sarcastic?" Bruce sighed.

"That's me saying no, Bruce!" Hayley said. "The Morning Glory is clear across town and the streets aren't plowed yet, and even if they were, the roads are so icy I'd probably lose control of my car and skid right off the town pier!"

"Man, Hayley, sometimes you can be such a drama queen," Bruce said, shrugging. "I just asked for some muffins. Maybe if you thought ahead, you would have considered the weather reports and whipped up some of your own muffins in your kitchen this morning, so you wouldn't have to go out in this nasty storm to buy us some now."

"You're not getting muffins, Bruce!" Hayley said.

Sal Moretti charged out of his office and bellowed, "Would you two pipe down? This is a newspaper, not a marriage counselor's office!"

Hayley and Bruce exchanged a look and called a silent truce. They both knew it was best not to tick off the boss right now because Sal was already on edge. His wife had left him for two weeks to go visit her mother in North Carolina, so there was no one at home to take care of him.

And this was painfully obvious. His shirts were wrinkled. There were a half-dozen empty bottles of TUMS on his desk from all the late-night gorging on pepperoni pizza. The poor guy was scattered and off his game. It was clear he missed his wife terribly and didn't like being on his own.

"They're saying on the Weather Channel that this storm's only going to get worse, so I think we should just call it a day and all go home," Sal said.

Stunned silence.

Sal was dismissing the staff for the day?

It wasn't even three o'clock in the afternoon.

Bruce did his best Rod Serling voice. "You're

about to enter another dimension. Next stop, the Twilight Zone!"

"Shut up, Bruce," Sal snapped. "I want everybody to be careful driving home. It's a mess out there."

Sal rubbed his eyes and ambled back to his office.

Hayley wasn't going to wait for him to change his mind. She quickly shut down her computer and grabbed her green L.L.Bean winter jacket from the office closet. She threw it on, laced up her black boots, and was out the door.

She carefully navigated the frozen walkway from the office to the street. Still, she nearly lost her balance on the slippery ice and had to wave her arms like a crazy person to keep herself from falling flat on her back.

Once she managed to reach her white Subaru wagon, which was parked up the street, she pulled on a pair of mittens her mother had knitted her twenty years ago and began brushing all the fresh snow off the car. She clicked the remote key to unlock the doors and then rummaged through all the kids' athletic equipment and empty fast-food cartons and discarded paper coffee cups in the backseat to find her red wooden-handled ice scraper.

Hayley began hacking at the clumps of ice that had formed on her windshield, clearing enough so she could at least see where she was going on the short drive home. Then she climbed behind the wheel, shut the door, started the engine, and cranked up the heat. She waited a few minutes for the car to warm up before slowly pulling away from the curb.

She could hear the wheels crunching through the snow and she hadn't even maneuvered the vehicle all the way into the street before the car hit a patch of ice and began slipping and sliding into the opposite lane. Luckily, no one was stupid enough to be out driving in this mess. There were no cars to collide with, so Hayley counted her blessings.

She stayed focused, never taking her eyes off the road, gently pressing her foot down on the accelerator not too much, just enough to keep the car going in a forward motion. She didn't want to chance losing control again and smashing into a tree or a fire hydrant or, God forbid, a storefront window.

What was normally a five-minute drive home took twenty minutes, but Hayley finally managed to get herself and her Subaru home safely. She turned into the driveway of her gray two-story house. Well, it was gray when she left for work this morning. Now it was completely white. At least the snow covered the fact that her house was in desperate need of a new coat of paint. Which she couldn't afford. Maybe she would get a nice tax refund this year, which she could use to paint the house in the spring.

Wishful thinking.

Lex Bansfield, the man Hayley had been dating on and off for the past year and a half, usually would clear her driveway with his snowplow truck during a storm. However, he hadn't had a chance to swing by yet, so Hayley assumed he was busy clearing the roads on the expansive seaside estate, where he worked as a caretaker.

It was slow going, the tires of her Subaru skidding through the mound of snow piled high in the driveway as she pulled in and opened the garage door with her remote. Hayley had to press her foot harder down on the accelerator to keep the car moving forward. Then suddenly, without warning, the tires freed themselves from the packed snow and the car took off, speeding toward the open door of the garage. Hayley slammed on the brakes and prayed her car wouldn't hurtle through the garage and crash right through the back wall and into her neighbor's adjoining yard. Luckily, the Subaru squealed to an abrupt stop just inches from the wall.

Hayley breathed a deep sigh of relief.

The last thing she needed right now was a costly repair. She got out of the car and was about to head into the house when she stopped.

She heard a creaking sound.

Hayley looked around.

Nothing appeared out of the ordinary.

She couldn't make out where it had come from.

She continued to walk out of the garage.

Another creak.

This time, louder.

What was that?

It seemed to be coming from the roof.

She looked up.

One of the wooden beams supporting the roof looked warped, as if it was bending and about to snap in half. That couldn't be.

She knew she would need to reinforce the roof at some point. Lex had warned her many times, but she just didn't have the money to do it right now. Besides, Lex told her she was probably fine unless there was a lot of weight on it. Only then might it give way to the pressure.

Wait.

Hayley suddenly realized there was about two-and-a-half feet of heavy snowfall on top of her roof.

The wooden beam suddenly snapped and Hayley heard a rumbling sound. Then she watched in horror as the entire roof over her garage caved in, landing on top of her white Subaru wagon and crushing it.

No. This was not happening.

Hayley just stood there in a state of shock. Flakes of snow landed on her rosy red cheeks. She was about to cry, but she choked back the tears. She was afraid if she did cry, the tears would freeze right on her face.

She heard Leroy, her white Shih Tzu (with a pronounced underbite), barking inside the house, undoubtedly spooked from the thunderous crash of the roof collapsing. Hayley decided to deal with the garage when the snow stopped. With her car buried underneath the rubble, she was probably going to have to borrow some snowshoes to get to the office in the morning.

Hayley entered the house through the back door into the kitchen. Leroy was there, jumping up and down to greet her. The sight of her devoted pup instantly put Hayley at ease. The little guy leapt into her arms when she knelt down to say hello. He began licking frantically at her face, attracted to the wet snow. Hayley noticed Leroy's nose was running and he was shivering. She set him down and took off her coat. That's when she realized the temperature inside the house felt like twenty degrees. Maybe even colder. She knew she had left the heat on when she went to work. What could have possibly happened?

Dear God, no.

Not the furnace.

Lex had also warned her that her furnace was barely hanging on and the odds of making it through another winter weren't very good. She had brushed off his comments, not because she didn't believe him, but mostly because she just couldn't bear the thought of having to invest in a new one. She simply didn't have the money. Hayley opened the door to the basement, snapped on the light, and descended the stairs. Leroy scampered behind her.

When she reached the bottom of the steps, she knew in her gut the situation was dire. She touched the furnace. Ice cold. She played with the buttons and readings. Nothing.

It was dead.

And she was screwed.

Unable to hold it in any longer, Hayley finally started to cry. Why was all this happening at once? How was she ever going to pay for all this? She sat down on the bottom step of the basement and let the waterworks flow.

She was going to allow herself a few minutes of self-pity, and then she would steel herself and work on solving the problems at hand.

Her cell phone rang.

Hayley reached into the back pocket of her snow pants and pulled out her phone.

It was Gemma.

Calling from her dad's in Iowa.

Hayley's two kids, sixteen-year-old Gemma and fourteen-year-old Dustin, were spending the winter break with their dad, Hayley's ex-husband, in Des Moines, Iowa, where he worked as a manager at Walmart.

Hayley got a lump in her throat. She missed them. The three of them were a team. Now faced with all this sudden adversity, she wished they were home with her to calm her nerves. Just having them around made her feel better. But they were so far away and she felt so alone right now.

Hayley wiped away the tears, cleared her throat, composed herself, and then clicked on the phone.

"Gemma, honey, how are you?"

"It's freezing here, Mom. I wish we were back in Bar Harbor."

"It's pretty much the same here, so you're not missing anything. How's your brother?"

"Still annoying. Dad's got a new girlfriend. Becky. She's nice, I guess, but totally trying too hard to impress us. Just like the last three. What's going on with you?"

"Not much," Hayley said. "I just got home from work."

"It's only three o'clock there. Are you sick?"

"No, I'm fine."

"You don't sound fine. You sound stressed," Gemma said.

"No, Gemma, everything's just fine. Believe me."

But things were not fine.

Not fine at all.

And they were about to get a whole lot worse because a collapsed roof, a crushed car, and a busted furnace would soon be the least of Hayley Powell's problems.

Chapter 2

Hayley was in desperate need of a strong cocktail. And pronto.

After hanging up with her kids, she placed a call to one of her two best friends, Mona Barnes, a local lobsterwoman, with an all-terrain vehicle that could get her to the nearest bar, which just happened to be owned by Hayley's younger brother, Randy. And with happy hour fast approaching, Hayley also knew at precisely five o'clock her other BFF, glam Realtor Liddy Crawford, would be seated atop the first bar stool nearest the entrance, sipping a Rose Kennedy and complaining about the weather to anyone within spitting distance.

Mona. Randy. Liddy. Her reliable support system. And she certainly needed them all now.

Mona was happy to leave her six kids—no, wait, seven—in the capable hands of her husband before dinner in order to hang with Hayley, especially after hearing her bestie's tales of woe. Her truck plowed through snow in Hayley's driveway at ten minutes to five; the palm of her hand was pressed down on the horn alerting Hayley to her arrival.

Hayley had wiped away her tears with a tissue, as well as some runaway mascara that had cascaded down her left cheek, and told herself everything was going to be okay as she zipped up her winter jacket and carefully made her way down the porch steps to Mona's truck.

She had quickly arranged a playdate for Leroy with the neighbor's rambunctious beagle so Leroy wouldn't have to stay cooped up in the freezing house.

As Hayley climbed into the passenger seat, Mona cranked up the volume of her car stereo. She was playing a Brad Paisley CD. The song was "Whiskey Lullaby," one of Hayley's favorites. And she could sure use one right now.

"Thought a little Paisley might cheer you up," Mona said.

"You're too good to me, Mona," Hayley said, smiling.

Mona cranked the car in reverse and backed out of the driveway. There wasn't another car in sight. Most people had the good sense to sit tight at home and wait out the nasty weather, but this was a cocktail emergency.

When Hayley and Mona entered Randy's bar, Drinks Like A Fish, and stomped the excess snow off their boots onto the welcome mat, Liddy spun around on her bar stool. With her half-empty Rose

Kennedy in hand, she wailed, "Can you believe this god-awful weather?"

Sometimes predictability can be a good source of comfort.

Hayley walked over and gave Liddy a hug.

"I hear you had a pretty bad day," Liddy said softly, patting Hayley on the back.

"Yeah, it really was." Hayley nodded, still fighting back tears. "But my kids are safe and everyone's healthy, so I guess I should be grateful."

"That's the spirit," Liddy said before she let go of Hayley and took a sip of her cocktail. "My day was the worst. Two canceled open houses and Eddie Grindle dropped out of an escrow because the pipes in the house he was buying froze up. I told him, 'You're buying a house in Maine during the winter. Pipes are going to freeze!'"

"Would you shut your piehole for once, Liddy, and let Hayley have our sympathy for at least five more minutes before we put the spotlight back on you?" Mona barked.

"Mona, it's all right," Hayley said, not wanting her two buddies to go at it.

"Well, excuse me, Mona, for wanting to share with my two best friends. Go ahead, Hayley, tell us about your terrible day and I will sit quietly and just listen so Mona doesn't go off and hit me or something."

Too late.

"I really don't feel like talking about it, actually." Hayley shrugged.

"See, Mona? I was being a good friend. I was just trying to get Hayley's mind off her troubles by sharing *my* problems."

"Yeah, I'm sure that was it," Mona said, rolling her eyes.

Hayley's brother, Randy, ambled over from behind the bar and slid a drink in front of her. "Hey, sis. Here's your Jack and Coke. And just in the nick of time, from what I hear."

Hayley smiled and nodded; then she took a big gulp and sighed. "Much better."

"Club soda?" Randy said, pointing at Mona.

"Yeah, whatever. I am so sick of not ever getting to partake in happy hour," Mona said, scowling.

"Wait, Mona, don't tell me," Hayley said, eyes popping out. "Are you . . . ?"

Mona thought for a moment, and then a smile crept across her face. "No! I'm not! I'm not pregnant! I just realized that I'm knocked up so much of the time, it just seems natural for me to lay off the booze! But I'm not pregnant now! My husband's back went out and he's been sleeping on the floor so he hasn't had the chance to climb on top of me in weeks. Randy, get me a Bud Light!"

"Great. Mona can slam down a six-pack and get even more loud and obnoxious and combative than she already is," Liddy moaned. "It's a glorious day."

Hayley chuckled. Despite the fast and furious insults, she knew Liddy and Mona truly cared about each other. They just didn't like to display their affection in public.

Randy popped the top off a bottle of Bud Light and placed it on a coaster in front of Mona. "On the house, Mona. To celebrate the fact there's not another baby on the way."

"I'll drink to that," Mona said, chugging down half the bottle.

Hayley felt happy to be among the people closest to her. And for a moment, she was able to put the dreaded thoughts of her situation out of her mind. She turned to Randy. "How are you doing?"

"I hate sleeping alone," Randy said.

Randy's partner, Sergio Alvares, was in Brazil visiting his family. Randy was unable to make the trip with him because he had no one to cover the bar in his absence. His manager, Michelle, was on vacation in Jamaica with her new husband, Ned, and her stepdaughter, Carrie. Sergio had only been gone a week, but Randy already desperately missed him and was marking off the days on his calendar until his lover's return.

"How many days left?" Liddy asked, sliding her empty cocktail glass over to Randy for a refill.

"Thirteen," Randy sighed. "I don't know how I'm going to make it."

The door to the bar swung open and a gust of bitterly cold wind blew a few napkins off the bar. Officer Donnie trudged inside, stomping his boots on the mat and slamming the door behind him.

"From what I hear, I don't know how Donnie's going to make it without Sergio either," Liddy said, cracking a smile.

Officer Donnie was a young, inexperienced cop in his mid-twenties. He was employed by the local police force, where Sergio was chief. Donnie was a towering, thin beanpole, with very little self-confidence and a permanent frightened look on his face. He tentatively made his way to the bar and put his hands down on the hardwood counter.

"I—I'll have a Coors, if you g-got one, Randy," Donnie stammered.

"Sure, Donnie," Randy said, sliding open the gray-topped cooler behind the bar and fetching a bottle.

"I certainly hope you're off duty, Officer Donnie," Liddy teased.

"I—I most certainly am, Ms. Crawford. I wouldn't be drinking alcohol if I was on duty!" Donnie hollered in Randy's direction, knowing he was his boss's partner in life.

Donnie had been put in charge while Sergio was away. That wasn't the original plan, though. Lieutenant Phil Jenkins, whom Sergio personally hand-picked to be acting chief while he was in Brazil, was hospitalized with gallstones two days before Sergio was scheduled to depart. There was talk of him postponing his trip, but Officer Donnie stepped forward and lobbied hard for the temporary position. Sergio was reluctant to put someone so young in charge, but Donnie argued that he could handle the responsibility and was ready to prove himself. Sergio finally agreed; and before the wheels on Sergio's plane were up as it left the runway of the

Bar Harbor Airport, Donnie's nerves collapsed faster than the roof over Hayley's garage.

Donnie was overwhelmed by the duties of chief. Being in charge of keeping an entire town safe and secure, he broke out with a case of shingles almost immediately. There was a discussion of summoning Sergio back. However, since there hadn't been a crime reported in Bar Harbor in several weeks, the city council decided just to let things be and crossed their fingers in hope that nothing bad would happen while Sergio was in South America.

Unfortunately, for the entire town of Bar Harbor, that would eventually prove to be a dangerous mistake.

Chapter 3

Hayley tried to be a trouper and sleep at her house that first night, bundled up in her long underwear, with a couple of heavy sweaters, and buried underneath a giant white down comforter. She snuggled up close with Leroy and shivered throughout the night. By morning her red nose was stuffed up and a nasty cold was coming her way.

Things just got worse once Billy Parsons arrived at the house shortly after seven. Billy was a local handyman in his early thirties, portly, with a scruffy face and an easy smile. There was a charm about Billy that a lot of the local single women found intoxicating. Now that Billy was going through a divorce and his copper wedding band had been removed from his pudgy ring finger, interest in Billy as a romantic prospect had recently spiked. Billy wasn't Hayley's type, but he was a hard worker, so he was the first person she thought to call when her furnace went on the fritz.

Billy showed up on time and trudged down the stairs to the basement; Hayley and Leroy followed behind.

Fearing the worst, Hayley had a knot in her stomach.

Billy snapped open his tool kit and grabbed a flashlight and a wrench and went to work inspecting the busted furnace. Hayley stood close behind him, arms tightly folded, eyes closed as she prayed for a miracle.

She had to bend down and pick up Leroy, who was sniffing around Billy's butt crack, which inched up from his scuffed belt as he crouched down to take a look.

Billy started to bang the side of the furnace and then stuck his head inside and looked around. When he pulled his face out, he had smudges of dirt all over his chubby cheeks.

"What's the verdict, Billy?" Hayley asked, taking a deep breath.

Billy shook his head, with a grim look on his face. "Not good, Hayley. This thing's beyond repair. Looks like you're going to have to buy a new one."

"How much is that going to cost?" Hayley said, still holding her breath.

"I'd say you're looking at three grand."

Hayley's heart sank.

She couldn't afford three hundred, let alone

three grand. She had just spent the last two thousand in her checking account paying her property taxes—and not only that, she needed to buy both her kids new ski boots when they returned from their dad's house.

Billy put a comforting arm around Hayley and squeezed tightly. "Now don't fret, Hayley. Ole Billy's here to help you. I know a guy who can get me a used one. That would knock off about fifteen hundred."

It was still more than she had to spend. She didn't even want to think about what fixing the roof was going to cost. She was afraid to ask, but sometimes she was just a glutton for punishment.

"Did you take a look at the roof before you came in?"

"Yes, I did," Billy said solemnly.

"And?"

"And I think it's best we deal with one thing at a time. And heating your house in February should be our biggest concern right now."

"Billy, I have to know what I'm dealing with," Hayley said, locking eyes with him.

Billy looked away and down at his Eddie Bauer boots. "I won't lie to you. It's going to be expensive."

"How much?"

"Another five, six grand."

Hayley's knees felt weak. She had to grab the furnace to keep from falling. Luckily, it was dead, so there was no chance of burning her hand from the heat.

"But I can throw some tarp over it for now and we can deal with it sometime this spring after the snow melts. Does that sound good to you?"

Hayley nodded.

"Like I said, the heater's more important. And your car."

"My car?"

"Yeah, it's pretty much totaled, I'm sorry to say." Of course it was.

"But you've got insurance, right, Hayley?"

"Yes," Hayley said, rubbing her eyes and shaking her head, grateful for that.

"Then you got nothing to worry about. You'll have another one parked in your driveway in no time," Billy said with his relaxed smile. "I'm partial to those Kia Sportage mini-SUVs myself."

If only she could afford one.

But maybe with the insurance money . . .

Billy was kind enough to give Hayley a lift to the *Island Times* office. When Hayley sat down at her desk, she immediately picked up the phone and called her car insurance agent, Gretchen Maxwell, a kind elderly local who had been handling her policy since Hayley first got her license at sixteen years old.

Gretchen adored Hayley and always commented

that Hayley's laugh was infectious and put a smile
on her face whenever she heard it at the bank or
in the grocery store or even on the street when
they were out walking their dogs. Gretchen swore
Hayley's distinct giggle echoed through town keeping Bar Harbor the happiest place on earth, a close
second to Disney World, where Gretchen took her
grandkids every Thanksgiving.

So Hayley knew Gretchen would do her best to
make the process of filing a claim as painless as possible. Hayley heard Gretchen type a few keys on her
computer as she chatted away about her recent hip
surgery and how she had to hire a dog walker to
take her poodle out to do her business because her
recovery was going too slowly.

"Here we go," Gretchen said. "I have your policy
right here in front of me. Now let's see. . . ."

Gretchen suddenly fell silent.

This wasn't good.

"Gretchen, are you still there?" Hayley asked.

"Uh, yes, dear. Your policy was due for renewal
on the fifteenth. That was a week ago."

"I know. I remember getting the bill in the mail
and I sent the check for the first installment of my
premium the day I got my paycheck, which was on
Thursday."

"We never received it."

"Well, I know I sent it," Hayley said confidently
as she fished through her bag and retrieved her
checkbook. She opened to the register and scanned

down the list of checks she had written. The last one was a deposit for Gemma's two-week cheerleading camp next summer. Before that, she wrote a check to Geddy's restaurant when she had taken the kids out for pizza. Nothing to the insurance company. But she distinctly remembered writing the check and stuffing it in the envelope and mailing it. She must have just forgotten to record it in the register.

Then it suddenly hit her.

She didn't have stamps that day and the post office was already closed, so she decided to do it first thing in the morning before work. But that was the day Dustin missed the bus for school because he couldn't drag his lazy butt out of bed and she had to drive him herself. She was running late for work and forgot to swing by the post office.

That could only mean one thing.

Hayley fumbled around the contents of her bag. Her fingers touched some paper and she instinctively knew what it was. An envelope. With the check for the insurance company inside it. She forgot to mail it.

"Gretchen, I am so, so sorry. I have it right here. I can run it by your office during my lunch hour."

"That will be fine, dear. Once I have it, I can reinstate your policy."

"Great, thank you. Now I need to file a claim for the damage to my car. Do you want to take down the information or have me fill out a form online?"

More silence on the other end of the phone. Again. Not good.

"Excuse me, dear, the accident happened yesterday?"

"Yes. The roof collapsed on top of my Subaru. There was no other car involved. I'm covered for something like that, right?"

"Of course, dear. The only problem is when your policy was a week past due, which would have been yesterday, it was canceled."

"I understand," Hayley said. "But I have the check right here in my hand and you said you could reinstate it."

"Yes. And you will be covered as of today. Unfortunately, and this is why I am so ready to retire next year, the vultures at this company will almost certainly deny your claim because at the time of the accident, you were technically not covered."

This could not be happening.

"But I've been on time with my payments for years. This was a onetime mix-up. I swear I'll never be late again."

"If it were up to me, I'd have you driving a brand-new Infiniti by the end of business hours tomorrow. But I'm not authorized to process this claim. I have to send it to corporate headquarters and they decide whether or not to cut you a check. Hayley, I'm telling you right now, this is the kind of loophole they always look for."

Hayley felt her eyes welling up with tears again. She couldn't take much more of this. She quietly thanked Gretchen for her time and hung up the phone. She sat in stunned silence the rest of the morning, robotically answering the phone and jotting down information from local businesses calling to place ads in the paper. She couldn't even begin to focus on her column, which was due by the end of the day.

Around noon Randy walked through the door in a stylish navy blue winter coat he bought while visiting a college friend in Denver and a scarf Sergio's mother had knitted for him last Christmas.

"Hey, sis, I've come to treat you to lunch. Want to go to Jordan's and split a large order of onion rings? I'm feeling naughty."

He instantly sensed something was wrong.

"What happened now?" he asked.

Hayley recounted the details of her conversation with Gretchen at the insurance company. And the devastating estimates from Billy Parsons to repair her roof and install a new furnace.

Randy rushed over to Hayley as she stood up and hugged her tightly. "You know I'd lend you the money, but we're cash poor right now because of the money pit we live in and our astronomical gas bill this winter. And Sergio cleaned out our savings to buy his plane ticket home to Brazil."

"I know, I know. This isn't your problem. I'm the one who got myself into this financial mess. I've been budgeting, but I just didn't include any unexpected problems. What am I going to do?"

"You're going to come stay in my drafty house

until we figure out how to get you a new furnace. We'll sit by the fire and wrap ourselves up in blankets and drink Irish coffee with whipped cream and we'll bake cookies until we both grow a belt size. It'll be like one big fun slumber party."

It sounded heavenly.

And Hayley really needed a lifeline right now.

Chapter 4

Randy picked Hayley up at the office promptly at five o'clock in his blue Prius and they drove straight to the grocery store to stock up on cookie dough, chocolate chips, coffee, and, most important, a bottle of Baileys Irish Cream before swinging by Hayley's neighbor to pick up Leroy, whose simple playdate had morphed into doggie day care.

When they finally arrived at Randy's large ocean-front house, Hayley made a beeline for the kitchen to prepare their feast of freshly baked cookies and warm drinks, while Randy lugged in an armful of chopped wood from outside and stacked them in the fireplace.

Leroy chose to curl up on the couch and fall into a deep sleep.

By the time Hayley carried in two steaming mugs of Irish coffee, Randy was stoking the roaring fire with an iron poker. He had already tossed some pillows on the floor, and they both sat down and toasted to a hopefully short winter before taking their sips.

"So, have you thought about what you're going to do?" Randy asked delicately.

Hayley shook her head. "The kids will be home soon. I'm going to have to figure something out quick."

"You can always go for the nuclear option," Randy said, smiling.

"No way! Absolutely not!"

The nuclear option was calling their mother in Florida and asking her for a loan. Sheila had some cash socked away for a rainy day, but the ordeal of asking was as painful to Hayley as the time she underwent dental implants. There had to be another way.

"You can at least try," Randy said, reaching for the cordless phone on the coffee table. "I know she's home. We chatted earlier."

"Randy, I've gone down this road before and she always makes me feel guilty for asking. I just don't want to go through that again. I'm not that desperate."

"Yes, you are, sis."

He had a point.

Hayley grabbed the phone out of Randy's hand and started punching numbers. "I have a very strong feeling I'm going to regret this."

Hayley shook her head and sighed as it rang. In her gut she just knew this was a huge mistake. But what choice did she have?

"Yes. Hello. Who is this?"

"Mom, I know you checked the caller ID before you answered. It's me. Your only daughter."

"Oh, hello, Hayley. You can't trust caller ID. The government has a lot of tricks up its sleeve. They can tamper with anything. In fact, this may not even be you. I'm sure with all the techno gizmos they've got, they can play with voice patterns and re-create the exact sound of your voice."

"Mom, I'm calling for a loan."

"Well, you've convinced me. It really *is* you."

Randy gave Hayley an encouraging thumbs-up.

Hayley took another sip of her Irish coffee to muster a little more courage. "I'll pay you back this time. I promise."

"Is that deadbeat ex-husband of yours late with the child support again?" Sheila cried out. She was never a fan of Hayley's ex, even when they were married.

"No, but I've had a couple of unexpected setbacks and I'm just not going to make it through the winter unless I get a little help."

"How much are we talking about?" Sheila said evenly and businesslike.

"Well, I'm not sure. I need a new furnace and a new roof on my garage, and my car is totaled, and . . ." Hayley was stalling.

The last thing she wanted was to give her mother an actual figure.

"How *much*?"

"Ten grand."

Dead silence on the other end of the phone.

Hayley's nerves suddenly took over and she began chatting incessantly. "I know it's a lot, and I normally wouldn't ask. Well, I mean, I would ask, because I've asked before. . . ."

"Multiple times," Sheila added.

"But I just don't know what I'm going to do. I never planned on any of those things happening, and—"

"Don't you have insurance to cover the cost of repairing your car?" Sheila asked, a cold tone to her voice.

"Well, yes, um, I mean, no. It's kind of funny. I sort of forgot to mail the check for the premium and they canceled my policy, and I didn't even know it. . . ."

More silence on the other end of the phone.

As Hayley predicted, this was one mother of a huge mistake.

"Hayley, I begged you to get yourself a financial planner, since you are so bad with money," Sheila said.

"I would, if I could afford one," Hayley said. She wanted to argue, but she couldn't. Her mother was right. And she always hated it when her mother was right.

"Hayley, I want to help you. Really, I do. And you know I came through for you the last four times you made this exact same call."

"Yes, but this time is different, because none of this was my fault. Well, except maybe the forgetting to mail the insurance check part, but it's been such a horrible winter, and I never expected—"

"I just don't have it, Hayley. You know I renovated my kitchen in the fall, and I got laser surgery on my eyes last month. You wouldn't believe how easy it is for me to read menus now in restaurants. Stan says I have X-ray vision like Wonder Woman."

"Wonder Woman doesn't have X-ray vision, Ma."

As if arguing over a comic-book character's superpowers was the best strategy to pursue at this moment.

"Well, you know what I mean!"

Hayley glared at Randy, whose smile slowly faded as he turned his thumbs-up into a thumbs-down.

Hayley nodded.

They both gulped down the rest of their Irish coffees.

"Look, I understand, Ma. Things are tight. No worries."

"By the way, Stan and I are taking a Mediterranean cruise. You know it's been my lifelong dream to see the Greek isles. Well, I'm not sure we'll actually go ashore, but I'm sure they will look lovely from the deck."

"That's so nice. Is Stan treating you?"

"Oh, please. Like he has two cents to his name. No, this one's on me. I always say, spend it while you've got it."

Hayley bit her tongue.

"I'd e-mail you the itinerary, but I don't want Homeland Security all up in my business," Sheila said. "They monitor our computers, you know, so you better make sure Dustin isn't going to any porn sites when you're not home."

"I will, Ma. I promise."

There was a *click* and Hayley noticed another call coming through.

It was Lex Bansfield, Hayley's boyfriend.

Or something.

She hadn't really defined it yet.

"Ma, I better go. Lex is calling."

"You should ask *him* for money," Sheila offered helpfully. "All those billions from that frozen seafood. I can't go into the supermarket without seeing that laughing lobster on all those boxes taking up most of the space in the freezer section. I just want a pint of frozen yogurt, for heaven's sake!"

"Ma, Lex is the caretaker on the Hollingsworth estate. It's not like he gets a cut from the sales. He just mows the lawn. Or this time of year, he plows the driveway."

"Well, he's closer to a giant fortune than most people."

"Bye, Ma."

Hayley pressed the flash button on the handset to switch over to the other line. "Lex, how did you know I was here?"

"Your boss, Sal, called and asked me to bring my plow over to his place and dig his car out of a snowbank, and he told me you had to move out of your house because your furnace is busted. I figured you'd end up bunking with your brother."

"You wouldn't believe the last couple of days I've had—"

"Listen, Hayley, I'm sorry to interrupt. I'm calling about our dinner tonight. . . ."

Dinner? Omigod. Hayley suddenly realized she was supposed to have dinner with Lex at Jack Russell's, a steak house just outside of town. She was so caught up in her personal drama she had completely forgotten.

"I'm going to have to cancel," Lex said, his voice shaky.

Hayley knew something was wrong. "Lex, what's going on?"

"It's Mr. Hollingsworth," Lex said.

Edgar Hollingsworth was Lex's boss and the billionaire owner of Hollingsworth frozen seafood. He was a kind man and treated Lex like a son, especially since his own son had died tragically in a car accident years ago. Lex thought the world of him. In the past few months, Edgar Hollingsworth had suffered from pneumonia and was resting at home under the care of a private nurse.

"He's taken a turn for the worse," Lex said solemnly.

"How bad is it?" Hayley asked.

Randy put down his empty coffee mug and scooted closer to Hayley, mouthing, "What?"

"He slipped into a coma this afternoon. We

called the ambulance and they took him to the
hospital. It doesn't look good," Lex said, his voice
cracking.

Lex was a strong man, not prone to showing
much emotion. Hayley knew he really had to be
hurting.

All she wanted to do at that moment was reach
through the phone and give him a big hug.

Chapter 5

After hanging up with Lex, Hayley put her winter boots on, wrapped a white wool scarf around her neck, buttoned up her still soggy winter jacket, and bolted out the door before Randy could stop her. She was headed to the hospital to be with Lex, who was holding vigil at his boss's bedside. Hayley worried about her relationship with Lex and where it was going. They hadn't talked about what they wanted out of it or if they were working toward something more serious in the future. Still, Hayley couldn't deny the feelings that she had developed in recent months for this strapping, soft-spoken man. When she sensed the anguish in his voice, she knew she just had to be with him.

It was a treacherous fifteen-minute walk to the local hospital, which was situated one block behind her office at the *Island Times*. When she stomped the excess snow off her boots and walked through the sliding glass doors into the hospital lobby, she quickly noticed how quiet it was. Behind the reception desk was Evelyn Tate, a short, stout woman who had a cherubic face and an infectious laugh. Hayley had known Evelyn since they shared a cubbyhole in kindergarten.

Evelyn looked up from her paperwork to see Hayley unzipping her jacket and wiping some wet flakes off her face with her scarf.

Usually, Evelyn would break into a wide smile and leap to her feet and grab Hayley in a hug and ask about her kids. Tonight, though, Evelyn wasn't smiling. She knew why Hayley was here.

"He's in room 216, Hayley. Lex is up there with him now," Evelyn said gravely.

"Thanks, Evelyn."

Hayley noticed Evelyn's eyes were brimming with tears. "Are you okay?"

"It's just that Mr. Hollingsworth is such a sweet and kind man. When I was eight years old, my father lost his construction job due to an injury and Mr. Hollingsworth paid the mortgage on our house until Daddy got back on his feet. Not many rich folks would do something like that."

Hayley took Evelyn's hand and squeezed it. "We both know Edgar Hollingsworth is a strong SOB. He's weathered a lot of storms. He'll beat this."

"I heard the doctors talking. They're saying this coma might be irreversible," Evelyn said, snatching a tissue out of the colorful flowery box on her desk and blowing her nose. "But I'm not supposed to say anything."

Hayley's heart sank.

She patted Evelyn's hand and hurried around the corner to the bank of elevators that would take her to the second floor.

As she counted down the numbers to room 216, her wet boots squeaked on the tile floor. Her arrival was much louder than she wanted it to be. Several RNs and orderlies at the nurses' station looked up from their work to see who was making so much noise. Hayley wanted to ditch the boots, but she was in too much of a hurry.

She spotted Lex standing outside room 216. He was still tall and handsome in his plaid work shirt, worn over a white undershirt, and khaki pants and black work boots. But his face was pale and gaunt. The sudden change in his boss's condition was clearly worrying him.

Hayley walked up to Lex, surprising him. He was in his own world, lost in his thoughts. He hadn't noticed her approaching, despite her squeaky boots. He grabbed and hugged her, holding her tightly, not wanting to let go.

Hayley rested her head on his broad chest and rubbed his back with her hand. "Have you spoken to the doctor?"

"Prognosis isn't good, I'm afraid. It's gotten worse since I called you. They got him hooked up to all sorts of machines now."

"Is there any way he might come out of this?"

"Depends on if you believe in miracles, I guess," Lex said, shrugging.

Hayley noticed a candy bar wrapper sticking out of Lex's pants pocket. She frowned. "I see you're taking care of yourself eating junk food. When was the last time you had a proper meal?"

"I haven't had time to think about eating," Lex said.

"Exactly. Which is why I'm here. Mr. Hollingsworth has a whole hospital full of doctors and nurses taking care of him. You need someone looking after you. Now sit tight. I'm going to go to the cafeteria and get you something decent to eat."

Hayley caught a quick glance inside room 216. Edgar Hollingsworth was lying in bed, a breathing tube sticking out of his mouth, a stack of monitors displaying all kinds of numbers and readings. His bone thin arms were at his sides; his wrinkled, gaunt face appeared lifeless; wisps of fine white hair flew off in all different directions on top of his head. Although he was in his eighties, Edgar Hollingsworth had always seemed so indestructible to Hayley. Ever since she was a little girl, he had appeared so strong and vital and wealthy and powerful. She hated seeing him like this.

As she pulled away from Lex, he clutched her hand and kissed her palm. "I'm glad you came over here to be with me, Hayley."

"Just try and keep me away," Hayley said, smiling. And then she squeaked down the hall in her annoying winter boots in the direction of the cafeteria.

The cafeteria was empty except for a high-school girl seated behind the cash register. The teen was busy texting her friends as two nurses, at a corner table on their break, were having a quick dinner.

One of the nurses was Candace Culpepper.

Candace was a couple of years older than Hayley. When they both attended Mount Desert Island High School, they had played on the same soccer team. Hayley remembered Candace being super-competitive. Whenever they were on opposing scrimmage teams during practice, Hayley would go out of her way to avoid Candace because Candace had no qualms about kicking shins, bodychecking, or giving her opponent a dirt facial in order to regain control of that black-and-white–checkered ball. It was because of Candace's fierce determination that the team wound up making it to the state championships. Unfortunately, during the final seconds in the fourth quarter, with the score tied three to three, Mona, who was also on the team, attempted a wide shot, which bounced off the goalpost, landing right in front of the other team's star player, who effortlessly kicked the ball back down the field to where the MDI goalie was wide open and exposed. Needless to say, the desperate goalie had little chance of stopping the ball. As the horn blared after the last few seconds ticked away, Candace's hopes of a trophy were dashed and she never forgave Mona. So, by extension, she blamed Hayley as well for the simple fact that Hayley and Mona were close friends.

Many years had passed since that fateful day; and Hayley waited patiently for the day Candace would finally decide to be at least civil to her, but she was still waiting. Things, it seemed, were not about to change on this cold Maine winter night in February.

Candace looked up from her soup and salad and saw Hayley scooping some chili into a plastic container for Lex. She just stared blankly at Hayley as if she didn't even recognize her. The other nurse, Tilly McVety, who spent a lot of time with Hayley at the PTA meetings at school, smiled and waved. When Tilly caught Candace glaring at her as if she were some kind of traitor, she quickly stopped.

Hayley acknowledged them both with a smile and then moved on to the bread section to grab a couple of rolls for Lex to have with his chili. She snapped the container shut and moved to the bored young girl behind the register, who rang her up and took her money.

Just as she was about to go, Hayley heard a gasp. She spun around in time to see Candace Culpepper spitting out her soup into a coffee mug.

Tilly got caught in the cross fire and some of the

broth splashed across her white nurse's uniform. She jumped to her feet in shock. "My God, Candace, what is it?"

Candace spoke in a low growl as she wiped her face with a paper napkin. "There are beans in this soup. I hate beans."

She grabbed the paper bowl with the soup in it and dramatically marched over and dumped it in the trash, glaring at Hayley and the girl behind the register as if the entire bean drama had been their fault. "Ida told me she was going to stop putting beans in her chicken chili stew. She said she'd use lentils instead."

"I know," Tilly said softly, "but people complained. They missed the old recipe, so she went back to the original. I'm sure she told you."

"No, she did not," Candace said, grabbing a glass of water and chugging it down in an attempt to erase any aftertaste of the offensive beans. "She knows I hate beans. Everyone knows I hate beans."

"I didn't," Hayley said, surprised the words spilled out of her mouth at that exact moment. She really needed to work on thinking before she spoke.

Candace slowly turned her head back to Hayley like some predatory cat who just noticed a mouse cowering in the corner. "Well, I do. I hate beans."

Hayley waited for her to continue with saying, "And I hate *you*!"

But Candace stopped short of that.

Tilly was desperate to change the subject. She didn't want Candace causing a scene. "So, did you apply online for the game show, Candace?"

"Yes, this morning," Candace said, throwing Hayley one last grimace before returning her attention to her quivering dinner companion and sitting back down at the table.

"It's so exciting. I watch that extreme coupon-clipping show all the time!" Tilly gushed. "I can't believe they're actually coming to do a show here in Bar Harbor."

Hayley's ears suddenly perked up.

A coupon-clipping game show?

Here in Bar Harbor?

Candace's eyes flared up and she put a finger to her lips. Tilly got the message immediately and obediently returned to scarfing down her own chicken chili stew. With beans. She was stuffing spoonfuls into her mouth to keep herself from talking anymore and making her fellow RN angrier than she already was.

But the cat was out of the bag.

And so was a possible solution to Hayley's problems.

If this was true—if there really was a coupon-clipping game show actually coming to the local market to tape an episode, and Bar Harbor residents were allowed to apply as contestants—then she was a shoo-in. Because nobody, *repeat nobody*, was as good at clipping coupons and cutting down her monthly grocery bill at the Shop 'n Save than

Hayley Powell. People marveled at her cost-savings skills. She was a master. And if she somehow managed to get on the show and win, well, then the cash prize just might be enough to pay all her repair costs.

An answer to her prayers.

Maybe there was such a thing as miracles.

Chapter 6

The following day after Randy dropped her off at the office on his way to the bar to do inventory, Hayley shed her winter jacket and scarf and booted up her computer. She googled extreme-couponing game shows and was quickly routed to the Small Town Life Network's website, where they were trumpeting a new season of episodes for their hit signature show, *Wild and Crazy Couponing,* one of which would be shot at the Shop 'n Save in Bar Harbor, Maine. Hayley clicked on the application page and began typing all her vital statistics, including name, address, phone number, and e-mail. There was also a section in which she needed to describe briefly why she loved couponing and why she was applying to compete on the show. Hayley didn't want to play on their sympathy in order to get selected. So, instead, she began talking about how as a single mother it was her duty to cut corners and find cost savings whenever possible.

Boring!

Hayley then remembered her mother talking about an old game show called *Queen for a Day* that Sheila had watched when she was a little girl in the 1950s. On this show women trotted out sob stories about how hard and sad their lives were. At the end of the program, the woman with the most pathetic life was crowned "Queen for a Day" and was handed prizes. Hayley deleted what she had written and started over. This time she detailed her collapsed roof, broken furnace, totaled car, and insurance woes. She didn't hold back. If she did her job right, the producers would actually hear her voice cracking with emotion and the sniffling nose of this desperate housewife as they read her essay. It was a calculated move, but it was worth the risk.

When she finished, she proofread the application for typos and hit the send button. She had no idea how many locals would be applying, and the deadline was today, as the show was scheduled to tape in less than two weeks.

She then read her work e-mails, which had piled up overnight. One was from Gretchen at the insurance company. Sure enough, Gretchen had spoken to her bosses and they were unwilling to help Hayley out. She was still on the hook for the cost to repair her car.

The front door of the office blew open and Sal and Bruce barreled inside, both bundled up, their noses a Rudolph red. Sal shed his army green parka and black stocking cap, hung them on a coatrack, and charged over to the coffeepot, which was percolating in the corner.

Bruce took his time taking off his coat, winking at Hayley, and presenting her with a paper bag.

"What's this?" Hayley asked.

"Blueberry muffin from the Morning Glory Bakery," Bruce said proudly.

"I'm speechless," Hayley said, her mouth open.

"I felt bad about the other day, so I thought I'd make it up to you by stopping by there on my way to work this morning."

Hayley opened the bag. "Bruce, I think this is the first nice thing you've ever done for me."

"I like to surprise you," Bruce said smugly.

She peeked inside.

"Um, Bruce, there's nothing but crumbs, an empty wrapper, and a wad of napkins in here."

Bruce snatched the bag from her. "What?"

He looked inside the bag. "I thought it felt light. Sal! Did you eat the muffin I bought for Hayley?"

"Yes, I did, while you were filling up your gas tank at the Big Apple. I was starving. My wife's still out of town and nobody's at home to cook me breakfast."

Bruce had been picking up Sal every morning as a favor. Sal's wife usually dropped him off at the office because Sal refused to operate heavy machinery before he had his morning coffee.

"So, when were you going to tell me?" Bruce barked.

"I didn't have to. Hayley already did," Sal said, pouring cream into his paper cup of coffee.

"I can't believe you!" Bruce said.

"You got a problem? Fire me. Oh, wait. That's right. I'm the boss. I'm the one who can fire you. Not the other way around."

Bruce decided to drop the matter out of self-preservation.

"While we're on the topic of you being the boss . . . ," Hayley said, treading gently.

"No raise, Hayley," Sal said, taking a sip of his coffee and then sputtering as it burned his tongue. "Damn it!"

"For your information, Sal Moretti, I was *not* going to ask you for a raise," Hayley said sharply, folding her arms and shooting him her best look of annoyance.

"Well, color me surprised," Sal said. "What is it, then?"

"I was going to ask for an advance on my salary," Hayley said, her voice volume dropping to a tiny whisper.

"An advance? How much of an advance?" Sal said, blowing on his coffee to cool it down.

"I was thinking . . . Oh, I don't know. . . ."

"Ballpark," Sal said suspiciously.

"Five months or so," Hayley said, not making eye contact.

"Five months! That's something like ten thousand dollars."

"Yeah, that's about right. It would be a huge help," Hayley said. The sinking feeling in her gut was telling her exactly where this conversation was going.

"You're kidding, right? This has got to be some kind of joke."

"You're right, Sal. I'm joking. Just lightening the mood around here," Hayley said, forcing a smile and returning her attention to her computer.

"Good. Because for a second there, I thought you were serious. Imagine. Me having that kind of money to throw around. If I did, I wouldn't be here. I'd be lying on a beach in the Bahamas drinking mai tais and laughing at all you poor saps braving this godforsaken Maine winter!"

Sal tried sipping his coffee again. Still too hot. It burned his tongue. Again. "Damn it!" Sal set the white paper cup down and stormed into the back bull pen toward his office.

Hayley could tell Sal knew she wasn't joking. He was just saving her the humiliation of having to say no to her.

Bruce hung back and waited for Sal to shut his office door before turning back to Hayley.

"I don't have ten grand in my account, Hayley, but I can probably float you half. And I'll give you a break on the interest. Say five percent?"

If it were anybody but Bruce Linney, Hayley would have considered it. But borrowing money from Bruce would inevitably come with strings attached. And she had no desire to find out what those strings might be.

Hayley shook her head and smiled. "No, Bruce, I don't think so. But thanks anyway."

"Well, I'm here if you change your mind," Bruce said, shrugging, before walking back to his own office.

She was tempted.

No. There had to be another way.

Wild and Crazy Couponing.

It was a long shot.

But right now, it was her *only* shot.

Hayley was determined to put the financial stress out of her mind and focus on her next column. But that was going to be next to impossible now that she had decided to do a series of columns featuring a variety of ways to prepare tasty meals on a budget. Every recipe would be a constant reminder that her future was about to be filled with a lot of Hamburger Helper.

Island Food & Spirits
by
Hayley Powell

Well, after the last couple of days I've had this week, the only words I keep hearing rolling around in my head are "I need a do-over!"

What a long week it's been! All of this snow we've been getting has me questioning why I chose to live in this town year-round! Oh, wait a minute, I didn't! I was born here, so I guess I can just blame my mother!

Although I do admit I love the spring, summer, and fall in our quaint little town of Bar Harbor, our winters can be brutal and unforgiving! Sometimes I think I should follow in the footsteps of my mother and become a snowbird in Florida. But then again, one thing I hate more than the snow is admitting my mother is right!

All this nasty weather reminds me of the afternoons when I was a kid and hanging out after school with my two best friends, Mona and Liddy, and we would plan our escape from our dreary, boring lives on this island! By the first snowfall, Bar Harbor looked like a ghost town! All the summer tourists were long gone, most of the restaurants and cute shops were boarded up, and the only businesses left open were the grocery store, the pharmacy, and one tiny Christmas decoration shop that opened just once a week on Saturday afternoon.

We were impressionable kids back then and yearned for the excitement of the big city of Bangor, where there were fast-food restaurants, a shopping mall, and more than one movie theater! To us, this was Mecca!

One cold day in February, the three of us had a sleepover at

Mona's house and we hatched a plan. It was simple. Sock away our allowances until the next snow day we had off from school. Then we would escape on the next plane to Honolulu, Hawaii, and sell t-shirts on Waikiki Beach and date hot Polynesian surfers. Once the logistics of that plan quickly began to fall apart, we decided on the next best thing! Sneak away to that bustling cosmopolitan Bangor! Since all of our parents would be working, no one would realize we were AWOL. By the six o'clock dinner hour, we would be happily munching on our Big Macs and French fries and living it up in the big city. Or so we thought. As usual, things didn't go exactly as planned.

First, our snow day came just two days later, so we hadn't had a lot of time to build up our fortune. We had roughly eight dollars and some change among the three of us. So there went the Big Macs. We'd have to settle for Happy Meals.

Then, after Mona and I trudged through the cold,

blowing wind and the heavy snowfall to Liddy's house, we found her waving frantically at us through a downstairs window and holding up a piece of paper that said, *I CAN'T LEAVE! MY MOM STAYED HOME FROM WORK TODAY!* She looked so miserable to be missing out on our great adventure. Poor Liddy. It was like leaving a wounded soldier behind during a combat mission.

Mona and I continued on for what seemed like hours, but was probably less than thirty minutes. Finally we arrived on Route 3. Our road to freedom. The plan was to hitchhike, but there wasn't a car in sight to pick us up, and the snowstorm was morphing into a full-blown blizzard. I didn't say anything to Mona, who was determined to carry out our plan and kept walking straight ahead. At this point, however, I just wanted to call it a day and go home.

After a few more torturous minutes, I finally opened my mouth to admit the truth to Mona, but a loud roaring noise from the top of the hill ahead of us drowned me out. We both looked up and saw the gigantic town plow truck barreling down the hill toward us! It took us a second to realize it wasn't just coming down the hill fast—it was actually spinning around in circles out of control. We saw Harry Smith, the head town plowman, desperately trying to straighten out the truck with all of his might, but it just kept picking up speed. We stood there, rooted to the spot in horror! Poor Harry suddenly spotted us and his eyes nearly popped out of his head!

At the last possible second, Mona regained her senses and gave me a giant shove and we both tumbled down the embankment as poor Harry and his truck roared past us. Mona and I struggled to our feet and scrambled back up to the road, relieved to see that the truck and Harry were still in one piece. Unfortunately for us, Harry, who later claimed to have seen his life flash before his eyes as his truck nearly mowed down two seventh graders, immediately radioed his boss, who, in turn, called our parents. (Another curse about living in a small town . . . everyone knows everybody!)

I swear, within moments my mother careened around the corner in her big brown Bonneville, slip-sliding all over the road, with Mona's mother riding shotgun next to her. Even from where we stood, hundreds of feet away, we could make out their panicked, angry faces and instantly knew this outcome was not going to be pretty. We also knew at that moment it would be a long time before we would be able to "do over" our adventure because we wouldn't be seeing the light of day for a long while to come. We didn't get dinner, nor were we allowed to watch that night's episode of *Beverly Hills 90210*! A punishment worse than death!

Well, times have changed, but the weather hasn't. We still have a couple more long months of winter left. I know many of you, like me, are on a tight budget because of the extra heating fuel and all the other unexpected costs that come along with winter. So I'm going to be sharing budget-friendly recipes for the next few weeks! This week we are starting off the week's meals with a "Meatless Monday"! If you ask me, after a long day there is nothing like a simple, uncomplicated yet satisfying meal. But don't panic! There is no reason for me, or anyone else, to sacrifice their nightly cocktail or two especially at a time like this when it gets dark at the ungodly hour of 4:30 P.M.! I guess the one advantage of the sun disappearing so early is that happy hour can start a little early! So let's all sit down and relax after work before fixing dinner with a special cocktail and close our eyes and dream we're on a beautiful beach somewhere in Hawaii. I promise you after a couple of these drinks, you will be searching for a grass skirt and a lei of flowers to do your own hula dance in the living room!

Warm-Me-Up Mai Tai

<u>Ingredients</u>
Ice
1½ ounces of your favorite
    dark rum
1½ ounces Cointreau
⅓ cup pineapple juice
Squeeze of lime juice
2 tablespoons grenadine
Nice pinch of sugar

Fill a cocktail shaker with ice.
Add your rum and Cointreau,
pineapple juice, grenadine, lime
juice, and sugar. Shake it up and
pour ice and all into a tall glass
and let the vacation begin!

Meatless Monday's Monterey Jack, Poblano, and Mushroom Quesadillas

<u>Ingredients</u>
1 tablespoon vegetable oil
2 poblano chilies, seeded and
    minced
1 large red or white onion, your
    choice, diced
8 ounces your favorite mush-
    rooms, sliced (about 3 cups)

8 six-inch flour tortillas
1½ cups shredded Monterey
   Jack cheese

In a 10-inch skillet, heat your oil over medium-high heat. Cook chilies, onions, and mushrooms in oil for about 10 minutes, stirring frequently until tender.

Divide your veggie mixture evenly onto 4 tortillas and divide cheese evenly among the 4 tortillas. Top with the remaining tortillas.

Wipe out your skillet with paper towels and spray skillet with nonstick cooking spray. Heat over medium heat. Place one quesadilla in skillet; cook 1 or 2 minutes or until golden brown on bottom. Turn and cook 1 or 2 minutes longer, or until golden brown and cheese is melted. Remove from skillet to your serving platter. Cover to keep warm until all remaining quesadillas are done. If you like, serve with a dollop of sour cream and a little salsa.

Chapter 7

"Did you arrange your coupons by sections? Produce, frozen food, breads and pastries, household cleaning supplies, canned goods?" Mona asked, pushing her grocery cart up next to Hayley's in the Shop 'n Save.

"Mona, please, I'm not an amateur," Hayley said, fanning through her stack of coupons to make sure they were in order and she was ready to rumble.

When Hayley discovered that Mona had also applied to be on *Wild and Crazy Couponing*, she suggested they do a dry run at the store to prepare in the event that one or both of them were chosen to compete on the show.

It had finally stopped snowing in Bar Harbor, but the temperature barely remained above zero and snow still blanketed the entire town. However, it was easier now for Hayley to get where she needed to go on foot, since she was without a car. Luckily, Mona owned a flatbed truck, so she could transport her purchases from this practice run back to the house. Even though she was broke, Hayley was confident enough about her couponing skills that she knew she would manage to buy three hundred dollars' worth of groceries for about seventeen dollars after discounts. If she couldn't pull that one off, Hayley had no business being on the show.

Although Hayley had been shopping at the Shop 'n Save for years, and knew every inch of the store, the owner had recently remodeled and added on. Therefore it was imperative that she and Mona use this practice couponing session as a refresher course and an opportunity to memorize every aisle that was reorganized and every new product that had been stocked. They were leaving nothing to chance.

Mona reached into her coat pocket and pulled out an old-fashioned gold stopwatch.

"I know, I know," she said. "My kids make fun of me for keeping this. They got all sorts of timers on their iPads and iPhones, but this belonged to my grandfather, so it has sentimental value."

"I think it's sweet," Hayley said. "Okay, how much time are you giving us?"

"Thirty minutes, and then we both have to be up front at the register ready to check out," Mona said, setting the watch. "Okay, ready, set . . . go!"

Mona pressed down the button on top of the stopwatch and stuffed it back in her pocket. Then she went flying down the breakfast cereal aisle with her cart. Hayley ran in the opposite direction. She was starting with pet food. She could feed Leroy for the next six months with the amount of Kibbles 'n Bits she was going to load into her cart; and if her calculations were correct, the final cost would be mere pennies.

Hayley skidded to a stop and began tossing boxes of dog food into the bottom of her cart. She almost cleared the shelf before she was off and running again. She veered around the corner to the next aisle, where she planned to work her upper-body strength by grabbing industrial-size bottles of laundry detergent. When she got there, another woman's cart was blocking her access.

"Excuse me, I'm trying to get to the laundry detergent!" Hayley said, trying not to sound bossy, but hyperaware she was on the clock.

The woman slowly turned around, holding two giant plastic bottles of All-Tempa-Cheer.

It was Candace Culpepper.

She was dressed in gray sweats, had her own stopwatch hanging around her neck, and wore a headband to keep her long brownish hair out of her eyes. She was also in Nike running shoes. She looked like she was in training for the Olympics.

And she was.

The Supermarket Olympics.

Hayley and Mona were not the only potential coupon-clipping queens in the market testing their abilities today.

Candace glared at Hayley, suddenly aware that

Hayley had indeed overheard her conversation with her fellow nurse Tilly and was now planning on horning her way in as competition. Candace dropped the two bottles of detergent in her cart with a loud bang and then turned to grab two more.

Hayley was silently counting in her head how many she needed. Maybe five or six to get the full discount. But it was quickly clear that Candace was going to upset her carefully planned strategy by grabbing them all.

"You mind leaving one or two for me, Candace?" Hayley asked.

Candace emptied the shelf of the Cheer and then started grabbing bottles of Tide. Hayley was not going to just stand around and let Candace outshop her. She stepped to the right in order to walk around Candace's cart and approach the detergent shelf from the other side, but Candace anticipated her move. With one foot Candace shoved her cart forward, blocking Hayley's maneuver. By the time Hayley forcefully pushed the cart to the side, Candace had her arms filled with all the available detergent and hurled them into her cart like a disc thrower.

Then she gripped the handle of her cart, knuckles whitening, and hissed at Hayley, "Get in my way again and I will take you down, bitch."

And then she was off, disappearing around the corner, heading for the meat-and-poultry section.

Hayley checked her watch. She had lost valuable time. Mona was probably already in the beverage aisle, hauling twelve-packs of soda off the shelf like she was stacking her lobster traps.

Think, Hayley, think.

She could still catch up if she made a beeline to the toothpaste and mouthwash. She had clipped coupons for about two dozen Crest and Listerine products. That would really add to her total, and end up costing her, after discounts, at tops maybe twenty-five cents.

Yes, she still had a fighting chance.

A pathway to victory.

Mona's Achilles' heel was subconsciously equating the bigger the product, the more it cost; so she was focused on heavy-duty items that filled her cart up faster. Hayley concentrated on lighter, more expensive products that would rack up her total faster and take up less room in her cart.

Hayley pushed her cart, rounding the corner at lightning speed, where the store owner, Ron Hopkins, was mopping up some spilled apple juice off the floor. Hayley gasped and tried to avert a collision by yanking the cart to the right. But she was too late and the wheels rolled right over Ron's foot. Hayley's cart tipped over on its side, sending all her items scattering across the floor.

Ron howled in pain and dropped his mop. Ron was a decent-looking man, but with a perpetual look of angst on his face. He never intended to be a small-business owner. He was kind of a screwup in school. Never had any real direction. So when his parents retired, it was either take over the family grocery store or enlist in the military. Kind of a no-brainer. His parents fled to the warmer climes of Florida, just like Hayley's own mother, and Ron was left to run the store. A job he detested.

He was planning to sell the store and use the money to travel, but then he met Lenora, a local middle-school teacher, and they married. Not long after that, Lenora gave birth to triplets, so Ron's dreams of blowing town and slumming around the world evaporated faster than Hayley's biweekly paycheck from the paper. Ron now had a family to feed. He put on a brave face. He loved his wife and children. But one night at Drinks Like A Fish, he let himself go, had one too many beers, and wept about the state of his life and how much he hated running the store and how things just didn't turn out the way he imagined.

Now that the kids were in high school, just one year behind Dustin, Ron saw a light at the end of the tunnel. Pretty soon the triplets would be off to college and Ron and Lenora would finally have the opportunity to finally travel a little bit. Ron still had hopes of selling the store and cashing out, so he decided to do some renovations in order to increase the value of the business.

Hayley was happy for him.

And sad for him.

Because at this moment Ron Hopkins was in an incredible amount of pain.

"Ron, I am so sorry. Are you all right?" Hayley asked, grabbing his arm.

Ron nodded. His face was flushed red, his eyes watery.

"I didn't even see you," Hayley said, simply because she didn't know what else to say. Secretly she was ticking off the precious seconds she was losing standing here talking to Ron.

"It's okay, Hayley. What's a couple of toes, right?"

Hayley stared at him, her mouth open in shock.

"I'm kidding. I think I'll live," Ron said, cracking a half smile. "But do you know how many collisions we've had in the store ever since that extreme coupon-clipping show announced they were going to shoot an episode here at the Shop 'n Save? It's been a free-for-all, and don't tell me you don't know what I'm talking about, Hayley. I know why you were in such a hurry. Half the town has been in here seeing how fast they can shop."

Hayley checked her watch again. She was done. There was no way she was going to beat Mona's time and total now. She sighed and turned to Ron.

"It's very exciting, you have to admit, Ron," Hayley said.

"You bet it is. A national promotion such as this is like hitting the lotto. Everyone's going to know this store. I even started a Twitter account so I can keep people informed about all the exciting things happening here. If I play my cards right, by this time next year, I'll be touring the ancient city of Petra in Jordan."

It was clear Ron saw *Wild and Crazy Couponing* as his ticket out of Dodge.

"What do you think of all the renovations, Hayley?"

"The place looks great, Ron. Really impressive," Hayley said, still smarting from mucking up her dry run at couponing. "Billy Parsons did a real nice job."

"I hear Billy was down at your place giving you an estimate to repair the roof on your garage the other day."

"How did you hear that?"

"It's Bar Harbor, Hayley."

Of course.

Small town.

No secrets.

"Well, let me tell you something. If this coupon-clipping show wasn't paying me a tidy sum to tape their episode here, I might be in bankruptcy court. Billy went way over budget and gouged me on everything. So be careful if you hire him."

"Not an issue, Ron. Even if I wanted to hire him, I just don't have the money. Which is a big reason I'm here with my coupons."

"Good luck to you, Hayley. I'd rather see you on the show than Candace Culpepper—the way she prances around this store, acting like she owns the place, barking orders at the stock boys and yelling at the cashiers. Sometimes I just want to snatch those coupons right out of her hand and shove them up her—"

"I can hear you," a deep, gravely, disembodied voice said.

Hayley and Ron swiveled their heads around, but there was nobody else in the aisle with them. Ron's eyes widened, a fearful look on his face. He reached over and pushed aside some bottles of Scope mouthwash so he and Hayley could look through to the next aisle. There, standing with an armful of Dove soap, was Candace Culpepper, and she did not look happy.

"It's a good thing I don't have a mean streak," Candace said, her voice lower and meaner than ever. "Or I'd be plotting ways to get back at both of you for all your trash talk."

Then she dumped the soap into her cart and moved on.

Hayley turned to Ron, who was physically shaking.

"Are you as scared of her as I am?" Ron asked in a meek voice.

"Of course not. She's all bark and no bite," Hayley said.

But Hayley didn't really believe one word she was saying.

No, Candace Culpepper had a vicious mean streak, and it was in everybody's best interest not to cross her.

Chapter 8

After listening to Mona gloat all the way back to Randy's house about her easy victory at the store, Hayley was feeling less confident about landing a coveted spot on *Wild and Crazy Couponing*. Once in the kitchen, she unloaded the ingredients for a beef stew she was going to prepare and take down to the Hollingsworth estate. Lex lived in a caretaker's house on the property, but she knew he was most likely at the hospital now, at his boss Edgar's bedside. However, visiting hours would be over at nine o'clock and he would probably just drive his truck back to the estate. That gave her plenty of time to whip up the stew and borrow Randy's Prius to delivery it to him personally. She knew he wasn't eating right. He never remembered to eat when something was worrying him.

Hayley couldn't relate. She always ate when she was worried. She also ate when she wasn't. Happy, mad, sad. Damn. Now that she thought about it, there wasn't one emotion or feeling that didn't cause her to want to eat. She just loved food.

Randy was working at the bar, so Hayley had the kitchen to herself as she prepared the stew for Lex. She checked her watch when she was done.

It was 9:15 P.M.

Lex was probably at home by now.

She ladled the stew into a large plastic Tupperware container and warmed some rolls, wrapping them up in Saran wrap and placing everything in one of her reusable bags. After feeding Leroy and leaving him a chew toy, she walked out the door to Randy's car. He was kind enough to leave it for her, in case she needed it, and bummed a ride to the bar from one of his employees.

Hayley drove the mile and a half to the sprawling Hollingsworth estate. The gate was open and she drove right through, veering left toward the caretaker's house. As she pulled up and looked through the home's window, she saw Lex in the kitchen. He was pacing back and forth, a hand over his mouth, his eye twitching. It was a habit she noticed whenever he got stressed out about something.

She hoped Edgar hadn't taken yet another turn for the worse.

When she rang the bell, and he answered the door, she instantly had a suspicion that Lex was not upset about his boss's failing health. In fact, his face was full of anger; he looked like he was ready to blow at any second.

"Did I come at a bad time?" Hayley asked, her voice almost squeaking.

"No," Lex lied. "Come in."

"I brought you dinner," she said with a smile.

He didn't smile back.

Lex ushered her inside. She noticed him glancing at the main house, Edgar's mansion, located across the property through a thicket of pine trees. Lex scowled and then slammed the door so hard behind her that she almost dropped the bag, sending the meal, which she had so lovingly prepared for him, sliding across the floor. Hayley managed to keep a grip on it as she jumped.

She knew Lex had a temper. It had gotten him into trouble before, but mostly during his heavy-drinking days. Hayley hadn't concerned herself with it much. As she crossed to the kitchen to unpack his dinner, she noticed a bottle of scotch on the table. It was opened and half of it was gone.

She averted her eyes from the half-empty scotch bottle and pulled a dinner plate out of the cupboard. Then she popped open the Tupperware container and began scooping out her stew onto the plate with a wooden spoon she found in a drawer. She could feel Lex's hot breath on the nape of her neck.

"You want to talk about it?" Hayley asked.

"Not really," Lex barked. The smell of alcohol on his breath wafted up into her nostrils.

"Something's gotten you riled up, Lex. You might as well tell me."

"Clark Hollingsworth showed up today."

"Edgar's nephew? He hasn't been here in years."

Clark Hollingsworth was the wealthy man's only living relative, with the exception of Edgar's twentysomething grandson, who was currently serving a life sentence in prison for murder.

Hayley had known Clark when they were kids and they attended the same summer camp. They were never close. In fact, she barely remembered what he looked like. He would only come to Bar Harbor with his parents—his mother was Edgar's sister—for a few weeks during the summer season. He would promptly be shipped off to a church-sponsored camp so he wouldn't be in his mother's hair while she visited all her relatives. It was the same camp where Sheila sent Hayley and Randy because Haylcy was a wild child and needed structure and Randy spent too much time in front of the TV watching cartoons during the summer months. Sheila was desperate to break him of the habit and expose him to a little sunshine.

Hayley loved the scenic camp on the lake and all the social interactions with the other kids. Randy, on the other hand, wrote a desperate letter to Sheila even before her station wagon had turned onto the main road back toward Bar Harbor after dropping him off. In his plea he threatened to hang himself if she didn't immediately return for him. He even took a Polaroid of his G.I. Joe dangling from his top-bunk bedpost, a piece of string serving as a noose, as an example of what the horrific scene might look like if she didn't come get him. Sheila called Randy's camp counselor and asked him to keep an eye on Randy. Their mother didn't make the two-hour drive back to the lake until the three weeks were over. By then, Randy had refused to shower out of protest and stank up the station wagon pretty bad. Sheila had to pull over into a gas station, drag him into the bathroom, and wipe all the dirt and grime off his face and arms.

Hayley had loved camp and had racked up at least a dozen new pen pals. She had even made a valiant effort to befriend the quiet, withdrawn Clark, but he didn't seem interested. She even stood up for him when some big, rowdy bullies picked on him, but even that didn't endear her to him. And that's pretty much all she remembered about him. She hadn't even heard his name again until now.

"He didn't even call first to let us know he was coming," Lex spat out. "Just showed up this morning, barking orders at my crew and yelling and pointing his finger in my face, saying he wouldn't tolerate me and my boys slacking off while his uncle was in the hospital. We'd been plowing and shoveling snow since five in the morning and just took a quick ten-minute coffee break, when he rolled up in a taxi and jumped out and started spewing insults at us, calling us a bunch of dead-beats!"

"That doesn't sound like the shy little boy I remember from summer camp," Hayley said.

"Well, he's not shy anymore. Prancing around here in his expensive winter coat and with those designer glasses that hung off the bridge of his nose like some snot-nosed fancy-pants professor!"

"Maybe he's just so worried about his uncle that he isn't being himself," Hayley said.

"You defending him, Hayley?" Lex said, eyes flaring.

Hayley threw her hands up in the air as a sign of surrender. "Nope. Not me. Guy sounds like a real jerk if you ask me!"

"You should've seen the way he talked to my guys. Made them feel so small and stupid, as if they were taking advantage of the boss and not busting their asses to get all the chores on the estate done. So if he does come home, he'd be proud of all their hard work."

"I'm so sorry, Lex."

"Then he marched inside the main house and started screaming at the household staff. I heard later he drove poor Ginnie Leighton to tears by complaining she hadn't changed the bedsheets properly. Ginnie's been Edgar's maid for years. A real sweetheart. Totally devoted to the old man. She didn't deserve that."

"What are you going to do?"

"Not much I can do until Edgar gets better," Lex said, pausing, his eyes drifting off and staring at nothing. "If he gets better."

Hayley walked up behind Lex and put her arms around his waist. She held him tightly, resting her chin on his back.

"I don't mean to rant and rave, but I got so riled up today and I just can't seem to shake it," Lex said softly.

"Have some beef stew. A hearty meal will make you feel better."

"Sure smells good, Hayley."

Lex was slowly calming down. Hayley released her grip and then went to work laying out the stew and bread for Lex's supper at a small table in a nook off the kitchen. Her phone in the back pocket of her jeans began buzzing with a text message.

She whipped it out and read the message.

It was from Randy: Get to the bar ASAP! Emergency!

Hayley's eyes popped open.

What could be happening now?

"Lex, I have to go. There's a situation at Randy's bar."

"Nothing serious, I hope."

"Me too."

She gave Lex a quick peck on the cheek and then hurried out the door, grabbing the railing on his front porch to make her way down the snowy, icy steps. She had no intention of falling flat on her back.

She jumped in Randy's Prius and sped off.

When Hayley walked into the bar, Mona was there, nursing a beer. A few locals were spread out at a couple of tables. One customer played darts, but it was otherwise a quiet night. Most people were at home warming up in front of a fire. Hayley didn't even bother taking off her coat. She scurried up to the bar.

"Randy, what is it?"

Randy was ringing up a patron's cocktail at the register. He counted out the correct change and slammed the cash drawer shut. He had a grave look on his face. He picked up the receiver of the bar phone and punched in some numbers.

"I just called home for my messages. You better listen to this one," Randy said.

Hayley grabbed the phone and listened.

After a beep there was a woman's cheery voice. "Hello, Hayley Powell, this is Christina. I work in the production office of *Wild and Crazy Couponing*, here in New York. Let me be the first to congratulate you on your selection to be a contestant on our show, which will be shot next Tuesday in your hometown of Bar Harbor, Maine, at the Shop 'n Save on Cottage Street."

Hayley glanced up to see Randy and Mona beaming from ear to ear. Randy was jumping up and down slightly on one foot, unable to contain his excitement.

She had listed Randy's home number on the application as an alternate contact number, since her cell service at his house was always spotty.

She couldn't believe they picked her.

She was Queen for a Day!

Now Hayley found herself jumping up and down. Randy raced out from behind the bar and enveloped his sister in a bear hug. They were both jumping up and down in unison. Hayley rolled her eyes over to Mona, who lifted her beer bottle and toasted Hayley before chugging down what was left of it.

"Mona, did you . . . ?"

"I'm first runner-up. That's what they called me, like I'm some airhead beauty pageant contestant. Though I do clean up pretty good and could probably win Miss Maine if I didn't have so much belly fat left over from popping out all those kids," Mona said.

"What does first runner-up mean?" Hayley asked.

"Anything happens to either of the two contestants they picked before the taping of the show, I take his or her place," Mona said.

"Well, do we know who else they picked?" Hayley asked, excited and breathless.

Randy shrugged. "Don't know. But if I were a betting man . . ."

"You *are* a betting man," Hayley said. "You drive

up to Bangor with me every weekend to play the slots."

"It has to be Candace Culpepper, don't you think?" Randy said.

Mona slammed her beer down on the polished-hardwood bar. "Looks like I'm going to have to take out Candace. Never liked that sourpuss anyway, ever since high school when she bad-mouthed me after that championship soccer game."

"Don't even joke about something like that, Mona," Hayley said, laughing.

"Who says I'm joking?" Mona said, gesturing to Randy to fetch her another beer. Her face was cold and expressionless. "I can't kill you. You're my best friend. That leaves Candace."

After a few seconds Mona broke into a smile and winked at Hayley and Randy.

Mona was only joking.

But the few customers in the bar seated behind her, eavesdropping, didn't see her smile or her wink. Just the back of her head.

And to them, she sounded dead serious.

Chapter 9

Hayley felt his lips press firmly against hers. His strong hands were gripping her upper arms, pulling her close to him. She thought he was going to suck her lips right off her face. She tried desperately to keep them shut, because her biggest fear at the moment was opening her mouth to scream and giving him the chance to thrust his purplish tongue down her throat. That was something she was never going to allow to happen.

He was tall and obviously worked out. He had a rock-hard chest, curly grayish hair, and a Tom Selleck mustache. He almost looked a bit like a younger version of Alex Trebek from *Jeopardy!* Which would make sense. They both made their living as game show hosts. But there was something seedier, less polished, about Drew Nickerson, who now held Hayley tightly and didn't seem to notice her trying to wriggle free from him.

It had all started so innocently.

* * *

Earlier that morning when Hayley arrived at work, Sal called her into his office and announced she would be interviewing Drew Nickerson, the dapper host of *Wild and Crazy Couponing.* Hayley was curious as to why she was qualified to interview a celebrity. Her job was food and cocktails. But ever since Hayley had fibbed her way into a hotel room last fall to meet her country music singing idol, Wade Springer, by posing as the *Island Times* entertainment reporter, Sal had decided she could fulfill that role on occasion. Hayley didn't protest because, after all, how many stars came to Bar Harbor? It's not like she would ever have to actually interview a famous personality. That was before *Wild and Crazy Couponing* had decided to tape an episode in town. Sal was elated at the prospect of one of his reporters, who also happened to be a contestant on the upcoming show, getting up close and personal with the suave, smooth-talking TV host.

Hayley just had no idea how "up close and personal" the interview would get.

Drew had arrived the night before and checked into the Captain's Arms, one of the few bed-and-breakfasts in town that was open during the winter. Sal gave Hayley a ride over at the appointed time of 11:00 A.M., giving Drew enough time to enjoy breakfast, lift his weights, which he always traveled with whenever he was on the road, shower and dress, gel his hair, and douse himself with some sweet-smelling but masculine cologne.

Hayley instructed Sal to swing by the B and B in thirty minutes to pick her up. She couldn't imagine her questions requiring any more time than that for Drew to answer. When she knocked on the door of his first-floor corner room, she could hear classical music playing inside. Vivaldi's *Four Seasons*. Something she actually could identify, which amazed her.

The door opened and Drew stood there. He was an impressive sight. Tall. Handsome. A jaw you could crack a walnut on. He smiled. The teeth were blinding. He would've made a much better Dudley Do-Right in a movie than Brendan Fraser. Except for his personality. He exuded arrogance. Entitlement. And he hadn't even spoken yet.

"Why are there no decent restaurants in this town?"

Suspicions confirmed.

"Well, Mr. Nickerson, it's February and most of the good ones are shut down for the season," Hayley said. "But if you come back in June or July, we have many fine establishments with creative gourmet menus—"

"I was told by some friends to come early before we taped the show to enjoy the pleasures of this quaint little town, and not a damn thing's open."

"Well, I'm sure your friends visited here in June or July or—"

"I thought Martha Stewart lived around here.

You would think if she had a house on the island, there would be some edible food somewhere!"

"Well, she's mostly up here during the summer, and like I said, it's February. . . ."

"I know what month it is. I'm not an imbecile."

"Well, things are pretty quiet around here this time of year."

"Even worse, I'm stuck staying in this dump. The sink clogs up, there is no mini bar, and the thread count on my sheets is lower than the owner's IQ."

This interview was not off to a good start.

But then something changed.

He fixed Hayley with a stare as if noticing her for the first time.

"Well, aren't you a cute little thing."

Hayley had been called "cute" before.

Even "thing."

But "little"?

Never.

Drew opened the door wider to allow Hayley to enter. A voice inside her head screamed at her to run, but she knew Sal would be disappointed if she failed to secure the interview. So she crossed the threshold with trepidation. The door slammed shut behind her.

Vivaldi's *Four Seasons* ended. She expected another classical piece to follow, but instead she heard Marvin Gaye singing his classic "Let's Get It On."

Drew Nickerson's iPod was on shuffle.

She spun around and he was staring at her with a wolfish grin.

"So, if, uh, you don't mind, I—I have a few qu-questions . . . ," Hayley stammered.

"Fire away," Drew said, moving forward and brazenly entering her personal space.

He was so close that her nose almost touched his Adam's apple.

"Okay, well, what made the show decide to tape an episode here in Bar Harbor?"

Drew exhaled his breath. Hayley was hit with a blast of mint. At least he brushed and gargled. For that, she was grateful.

"I've always been a fan of this beautiful little hamlet. I've spent many summers boating around the island, browsing the gift shops, enjoying your famous lobster rolls, but here, now, in the dead of winter, I am happy to report Bar Harbor is just as charming and inviting."

Hayley looked up at him, her mouth agape. "Didn't you just say . . . ?"

"That was off the record. This is on the record."

"Oh. Okay."

"In fact, there are fun little surprises to be found everywhere in this town," Drew said, stepping closer to Hayley as she tried casually backing away from him.

Did he just call her "little" again?

"Great. I think I've got what I need," Hayley said quickly, eyeing the door.

"That was just one question. I'm all yours. Ask me anything."

"No. I think that will do it."

"Then let me ask you a question."

"Uh, I really should go. . . ."

"Are you as hot with desire as I am?"

"Probably not, to be honest."

"Those adorable rosy cheeks tell another story."

"I'm just embarrassed for you, that's all."

"I know all about you shy small-town girls. You just need a little push."

He called her a "girl." Okay. Points for that one. No, on second thought, he was too disgusting. No points at all.

And that's when he grabbed Hayley by the arms and rammed his lips into hers, and now she was caught in an impossibly grotesque situation.

Hayley would've preferred Alex Trebek making a pass at her.

Not this scumbag.

She struggled in his strong grip. It just made him even more excited.

He was backing her toward the blue-and-white canopy bed.

She reached up with her right hand and grabbed his dimpled Dudley Do-Right chin, yanking it down hard. His tongue snaked out of his mouth; he shut his eyes tightly, as if he assumed this was foreplay.

Hayley grabbed hold of his tongue and pulled hard. His eyes suddenly popped open in surprise and he tried saying something. He couldn't, though, because Hayley was holding on to his tongue like some slippery, flopping fish on the deck of Mona's boat. When she let go, he retracted his tongue and immediately began rolling it around in his mouth to check for damage.

That's when Hayley slapped him.

Hard.

He stumbled back, caught off guard, throwing a hand to his cheek.

"What the hell do you think you're doing?" he wailed.

"Teaching you some manners," Hayley said. "I'm sure where you come from, girls fall over themselves to get your attention. Here in Maine, we don't give a rat's ass about how much money you have or how many people know you."

He stood there silently, sizing her up and down, deciding on his next move.

Hayley didn't wait for it.

She whipped her head around and hightailed it out of there.

She had only been in the room for ten minutes. Sal wasn't scheduled to swing by and pick her up for another twenty. So she trudged on foot through the mud and snow back to the office.

She had really done it this time. Her genius plan to win the show, collect the cash prize, and pay off all her hefty expenses was suddenly in jeopardy.

Now that she had completely alienated the host of *Wild and Crazy Couponing*, who would inevitably discover that she was also one of the two contestants competing on the show, she was totally screwed.

Because Drew Nickerson was definitely the type of man who would not soon forget she had done him wrong. And it was more than likely he would find a way to sabotage her chances of even being on the show, let alone winning.

Chapter 10

After her ill-fated interview with the detestable Drew Nickerson, Hayley was too upset at the office to concentrate on her next column, so she put it off until that evening. She knew Randy would be working late tending the bar, so she would have the whole house to herself. After a bowl of her leftover beef stew, Hayley washed the dishes and sat down in front of the crackling fire with her laptop. She stared at the blank screen while Leroy slept next to her, snoring softly.

She hadn't even thought about a topic. Hayley knew she was the queen of procrastination, but this column was due today, which technically gave her another three hours before midnight, so she had to focus.

Meals on a budget. Meals on a budget.

She barely had begun typing when the house phone rang. Hayley sighed, stood up, and picked up the receiver. She checked the caller ID. It was Randy calling from Drinks Like A Fish.

Hayley picked up. "Slow night? You bored and calling to bug me?"

"No, sis, this is bad."

Hayley's heart nearly stopped beating as she clenched the receiver more tightly. "What? What is it now?"

"Officer Donnie was in here again tonight, calming his nerves with a beer, when he got a call on his radio."

Hayley took a deep breath. "What?"

"Bad accident on Mount Desert Street. Two-car collision."

"Anyone hurt?"

"I'm not sure. He ran out of here so fast. But one of the drivers was Imogen Tubbs."

Imogen Tubbs. Hayley had a soft spot for the eighty-five-year-old church organist. Seven years ago her husband had passed away of natural causes. He was ninety-three. Because they had no children and had been married for over sixty years, most people in town naturally assumed his loss would be too much for her and she would wither and die soon after. Imogen, however, surprised everyone. She poured her energies into fundraising for the church and feeding poor people in need all over the island. She was a spitfire and didn't allow her age to hinder her in any way. She powered around town in her giant 1982 Cadillac, driving as if she were racing in Le Mans. There were a few whispers that it might be a good idea for the police to confiscate her driver's license, given Imogen's advanced age, but she swept that ridiculous talk aside as malicious gossip. She had too much to do and didn't need to waste her time thinking about her detractors. Hayley had always liked Imogen.

"Who was in the other car?" Hayley asked.

"I don't know. That's all I got before he left."

"Thanks, Randy."

Hayley hung up and immediately called the hospital.

Evelyn Tate, the hospital receptionist still on duty, answered the phone. "Bar Harbor Hospital, how may I help you?"

"Hi, Evelyn, it's Hayley Powell."

"Hello, Hayley. Lex isn't here. He left ten minutes ago. I'm afraid there has been no change in Mr. Hollingsworth's condition. The doctors insisted Lex go home and get some rest and come back in the morning."

"That's not why I'm calling, Evelyn. I need to know if anyone was brought in by ambulance in the last hour."

"Yes. Mrs. Tubbs. Poor thing. Rammed into a car on Mount Desert Street. I heard she was driving on the wrong side of the road. She's eighty-five, you know."

"Is she going to be all right?"

"I don't know. I was on my break when they brought her in. I just heard the nurses talking."

"I'm coming right over," Hayley said, hanging up and scurrying over to the closet to grab her coat and boots.

When Hayley rushed through the doors of the hospital twenty minutes later, Evelyn was still at the reception desk. She waved her on up to the third floor, where they had taken Mrs. Tubbs. Upon reaching the nurses' station, Hayley was greeted by a smiling Tilly McVety.

"Congratulations, Hayley. I hear you were picked to be a contestant on my favorite show, *Wild and Crazy Couponing*. I can't believe they're coming to Bar Harbor! It's the most exciting thing that's ever happened to me, and it's not even happening to *me*!"

"Tilly, I was hoping you could tell me—"

"I'm just dying to get a glimpse of that gorgeous hunk of a man Drew Nickerson. I wonder if he's as handsome in person as he is on TV?"

Hayley didn't have time to give her the lowdown: Drew Nickerson was about as charming as Officer Donnie's case of shingles.

"Tilly, I'm here to see Mrs. Tubbs. I heard she was brought in here by ambulance. Do you have any idea how she's doing?"

"Oh, she's fine," Tilly said, picking up a file folder and thumbing through it. "Do you believe they still let her drive? They're checking to see if she has any broken bones."

"Can I see her?"

"Oh, sure. She's right across the hall. Room 305."

"Thanks."

"I know Candace is one of my coworkers, but I really hope you beat her," Tilly said in a whisper, followed by a burst of giggles. "Don't tell her I said that."

So it was finally confirmed.

Her competition was Candace.

Hayley smiled and then crossed to room 305 and gently knocked on the door.

"Come in," a frail, raspy voice said.

Hayley pushed open the door. As she entered, she saw Imogen Tubbs in a pale blue hospital gown, sitting up in her bed, clutching her red purse to her bosom. Imogen was usually immaculate, with perfect hair tied in a bun and flawless makeup. She had been crying, so her makeup was smudged and wisps of her fine white hair were flowing in all different directions. She looked smaller than Hayley remembered. Almost helpless.

"Don't let them take away my driver's license, Hayley. Officer Donnie tried to take it out of my purse, but I grabbed my purse back from him and swatted him in the face with it. His nose started to bleed. Do you think I'm going to have to go to jail for assault?"

"I don't think Officer Donnie wants to lock you up, Mrs. Tubbs. He's probably more embarrassed that you got the better of him. How are you feeling?"

"I'm perfectly fine. But the doctors think I may have a broken bone or two. I just want to go home."

"Do you remember what happened?"

"I don't remember much. I went to practice on my organ at home for Sunday's service, but I forgot my music sheets at the church. I decided to drive back over there and pick them up, and the rest is a blur. I'm so confused. Do you think I have early onset of Alzheimer's?"

Early onset? The woman was eighty-five!

Hayley shook her head. "You're as sharp as ever, Mrs. Tubbs. Trust me."

"I do remember the roads being just so dang slippery, and I thought I might have to pull over. But then the next thing I knew, I was being loaded into the back of an ambulance by that sweet paramedic, Jay Higgins. He's so big and strong and quite the looker. If I was ten years younger . . ."

Ten years younger?

Jay was thirty-seven.

Mrs. Tubbs reached out and squeezed Hayley's hand. "Please, Hayley, you have to go over to my house and check on Blueberry."

Blueberry was her Persian Blue cat, hence the name.

"Don't worry," Hayley said softly. "I'll make sure he's okay."

"He's probably torn up my couch with his claws—he's so worried about me. I never leave him alone for this long. Oh, and while you're there, could you also pick up some personal items for me?

My makeup, a hairbrush, a few magazines from my coffee table? There's no telling how long they're going to keep me here."

"Absolutely," Hayley said, bending down and kissing Mrs. Tubbs on the forehead. "I'll take care of everything."

Hayley had a soft spot for feisty old women like Mrs. Tubbs. Perhaps it was because she was hoping to be just like her someday.

Hayley walked out of the room and past the nurses' station. Tilly McVety was on the phone.

"She's over two hours late for her shift and I can't reach her," Tilly said breathlessly, her face scrunched up with concern.

The elevator doors opened and Hayley stepped inside. As the doors closed again, she managed to hear Tilly say, "It's so unlike Candace not to at least call with an excuse."

Hayley left the hospital to make the three-block trek to Imogen Tubbs's house. Trudging through the snow, bundled up, breathing in the blistering cold night air, she suddenly realized Mrs. Tubbs was Candace Culpepper's neighbor. Hayley was burning with curiosity as to why Candace blew off work. Maybe after feeding Blueberry and packing up a few of Mrs. Tubbs's belongings, she would peek inside Candace's windows to see if she was just playing hookey from work.

Not because she was nosy.

Just out of neighborly concern.

Yeah, right.

As Hayley rounded the corner onto Hancock Street, she noticed all the lights on in Mrs. Tubbs's house. Candace's house next door, on the other hand, was pitch-black. Clearly, nobody was home. As she approached Mrs. Tubbs's driveway, she noticed something on the edge of Candace's snow-covered lawn, like a fallen tree branch. However, since the streetlight closest to the house was out, she couldn't be sure.

As she got closer, she stopped suddenly, nearly losing her balance on the icy sidewalk.

Was it a deer?

What was it?

It was so dark that Hayley couldn't see much except the outline in the snow. She fished inside her coat pocket and fetched her iPhone. She pressed the button and a light snapped on, illuminating the figure in the snow.

It wasn't a deer.

It was a person.

Facedown in the snow, his arms and legs splayed as if making a snow angel.

Hayley stepped closer.

The head was turned to the side, facing her.

It wasn't a him.

It was a her.

It was Candace Culpepper.

Her glassy, dead eyes stared at Hayley.

Hayley tried to scream, but it got caught in her

throat. It was so cold that she was having trouble breathing.

As the winter winds kicked up, coupons began flying up from the ground like a flock of birds disturbed by an approaching car.

And then the light from her phone caught a glint of something.

A large pair of industrial-size scissors sticking out of Candace's back.

Island Food & Spirits
by
Hayley Powell

All my closest friends will tell you that I am never one to toot my own horn. So they're going to be shocked today when they read this because I'm about to indulge myself and brag a bit. Okay. Here we go. I can say with certainty that I am a pretty darn good coupon clipper.

Over the past couple of years, I have been honing my skills, and—dare I say it—I am now at a competition level. And I am so thrilled to be able to tell you that I have been selected to compete on that breathlessly exciting cable-TV game show *Wild and Crazy Couponing*! Be still, my heart! They're going to tape an episode right here in our very own Bar Harbor, Maine! Needless to say, I am just beside myself to finally have a venue to showcase my impressive couponing talent!

However, it wasn't always like this. Not by a long shot. A couple of years ago, I was sitting in my living room where I watched a TV show about couponing. I found myself mesmerized, watching all these obsessed, bargain-hunting families saving huge amounts of cash and filling their houses with giant stockpiles of practically free stuff. Just looking at the tall metal shelves in their garages or extra bedrooms piled high with tons of toilet paper, paper towels, toothpaste, snacks, pastas, and so much more just about made me swoon with excitement! No more worrying about natural disasters or nuclear attacks! These families were fully stocked and prepared! My head was spinning with thoughts of how much money I could save and how much less time I would have to spend at the grocery store.

How hard could couponing be? Especially since every year, the whole week before Thanksgiving, Mona and I pore over every sale flyer that we can find, chart our driving course from store to store in Bangor, map out the aisles for the fastest way to get to the items that we want, and even schedule in a break or two. Then, the day after Thanksgiving, when most people are still stuffed with turkey and unable to move, Mona and I are in her truck by five in the morning, armed with thermoses of coffee, home-made blueberry muffins, and our Christmas shopping lists. We head off to the stores; our lists are mapped out with military-like precision, to make the most of "Black Friday" shopping. By the end of the day, we're tired, happy, and completely loaded down with this year's Christmas gifts, congratulating each other on the way home on a job well done as we immediately begin strategizing for next year.

So couponing seemed like a natural for me. I began clipping stacks of them from wherever I could find them. Just browsing all the items I could save money on kept me clipping away and preparing for my first shopping trip later in the week. Finally, when I felt I had enough to work with, I marched into the Shop 'n Save with my envelope stuffed with coupons and visions of dollar signs dancing in my head.

I grabbed a cart and practically did a jig as I headed up and down the aisles, boldly tossing items into my cart. I made a beeline for the meat department and, sure enough, there was a sale on ground beef. I had at least four coupons! I had never been able to buy lean ground beef for the amount I would pay today. It was a miracle!

Since this was my first shopping trip with all these coupons, I overprepared by bringing fifty dollars to spend, because I figured I wasn't practiced enough to walk away with hundreds of dollars' worth of groceries for just ten or twenty dollars. I would have to work up to that. But in my head I was calculating the amount I would save with the coupons and was feeling very confident and excited. With all the extra money, I just might eventually be able to afford for the living room that new recliner, with its very own cup holder, I had been coveting at Merrill's Furniture in Ellsworth.

With my cart overflowing, I patiently waited my turn in line, and then began unloading my haul. Bethany, the cashier, kept ringing up my purchases until I proudly set down my last item with a flourish on the conveyor belt, and Bethany hit the total button.

The grand total came to $353.42. I think my jaw hit the floor. But then Bethany asked if I had any coupons today and I said, perhaps a tad too loudly, "Why, yes, Bethany, I do!" I handed over my stack of coupons to her while glancing around with a big grin on my face. That's when I noticed there were more than the usual number of people standing around the checkout line. I may have mentioned to a few people how good I was at this couponing thing and I was going to save hundreds of dollars, so that may have drawn a few spectators.

At first, I was elated when I saw the total begin to drop dramatically, but then as she kept scanning, my heart started pounding. The stack of coupons was dwindling fast, but my grand total was still over three hundred bucks. I didn't dare even look at the small crowd gathered to witness my miraculous feat. I watched, horrified, as Bethany swiped the last coupon through and hit the total button again: $298.18.

Inside, I was screaming. And as I looked around at all the startled faces staring at me, I suddenly realized I wasn't screaming to myself. I was actually screaming out loud. My high-pitched screeching even made a baby in the nearby express checkout line cry. What in the world was I going to do? Where did I go wrong? Well, I would later learn I needed to focus on the sale amounts of products and practice using double coupons. But that wasn't going to help me now when I only had a measly fifty dollars in my wallet.

At that moment the automatic door to the store swished open and in walked an angel from heaven. Well, at least an angel from down the street. One of my best friends, Liddy, stopped in the doorway and surveyed the silent crowd of gawkers. She then took in the frozen, panicked look on my face and rushed over to see what was happening. After I quickly explained my predicament, Liddy opened her wallet and paid my balance, and then we left the store, almost forgetting the huge cart of groceries I had just bought. Despite this minor setback, in my head I was already planning my next couponing adventure, hoping the next time would yield better results! And I'm happy to report it did.

The upshot from that first day was how much I did save on twelve pounds of ground beef, which I could freeze and use throughout the winter. So as part of our budget-friendly meals for today, it's going to be "Taco Tuesday"! And nothing goes better with Mexican food than a large pitcher of jalapeno margaritas. These will definitely help you ward off the chill in the air!

Jalapeno Margaritas

<u>Ingredients</u>
1 thin slice of jalapeno
1 handful of celery leaves
6 ounces fresh lime juice
1 spoonful confectioner's sugar
16 ounces of your favorite
   tequila
8 ounces of orange liqueur
Salt for rimming the glasses

In a blender add the jalapeno, celery leaves, fresh lime juice, and sugar and blend well. Mix with the tequila and orange liqueur in a pitcher; chill and serve on the rocks with salted rimmed glasses. Salute!

There is nothing more comforting than homemade tacos to warm you up on a cold February night in Maine. You can double or even triple this recipe depending on how many people you want to feed:

Taco Tuesday's Warm-Me-Up Tacos

<u>Ingredients</u>
2 tablespoons canola oil
¾ cups chopped onions
1 pound ground beef
2 to 3 cloves garlic, chopped
1 tablespoon chili powder
2 teaspoons cumin
2 teaspoons ground coriander
½ teaspoon kosher salt
½ teaspoon ground pepper
8-ounce can of tomato sauce
1 fresh jalapeno, seeded and minced (I like to keep some seeds for heat)

In a skillet heat your canola oil on medium heat and then add the chopped onions and minced jalapenos, cook for 2 minutes, then add the chopped garlic and cook one minute. Add the ground beef, breaking it up with a wooden spoon, and cook until browned.

When the ground beef is browned, drain off the grease and add the rest of the ingredients, stirring well to incorporate them, then simmer on medium heat for 10 to 15 minutes for flavors to meld together.

Use your favorite taco shells or flour tortillas and your favorite taco toppings and enjoy your own Cinco de Mayo in February!

Chapter 11

When the Bar Harbor police cruiser pulled up to the crime scene and Officer Donnie stepped out, Hayley audibly gasped. Donnie's face was pockmarked all over with red splotches. It looked like his face was swelling.

"Donnie, are you all right?" Hayley asked, touching his arm with her hand, but quickly retracting it out of fear that whatever he had was infectious.

"Isn't it obvious?" Donnie said, scratching his face. "I'm breaking out in hives. This hasn't happened since I was a kid. I used to get them before I had to take a geometry test."

Yes, stress often caused hives. And Officer Donnie had been under an incredible amount of it since taking over for Chief Sergio Alvares.

"So, what happened here, Hayley?" Donnie asked, still scratching.

Hayley glanced down at Candace Culpepper's body, the pair of scissors sticking out of her back.

"Um, well, Donnie, I think it's fair to say there's been a murder."

Donnie looked down and nodded. "Yes, looks like it."

Hayley waited for Donnie to take charge, but he just stood there, averting his eyes away from the body and stepping back.

"Did you call forensics, Donnie? Are they on their way here?"

"No, I should have somebody do that."

"Yes, I think that would be a good idea," Hayley said.

Donnie pulled out his cell phone, but he just held it in front of his face for a few moments, staring at it. "I don't know the number. Do you know the number?"

"Why don't you call the station and have the dispatcher contact them? They're going to need to do a full sweep of the crime scene."

"Right. I'll do that. Meantime, maybe you ought to get those scissors out of her back. I'd do it myself, but I've never actually seen a dead body before, and it's really kind of freaking me out."

"Donnie, if we remove the scissors, then we're tampering with the crime scene, and that's not really a good thing, so let's not touch anything, okay?"

"Yeah, okay, that makes sense," Donnie said, holding the phone to his ear, his hand shaking. "Damn, my face itches!"

Hayley was still in a state of shock over Candace's

dead body lying only a few feet away from her. Who would commit such a horrific violent act? How could anyone literally stab her in the back?

Donnie mumbled something to his dispatcher and nodded before ending his call and stuffing his cell phone back in his pocket. Then he just stared numbly at Hayley.

"Donnie?"

Nothing.

"Donnie?"

He finally snapped out of his dazed state. "Yeah? What?"

"Now that forensics is on their way, you might want to think about cordoning off the crime scene with police tape."

"Is that the yellow tape with the black writing on it that says something like 'Do Not Cross,' or words to that effect?"

"Yes, that would be correct."

"I don't think I brought any. You think maybe the hardware store sells it? Are they still open this time of night?"

"Probably not. But perhaps you could check in the trunk of your cruiser? There might be some in there."

Donnie thought about this for a second, then nodded, and crossed over to the police car and popped open the trunk. He peered inside.

Sure enough, there was a roll of tape in plain view. He scooped it up and handed it to Hayley.

"You think you could do it? My hands are a little shaky."

Hayley nodded and took the tape from him and began unraveling it.

"Damn. A car crash and a murder, all in one night. We might as well be living in Boston. This is just too much for a small town."

What he meant to say was this was all too much for *him*.

Cars began arriving on the scene—mostly curious onlookers who had heard about the murder from their police scanners, just like the one Hayley kept on top of her refrigerator to monitor all the goings-on in town.

When she finished tying the yellow crime-scene tape around the trees surrounding Candace's body, she walked back over to Donnie, who was yelling at the gawking residents to step back and keep out of the way. His face was getting redder and redder, and not just from the hives.

Hayley spoke softly, hoping not to make his meltdown even worse. "Why don't you question me now, Donnie."

"What? Why?"

Hayley sighed. "Because I'm the one who discovered the body."

"Oh, right," Donnie said, staring at her blankly, not exactly sure how to proceed.

Hayley decided to take the lead. "I was visiting Mrs. Tubbs at the hospital after her accident earlier tonight and she asked me to come by and feed her cat and pick up a few of her belongings that she might need. When I arrived, I saw a figure lying facedown in the snow and I immediately thought it was Candace."

"The body is facedown. How could you tell it was Candace Culpepper?"

Finally.

A reasonable question.

"I recognized her jacket, and her white pants are obviously part of a nurse's uniform, and I found her body on her front lawn, so I thought it was safe to assume it was Candace."

"Have you ever heard of the phrase 'When you assume, you make an ass of you and me'?"

"Yes, Donnie, but her face was also turned in my direction, so I was pretty sure it was Candace."

Donnie inched closer to the body, knelt down, and was about to turn the head toward him before Hayley stopped him.

"To reiterate, Donnie, I don't think it's a smart idea to touch the body just yet."

Donnie glowered at her, but he nodded; then he stood back up. "Don't matter. I'm pretty sure it's Candace Culpepper."

"I think you might be right, Donnie," Hayley said. "Do you have any more questions for me?"

"No. Not at the moment. But don't be thinking of leaving town just yet."

"I live here, Donnie. I'm not going anywhere."

"I know. But sometimes suspects take off without warning, to avoid being arrested."

"Am I a suspect?"

"Everyone is a suspect, or at least a person of integrity."

"'Person of interest'?"

"Yeah, isn't that what I said?"

Well, at least Officer Donnie was like Sergio in one respect. Mixing up his words. But fortunately for Sergio, English was not his first language, so he had a decent excuse. As for Officer Donnie, well, it was best just to assume his nerves were getting the best of him.

However, when you assume . . .

Chapter 12

When Hayley finally made it back to the Bar Harbor Hospital with a tote bag filled with some makeup, a nightgown, and a few books of crossword puzzles for Mrs. Tubbs, word had spread fast about the fate of Candace Culpepper. There was an eerie silence in the main lobby as Hayley entered through the automatic sliding glass doors and approached the reception desk.

Evelyn Tate was at her station, dabbing at her eyes with a tissue, a lost look on her face.

"Isn't it just terrible, Hayley? Candace, of all people? Such a kindhearted, sweet woman. She just radiated goodness and light!"

Hayley nodded, not quite sure what to say. "Yes. Terrible. Just terrible."

"The patients are simply devastated. She was their favorite nurse in the whole hospital. Always going that extra mile to make them feel comfortable."

Now that was a stretch. Hayley knew for a fact that Candace had at least a dozen patient complaints lodged against her for her rude manner and penchant for telling the sick and tired to stop feeling sorry for themselves.

Evelyn buried her face in her balled-up tissue as Hayley awkwardly reached over and patted her on the back before she hurried to the elevator.

When Hayley arrived at the nurses' station near Mrs. Tubbs's private room, Tilly McVety was also in tears, shaking her head. Hovering around were a few of the night shift nurses, all of them in a state of shock.

Hayley tried to slip past them, unnoticed, hoping to leave them to their grieving, but Tilly spotted her and grabbed a fistful of her winter coat.

"Oh, Hayley, tell me this isn't happening! Tell me Candace isn't really dead!"

Before Hayley could respond, Tilly threw her arms around her and began weeping uncontrollably, dampening Hayley's coat with tears and phlegm.

Again, the only thing Hayley could think to do was gently and awkwardly pat Tilly on the back. She didn't dare say anything, because she knew it would come out wrong and make her look insensitive or unconcerned about Candace's sudden death.

The fact was, Hayley was gravely concerned. She just didn't buy all this outpouring of emotion from

Candace's coworkers. They all knew she was not the warmest person and had a vicious competitive streak. But perception always changes with someone's passing and Hayley accepted that.

"She was such a free spirit. So happy and calm about everything. She never let anything get to her," Tilly said, sobbing.

Except competing in an extreme coupon-clipping show and wanting to win at all costs.

No, it was best not to bring that up.

"I know, Tilly. So tragic," Hayley said, trying to wriggle out of her iron-like grip. But Tilly wouldn't let go. Finally, after what seemed like an eternity, Tilly relaxed her arms. Hayley leapt at the opportunity to scoot away from her. Tilly eyed her suspiciously, like she was gauging Hayley's sincerity about losing such a dear, beloved friend.

Hayley sensed this and slowly shook her head. "Such a senseless loss."

She was being honest. It was senseless. What could have possibly driven someone to take a pair of industrial-size scissors and plunge them right into Candace's back? It was so vicious. So cold. She just wished Sergio were not in Brazil and could properly investigate, instead of relying on a nervous rookie with a case of shingles.

"I better get this bag to Mrs. Tubbs," Hayley said softly. "She's probably wondering what's taking me so long."

"Oh, dear. Mrs. Tubbs, she was Candace's neighbor. This is going to kill her," Tilly cried, scurrying off to the ladies' room to find some toilet paper to cry into.

When Hayley entered Mrs. Tubbs's room, the octogenarian was sitting up in bed, watching the local news on TV. They were already reporting the murder and trying to interview Officer Donnie, who seemed to be running away from the scene to avoid the cameras.

"Who would do such a thing, Hayley?" Mrs. Tubbs said, staring at the television.

"I don't know, Mrs. Tubbs," Hayley said. "But I'm sure the police will find out."

Mrs. Tubbs gave Hayley a disbelieving look. "If you think Dennis the Menace there is going to solve anything, then you need a reality check, my dear."

Hayley smiled for the first time since stumbling across Candace's dead body.

"I hate to say this, but I feel a lot safer here in the hospital than at home with a mad killer on the loose in the neighborhood," Mrs. Tubbs said, pulling a baby blue hospital-issued blanket up over her chest. "You never know who could be next."

"Well, I'm not sure this was a random killing," Hayley said. Her eyes were fixed on the television as the news broadcast showed a picture of Candace in her nurse's uniform.

"Do you think it was somebody she knew?"

"Maybe. I don't know. You lived next door to her. Did you ever see her fighting with anyone?"

"No. Never. But then again, I never saw her too

much. She worked all the time, and I go to bed at eight, right after *Jeopardy!* before she even gets home. And I take out my hearing aid and can sleep through a category-five hurricane."

Hayley couldn't help but focus on the fact that the killer used a pair of scissors to stab her—scissors that someone would use to clip coupons. There was an irony about the murder weapon that kept gnawing at her.

Mrs. Tubbs reached out and touched Hayley's arm. "Hayley, I'm so worried."

"Don't worry, Mrs. Tubbs. You're perfectly safe here."

"No. I'm not talking about the murder. Officer Donnie, that little prick, came by again, insisting I'm too old to drive and saying he's going to take away my license one way or the other. What will I do without my car, Hayley? I need to get to the grocery store, the bank, the post office."

Hayley resisted the urge to ask Mrs. Tubbs, in the event that the police did confiscate her license, if she would be willing to sell her car real cheap. No, that would not be appropriate at this time, not when Mrs. Tubbs was on the verge of tears and feeling so vulnerable.

Still, it was something to keep in the back of her mind.

"I'm sure once they review all the facts of the accident, you'll be cleared to drive again. And if not, you have lots of friends. We'll all pitch in and get you where you need to go."

Hayley handed Mrs. Tubbs the tote bag. "Now I got you everything you requested. If you need me to run to the store in the morning before I go to work, I'd be happy to pick up whatever you need."

"But tomorrow is Saturday."

"Sal's making us work because of the snow day earlier this week."

"Slave driver."

"Tell me about it," Hayley said, chuckling.

"What about Blueberry? Did you see Blueberry when you were at the house?"

"No. But I left a big bowl of food and some water in the pantry off the kitchen. He should be fine until I can get back over there tomorrow."

"He was probably hiding under the bed. I'm sure he's so scared right now. He doesn't know what's happening and why I'm not there. I'm so worried about him. Hayley, please don't leave him alone in that cold, dark house."

"I'm not sure what I can—"

"Can you take him home with you? Just until I get out of the hospital?"

"Well, the thing is, Mrs. Tubbs, I'm not staying at my house right now. I'm actually at my brother's, and—"

"That big, rambling house on the shore? Oh, Blueberry would love staying there. Exploring all the nooks and crannies. Oh, please, Hayley, I'm begging you. Is your brother allergic to cats?"

"No, it's not that. I'm just not sure if he wants me to bring home . . ."

Mrs. Tubbs's eyes brimmed with tears; her finger twisted around her thin, gray hair; she looked so helpless and worried.

Hayley just hated herself for falling for it, but she found herself saying, "Sure. I'll go by there now and pick him up."

Suddenly the tears were gone and Mrs. Tubbs was smiling, satisfied her performance got her exactly what she wanted. "Thank you, Hayley. You're a peach."

Hayley tried Randy's cell to warn him of their four-legged houseguest, but he didn't pick up. He was still at the bar, busy serving the rowdy fishermen blowing off steam after a long week of hauling traps.

But Hayley wasn't too worried.

Not really.

How much trouble could one cat be?

Worst. Decision. Ever.

Unfortunately, Hayley underestimated the bloody battle it would take to get Mrs. Tubbs's fat, nasty Persian cat, with satanic yellow eyes, out from under the bed and into a plastic carrier. Making kissing sounds and reaching under the bed to coax him out was her first mistake. Blueberry hissed and howled and used Hayley's arms for a scratching post.

Hayley was about to give up, but then went through Mrs. Tubbs's kitchen drawers and found some Christmas-themed oven mitts with reindeer embroidered on them. She slipped them on and was able to get a grip on the struggling ball of fur. Getting him into the carrier took another agonizing thirty minutes with him slipping out of her covered arms and racing around the house. Luckily, Blueberry's massive weight slowed him down considerably and Hayley managed to corner him with the carrier and force him inside. He continued hissing as she slammed the metal door of the cage shut and locked it into place.

She was out of breath by the time she secured Blueberry and finally got Randy on the phone to pick her up on his way home from the bar. Randy was more than a bit wary about hosting a demon cat in his house. He relented, however, because there wasn't much choice in the matter, since neither of them wanted Mrs. Tubbs to worry.

The one other factor neither considered was Leroy. Leroy loved chasing cats, and there was some concern that he might terrorize the poor kitty. But that theory was quickly put to rest when the carrier was unloaded and Blueberry flew out like a shot. Rather impressive for such a huge, flabby cat.

No, Leroy was not going to scare Blueberry.

First of all, Blueberry was almost twice Leroy's size.

And the moment Leroy came running at Blueberry, full of excitement and expecting a fun romp around the house, the cat's claws came out, the teeth were bared, and Blueberry slashed Leroy across the nose.

Leroy went yelping in the other direction, and the demon cat followed him, slowly, methodically, determined to keep the tables turned on this rather annoying yapping little adversary.

Keep him on the run.

That was Blueberry's plan.

And it worked.

Leroy hid behind a door as Blueberry finally turned away and decided to get comfy on Randy's expensive, hand-printed Oriental rug near the fireplace.

And that's where he settled before peeing all over it.

Chapter 13

Hayley was almost relieved to have to work on Saturday, if only to get out of Randy's house, where Blueberry was wreaking havoc like some evil presence in those *Paranormal Activity* movies—except this wasn't some unseen apparition moving furniture and flipping lights on and off. No, this was a twenty-five-pound cat—right out in the open—with killer claws, and a really bad attitude, who was determined to keep everyone around him on edge.

Hayley felt bad about slipping out of the house just as Randy stepped in yet another pool of urine with his bare foot on his way to make a pot of coffee in the kitchen. Leroy, meanwhile, was hiding under the bed in Randy's room, whimpering softly, terrified Blueberry might sniff him out.

After trudging through the snow to the office, Hayley blew through the front door; her cheeks were red from the bitter cold. She found Bruce sitting at her desk, typing on her computer. He didn't even bother to look up as she shook off her coat and kicked off her winter boots.

"Before you ask, I didn't pick up any muffins at Morning Glory," Hayley said, blowing into her hands to warm up her face. "Maybe I'll go later. It's finally supposed to warm up today."

Bruce shrugged and just kept on typing.

"Is something wrong with your own computer?" Hayley asked.

"Yeah, it's on the fritz and I want to file this story by noon so we can upload it on the website."

"Okay," Hayley said, crossing to pour herself a cup of coffee. "Is Sal in yet?" she asked, searching for the vanilla creamer. She noticed the last few packets were ripped open and empty. She glanced over as Bruce stopped typing momentarily to slurp his Styrofoam cup of light brown coffee.

Guess who used up the last of the creamer?

Hayley sighed and decided that today she would refrain from comment and just take her coffee black.

"He's on his way. He wanted to get an interview with Eddie Phippen and decided to do it himself," Bruce said, setting his coffee down and continuing to type furiously.

"Who's Eddie Phippen?"

"The producer of that extreme coupon-clipping show you're going to be on. He flew into Bangor last night and just arrived on the island this morning," Bruce said, stopping to read over his last paragraph.

He grimaced and then started tapping the delete button to erase his last sentence.

"I suppose he knows all about Candace Culpepper's murder," Hayley said.

"Duh. Everybody does, Hayley. He's thinking about canceling the whole show."

"What?" Hayley said, her heart nearly stopping.

She knew it might be the right thing to do, considering the controversy surrounding the murder—and, of course, out of respect for Candace, who was slated to appear as Hayley's opponent. But that show was Hayley's chance, perhaps her only opportunity, to dig herself out of crushing debt, and now it was quite possibly slipping through her fingers.

"You might want to rethink taking me up on that loan offer," Bruce said, grinning, knowing how much he would enjoy Hayley having to grovel.

"No, thanks, Bruce, I'll be fine either way," Hayley lied.

"Suit yourself. So, does Mona go by 'Barnes,' or is she one of those feminazis who insists on being called by her maiden name? It's something Irish, right, like 'MacDonald' or 'McDuffie'?"

"It's Mona McDuffie, but she uses her husband's name. Why?"

"Just confirming for my column."

"Mona's in your column?"

"She's not just in my column. She *is* the column."

Hayley nearly choked on her coffee. She marched over to her desk and looked at what Bruce was typing on her computer screen. "Please don't tell me . . ."

"Yup. Mona Barnes is a suspect in the Candace Culpepper murder."

This was not the first time Bruce accused one of Hayley's friends—let alone Hayley herself—of a local murder.

"Why do you insist on constantly painting me and my friends as world-class criminals in your columns, Bruce? This is becoming a pattern!"

Bruce had written about both Hayley and Liddy in previous columns, offering tantalizing but ultimately misleading details about their connection to a couple of local crimes.

"It's only becoming a pattern because you and your little girl posse always seem to be in the thick of things whenever there's a murder in this town."

"You have no proof."

"I have several witnesses who clearly overheard Mona making public threats against the victim at Drinks Like A Fish."

"She was joking!"

"That's your interpretation. Look, I didn't go looking for these people who were at your brother's bar. They all came to me. And according to them, it didn't sound like Mona was joking."

"You know as well as I do that Mona is no killer," Hayley said, resisting the urge to punch him in the face.

But losing her job at the paper because of assault was not an option at the moment.

"Maybe. But I don't have the luxury of pulling a chicken marsala recipe out of my mother's scrapbook and writing about how some dandelions in the backyard help spruce up my tablescape. I'm a serious journalist."

"Writing about the town drunk mowing down a stop sign doesn't make you a 'serious journalist,' Bruce. You're a muckraker who will stoop to any level to titillate and get some attention, and it doesn't matter who you hurt."

"Maybe Sal will let you write Monday's op-ed piece and you can get all that off your chest, Hayley. But by then, it will be too late because this column is being posted on the website today."

Hayley knew there was no stopping Bruce, and she was done trying. She would call Mona and warn her. Mona was a sturdy brick wall. Unlike herself and Liddy, she could weather any kind of storm—both literally and figuratively. She hauled traps for a living and had rough skin and calloused hands, and her spine was made of steel. Handling petty accusations and town gossip would be a cakewalk. But it still angered Hayley that Mona would have to go through it at all. It was so unnecessary. Just an excuse to give Bruce something to write about. Officer Donnie hadn't even interviewed her yet about that night at the bar, and now the whole town would just assume she had something to hide.

The door to the office burst open and Sal plowed inside. "Christ, it's cold out there. I can't even move my face. I'm talking right now, but are my lips even moving?"

"Let me pour you some coffee, Sal," Hayley said, scooting back over to the pot. There was just enough left to fill one more cup.

"How was your interview, Sal?"

"Fine. I'm always wary of talking to showbiz types, but Phippen wasn't an a-hole like most of 'em," Sal bellowed as he tried extracting himself, with little success, from his bulky wool coat. He managed to get one arm free before Hayley handed him his coffee and helped him get his other arm out. Then she took the coat, brushing off the flecks of snow with her hand, and hung it in the closet.

"So, is he canceling the taping?" Hayley asked, almost not wanting to hear the answer.

"No, they may delay it a few days, but otherwise it's full steam ahead. He wants the show to be a tribute to Candace."

"That's sweet," Hayley said, trying not to sigh audibly with relief.

"It's bull puckey, is what it is. He may be a nice guy, but he's still a TV producer. The murder is all over the news. Do you know how much free publicity he can milk this episode for? It'll be a ratings bonanza for him. And a boon for us. This is an exclusive. We're going to scoop the *Herald*. I'll be in my office writing up my interview so we can post it immediately."

Sal headed for his office, but he stopped long

enough to check the area around the coffee station. He frowned. "No muffins?"

"Hayley didn't pick up any," Bruce offered quickly.

Hayley scowled at him.

Sal kept going, exhaling a big, disappointed moan.

Hayley heard a click. She swiveled around and saw Bruce stand up from her desk.

"All done. Uploading," he said, winking as he brushed past her and ambled back into the bull pen.

Hayley was not going to stand by and just do nothing as Bruce's column indicted her best friend Mona.

No.

She was going to be there for her best friend, and she was going to start by looking into the facts surrounding Candace Culpepper's murder herself.

That's right. Here we go again.

Chapter 14

"There's no way I'm letting you in here," Officer Donnie said. His lean, lanky frame filled the doorway of Candace Culpepper's small two-story house.

"But I brought almond fudge brownies. Your favorite," Hayley said, holding out a white plate stacked with brownies and covered with plastic wrap.

Actually, she hadn't made them. She had bought them at the Morning Glory Bakery. But these were just as good as hers, and Officer Donnie would never know the difference. Hayley had babysat Donnie when he was a little kid and remembered he had an insatiable sweet tooth. She was hoping to take advantage of that weakness for chocolate to gain entry into Candace's house.

So far, it wasn't working.

"How did you know I was even here?" Donnie asked, with a raised eyebrow.

"I called you at the station to get an update on

the case, and Earl, who was working dispatch, told me where I could find you." Hayley thrust the plate up into Donnie's face. "Don't be shy. Take one."

Donnie was trying hard to resist the urge. The brownies looked warm and inviting; he sniffed a few times as the cold air made his nose run. Finally he couldn't help himself and reached out, ripped open the plastic wrap, grabbed the brownie on top with his gloved hand, and stuffed half of it into his mouth.

"Technically, this is a bribe," Donnie said, his mouth full, bits of brownie flying out so fast that Hayley had to duck to avoid getting hit in the face.

"I just thought you'd like a snack while you were searching Candace's house for any clues that might point you in the direction of her killer," Hayley said, trying to sound as innocent as possible.

Donnie eyed her suspiciously. He knew her history of poking her nose into crime scenes, and he didn't want to do anything to make Sergio mad.

Hayley could tell his mind was racing as he debated with himself. He looked like he was about to crack, especially since he had just finished downing one brownie and was glancing at the plate, hoping she'd offer him another.

Hayley raised the plate even closer to his nose. "Go on, Donnie. I won't tell if you won't."

He slipped off his glove and picked up another,

popping the whole thing into his mouth this time. "They're really, really good."

Hayley knew she was in when he casually stepped aside as he licked chocolate off his fingers. Sergio would never allow her to enter the house of the victim. In the past she had tried to do it under his nose, with disastrous results. But right now, Sergio was thousands of miles away in Brazil. What harm could it do? Poor Donnie was an emotional wreck being in charge. She convinced herself that she was actually helping the chief by holding Donnie's hand and guiding him along so he didn't miss any important clues.

"Now don't touch anything," Donnie said, closing the door behind them.

Hayley looked around. The house was dusty and unkempt. Candace worked a lot of double shifts, so she wasn't home a lot to do much cleaning. Hayley made her way to the kitchen and opened the refrigerator. A half bottle of white wine. Some mustard and ketchup. Not much else. Candace probably ate most of her meals at the hospital, which would explain why she complained so hard about the beans in her chili. She didn't do her own cooking and relied on the cafeteria to make sure she got what she wanted to eat.

"Hayley, I told you not to touch anything," Donnie wailed as he followed her into the kitchen.

Hayley slammed the refrigerator door shut

and threw up her hands. "Sorry." Then she handed Donnie the plate of brownies. "You mind holding this while I check upstairs?"

Donnie opened his mouth to protest, but then decided to silence himself by popping a third brownie into his mouth. Hayley seized the opportunity to slip out of the kitchen and up the staircase.

She had reached the second floor and was halfway into the bathroom when Donnie called to her from the foot of the stairs. "I already did a sweep up there. I didn't find anything. So, why don't you just come back down here? I'm starting to think letting you in the house wasn't such a good idea."

"Okay, let me just use the bathroom first," Hayley said, sneaking into the bathroom and closing the door before opening up the medicine chest. There was blood pressure medicine, some Advil, a half tube of toothpaste, and what looked like a bottle of birth control pills. Hayley checked the label. Definitely birth control pills. She was about to close the cabinet, when she noticed something odd. The back of the cabinet was lined with newspaper pinned down with Scotch tape. She pulled at a small piece and tore it away. It was covering some kind of mirror. Hayley started ripping the newspaper off. When she had removed half of it, she realized it wasn't a mirror at all. It was a small window, which looked into Candace's bedroom. She flushed the toilet and turned on the faucet and let water run into the basin so Donnie would have the impression she was washing her hands.

She quietly opened the bathroom door and tiptoed down the hall into the bedroom. There was a mirror hanging on the wall in the exact spot as the window in the medicine cabinet.

Omigod.

It wasn't any regular old mirror.

It was a two-way mirror.

Why on earth would Candace need a two-way mirror pointing straight at her bed?

Unless . . .

Hayley didn't even want to think about it, but she couldn't help herself. Was Candace making sex tapes when she wasn't busy working as a nurse? Hayley knew that once the image got into her head, there would be no way of ever getting rid of it.

Too late.

Hayley searched the dresser drawers and found some camera equipment; she then began rummaging through Candace's closet. Hidden deep in the back was a box filled with DVDs. Most of them were boxed sets of Candace's favorite TV shows, such as *The Sopranos*, *True Blood*, and *Game of Thrones*. Nothing sordid or out of the ordinary about those. But as she opened one of the cases, Hayley noticed the DVDs didn't have any labels. The distributor would certainly have labeled the DVDs. The only thing written on them were dates.

It suddenly struck her.

Were the TV cases a way to disguise Candace's homemade tapes?

She grabbed one made a month ago and hurried over to a small desk and inserted it into Candace's laptop.

Sure enough. It was a recording of Candace's wild romp with the local pharmacist.

The local *married* pharmacist.

Hayley ejected that one and put in another from six months ago, during the summer. Some rather erotic foreplay of Candace with a man wearing nothing but a Chicago Bulls basketball team cap. Probably a tourist she had picked up.

Hayley knew the clock was ticking.

Even though Donnie wasn't exactly a Rhodes scholar, pretty soon he was going to realize it would never take Hayley this long to wash her hands. She was about to head out when she noticed a DVD left out on the desk; it was almost buried underneath some of Candace's bills.

This one had been made just two days ago.

"Hayley, what are you doing up there?" Donnie yelled as he began stomping up the stairs.

She was out of time.

But she had to know.

She waited for the DVD to load and play.

Outside in the hall she heard Donnie banging on the bathroom door.

"Are you okay in there?"

An image of Candace, topless, came up on the screen.

She was with a man; his bare back was to the

camera as he grabbed Candace and began smothering her with kisses. He pushed her down on the bed, turning just enough so he could straddle her. It was at that moment Hayley saw a glimpse of his face and instantly recognized him.

It was Drew Nickerson, the pompous, overbearing, and sex-crazed host of *Wild and Crazy Couponing*.

Chapter 15

Steffie Blackburn's jaw nearly hit the hardwood floor when she spotted Hayley walking into her small, low-lit yoga studio, which was located on the second floor of some retail space in the middle of town. Most of the shops were closed up for the winter, but Steffie had enough clients to continue her various yoga and meditation classes year-round, except for the month of April, when she traveled to Arizona to visit her parents in Scottsdale.

Hayley shed her coat and hung it on a wooden rack. She was in a roomy t-shirt and sweats and stood out among the five other much thinner women in mesh tank tops and wrap-waist yoga pants that accentuated every curve of their lean bodies. They were drinking bottled water and gossiping as they laid out their mats and set down their towels. Hayley realized she had come totally unprepared.

Steffie made a beeline for Hayley, still in somewhat

of a state of shock. "Hayley, what are you doing here? How can I help you?"

"I've come to take your restorative yoga class," Hayley said, smiling.

Steffie's jaw hit the floor again.

Hayley fished in the pocket of her sweatpants and pulled out a crinkled ten-dollar bill and handed it to Steffie. "Ten dollars, right? That's what it said online."

"You actually went to my website and looked it up? Is this some kind of joke?"

"I know it's been a while since I've come to your class, and I'm aware that the last time didn't go so well."

"It was a disaster," Steffie said, nodding.

"Well, I don't know if I'd go that far," Hayley said defensively.

"Hayley, you couldn't hold a simple warrior pose and fell into Kim Lankford, who was next to you, who then fell into Liz Beard, who then fell into Sue Farley, who sprained her ankle and had to be taken to the hospital."

"Okay, maybe your choice of words actually does describe the last time I took your class. But I'm not one to give up. I'm here to try again."

"It took you three years to come to this decision to try again?"

"Yes. I've always been a late bloomer and, well, I've put on a few pounds this winter, I'm sure you understand," Hayley said, glancing at Steffie's perfect body. "Or maybe you don't. Anyway, I've decided it's time for me to get serious and get back into shape, and I know your class does wonders for Liddy. She's always singing your praises and telling me how much she loves how you teach."

"Liddy hasn't been to my class in almost two years."

"Maybe it wasn't Liddy," Hayley said quickly.

Hayley knew she couldn't say it was Mona. Mona wouldn't be caught dead doing a downward-dog pose. The only exercise she got was lifting a beer mug, and only when she wasn't pregnant.

"But the point is, I'm here, Steffie, and I'm ready to get to work," Hayley said.

"Well, if you're sure you really want to do this," Steffie said, more than a hint of reluctance in her voice.

"Yes, I'm ready."

"Did you bring a mat?"

"No."

"Water?"

"No."

"A towel?"

"No."

"Okay, well, next time I suggest you bring all of those things. But just for today, I'll provide you with everything you need."

"Thanks, Stef. Appreciate it," Hayley said, knowing full well she was never, ever going to be coming back to the class after this day.

She was on a mission.

She was here to talk to one of Steffie's regulars,

but Sabrina Merryweather, the county coroner and Hayley's former high-school rival and resident mean girl, hadn't shown up yet. If she didn't, then there was no way Hayley was going to stick around and torture herself by twisting her body into all kinds of unnatural positions.

Steffie eyed Hayley suspiciously, not entirely convinced her motives for being here were pure, but she padded over to the other side of the room to fetch a mat and towel and some bottled water.

Hayley checked the clock.

Two minutes past eleven.

She knew Sabrina went to morning church services at nine-thirty and then usually drove right over to the class. She should have been here by now.

Steffie returned, handing Hayley her yoga essentials. "Why don't you come up front near me, Hayley, so I can work closely with you and make sure you don't fall again. I don't want to be liable again for any injuries."

Hayley nodded and followed Steffie past the other women, who were now on their mats and stretching and contorting their perfect bodies into various pretzel shapes in order to loosen up before the class began.

Near the front of the room, as instructed, Hayley rolled out the sticky, stained purple mat, which Steffie had given her, and then took a swig of her water, ready to plan a quick escape if Sabrina was a no-show. Suddenly the door to the yoga studio flew

open and Sabrina breezed in. Her blond hair was
in a ponytail; a wide smile was on her face.

"Morning, everybody, sorry I'm late. The reverend went a little long today, talking about his trip
to Nigeria building toilets for poor people. I was
like, 'Yuck, wrap it up, Rev. Why not just write a
check?' Am I right, people?"

A couple of the women giggled.

The others just looked at Sabrina, horrified.

Although she was a respected county coroner
and took her work seriously, Sabrina was still as
shallow and as stuck-up as she had been in high
school. Sabrina had conveniently forgotten how
mean she had been to Hayley when they were
teenagers and now considered her to be one of her
besties. Hayley played along because she never
knew when Sabrina's expertise, when it came to
autopsies, might come in handy.

Like today.

Hayley raised her hand to wave Sabrina over, but
she wasn't fast enough. Sue Farley had already
made room next to herself for Sabrina's mat. They
were chatting amiably and Sabrina hadn't even
spotted Hayley yet.

Meanwhile, Steffie was dimming the lights even
further to the point where Hayley couldn't see anything. Steffie then plugged her iPod into a speaker
and started playing soothing, soft music about
grace and gratitude, and then turned the heat up

so high Hayley began sweating even before she could get into her first pose.

"Let's get into position, ladies," Steffie said, assuming the lotus position.

The other women followed suit. Hayley had to use her hands to get her right leg over her left; then she had to wipe the sweat off her forehead.

This was not starting well.

"Everyone, close your eyes and let's take this opportunity to release the tensions of our lives and be present and centered and grateful for this opportunity to restore our body and our mind and to be strong and clear."

Hayley cranked her head around to get a look at Sabrina.

Damn.

She had her eyes closed.

Leave it to kiss-ass Sabrina to follow the teacher's instructions to the letter.

Hayley cleared her throat.

Sabrina didn't hear her or was ignoring her.

However, Sue Farley popped one eye open, noticing Hayley for the first time. Her face was suddenly full of concern. Or was it outright fear? She was probably afraid of spraining her ankle again. Hayley signaled Sue to get Sabrina's attention. Sue looked at Sabrina and then at Hayley, who was now sighing loudly out of frustration and pointing at Sabrina. Sue finally got the message and nudged Sabrina, who eventually opened her eyes.

"Omigod, Hayley, I didn't even see you here. How are you doing, girlfriend?" Sabrina asked, her voice raised as she talked over the soothing music.

"Ladies, please, class has begun," Steffie said, trying hard not to throw a hissy fit.

It was important for a yoga instructor to remain calm and collected.

Hayley stood up and picked up her mat and towel. "I'm just going to move next to Sabrina."

Before Steffie could protest, Hayley was scurrying over to Sabrina, her mat slapping Sue in the head as she stepped over her. Sue was forced to move her own mat a few feet to make room for Hayley as Steffie just glared at her, not sure how to handle this rude disruption of her peaceful and restorative class.

Once Hayley settled in, Sabrina reached over and gave her a quick hug. "It's so good to see you. We don't hang out enough."

"I was hoping we could talk for a bit after class," Hayley whispered, keeping one eye on Steffie, who was close to ejecting her from the class.

"Sorry, my deadbeat husband has an art show at the library. Like selling one of his crap paintings to his eighty-year-old aunt is going to pay for our two-week trip to Fiji next month. But I'm not bitter about being the sole breadwinner in the family."

Steffie started chanting.

Really loud.

To make a point.

And that was for the two of them to shut up.

Sabrina closed her eyes and readjusted her position and joined in the chanting. "Ommm . . ."

Hayley opened her mouth to ask Sabrina a few questions about Candace Culpepper's autopsy, but she noticed Steffie staring at her, stone-faced, just waiting for any excuse to kick her out. Hayley knew she couldn't take that chance. She had to get information out of Sabrina in the next forty-five minutes. Once Sabrina was at the art show berating her husband, there would be no talking to her.

Hayley tried her best to keep up with the other women as they held various yoga positions. Some were so torturous and painful, she felt like an insurgent at an Iraqi prison during the Bush administration.

Steffie hovered over her the entire time, helping her adjust her position, taking extreme pleasure in the shooting pain that Hayley endured as she twisted her legs, arms, and head in all different directions.

In fact, Steffie could barely contain her glee.

And with Steffie on top of her the entire time, there was zero opportunity for Hayley to speak with Sabrina.

Until the final minutes of the class, when all the hard work was done and it was time for everyone to stretch out on their backs and enjoy five minutes of meditation.

This was her chance.

Hayley turned her head in Sabrina's direction and talked in a low whisper. "Sabrina, I know you're not supposed to talk about anything related to an open murder case because you're a professional, but I was just wondering—"

"Candace was stabbed three times. Twice in the back. And once in the chest. She could've survived the two in the back, but the one in the chest punctured her lung, killing her almost instantly," Sabrina said in a normal voice.

Sabrina was a professional all right.

A professional gossip.

The entire class was riveted to her story.

"I'm guessing the killer came up behind her and stabbed her once in the back," Sabrina said, sitting up from her prone position and reenacting the murder for Hayley, as well as the rest of the class, all of whom could no longer pretend they were meditating. "Candace then spun around in surprise and was suddenly face-to-face with her attacker. That's when the killer stabbed her again in the chest. Candace probably had time to turn back around and try and run away and that's when the killer stabbed her in the back once more, leaving the scissors lodged there as Candace fell face-first to the ground and died."

So much for peaceful meditation.

None of the women in the room would ever be able to clear their minds and meditate after that grotesque, violent image Sabrina had just planted in all their heads.

Steffie sat up, ready to explode.

Hayley quickly closed her eyes and pretended to be deep into her own meditation. After a few moments she opened her eyes and saw Steffie turning up the music, hoping to drown out the troublemakers.

"So, do you know the exact time of death?" Hayley whispered urgently.

"Of course I do, honey, because I'm damn good at my job. Based on the body's decomposition, I would put the time of death around nine o'clock."

Sue Farley couldn't take it anymore. She stood up and wiped her face with her towel and quickly rolled up her mat. "This is not appropriate conversation for a Sunday. I am out of here."

Sue stomped off, her hand covering her mouth as if she was going to be sick.

Hayley had gotten exactly what she came for.

An estimated time of death.

That meant she could start lining up alibis and figuring out who had one and who didn't.

Her foray back into the world of yoga was officially over.

Especially since Steffie quietly informed her that she was banned from her class for life.

It was actually fun for Hayley pretending to be crushed.

Island Food & Spirits
by
Hayley Powell

What a busy week it's been—
what with work, coupon clipping,
and cat sitting for Mrs. Tubbs!
I'm sure most of you know by
now that poor Mrs. T had an un-
fortunate car accident, and is recovering in the hospital. She
wanted me to let everyone know
that she is on the mend and will
be up and about and back on the
road in no time! So watch out!
Kidding.

Anyway, the other evening,
shockingly enough, I found
myself with a little spare time, so
I decided to clip some more
coupons for the upcoming extreme-couponing show to be
filmed here in Bar Harbor. Whenever I decide to clip coupons,

I find myself turning the house upside down to find my favorite pair of scissors, which I swore I had placed back in the top left drawer in my brother's kitchen. I'm staying with him while some issues at my own house are being worked out.

I just love his kitchen drawers, mostly because they are so neat and orderly. Everything has its place—unlike my own kitchen drawers at home, which look like the aftermath of a small grenade.

Of course the scissors were nowhere to be found, so I glanced around the room, taking in the beautiful pristine white walls, lovely built-in cabinets with the open fronts, not to mention the beautiful black-and-white checkerboard-tiled floor, which he and Sergio painstakingly put in themselves.

I happened to spy some cans of paint sitting next to the doorway of the pantry and I remembered that my brother had told me they were going to paint the walls. They hadn't been able to find the time yet, since Sergio

was away visiting family and
Randy was so busy at his bar.

That's when a genius idea
struck me! It was only 5:30 P.M.
and Randy wouldn't be home
until after 2:00 A.M. If anyone
knew how to paint, it was me, especially given the fact I had recently updated every one of my
rooms in my house in a variety of
colors! What a wonderful way to
repay my brother's kindness for
allowing me to crash at his place!

I quickly emptied the pantry
shelves; then I searched the
garage and found all the rollers,
canvas for the floor, and even an
old pair of extra-large white dun-
garee overalls to protect my favorite slacks from JCPenney. And
so I began painting the white
pantry walls the bright cherry
red they had chosen, while
singing along at the top of my
lungs to some Trace Adkins I
was blasting through the stereo
speakers from the living room.
That's another great thing about
my brother's house. It sits
right on the water; so during

the winter, with the howling winds gusting in from the ocean, no one can hear my atrocious singing voice!

I realized much too late that because of the cranked-up music, I couldn't hear a commotion brewing down the hall in the living room.

I managed to finish painting the first coat, and figured I could do the second coat tomorrow night. Time for a break. I grabbed the half-full can of paint and stepped backward out of the pantry door to survey my work.

With the music still blaring, I didn't hear Leroy barking as he barreled down the hall toward the kitchen. But then, I suddenly sensed something and turned to my left just as poor Leroy came crashing into the kitchen, a wild-eyed look of terror in his eyes! Right behind him, hissing furiously, in hot pursuit was Mrs. Tubbs's Persian cat, Blueberry, whom I've been looking after for her. Leroy launched himself right into the air, straight at me.

Without thinking, I let go of the can of paint to catch him! What happened next unfolded in slow motion. The paint can hit the floor and tipped over and a torrent of cherry red paint spilled out.

Blueberry tried skittering to a stop, but he couldn't slow down fast enough and slid right into the ever-growing circle of paint, his flabby body skidding to a stop right in the middle, his fur sopping up the paint like a giant sponge. I dropped Leroy, who scampered away from the scene to hide in another part of the house. Blueberry, I believe at this point, was in a mild state of shock. He was on his belly, frantically trying to escape the sticky paint, unintentionally soaking up so much of it that he began to resemble Elmo, the furry red Muppet, from *Sesame Street*! Only not as adorable.

In the silence that followed, my head was filled with disturbing visions of a fat cat bounding away, tearing through the house,

painting everything in sight
with his long, dripping red fur. I
hurled myself on top of the
startled cat, who let out a blood-
curdling screech. He flipped
open claws so long and sharp
that he reminded me of sexy
Hugh Jackman in those *X-Men*
movies! Again, only not as
adorable.

That's just about the time my
brother, who made the fateful decision to leave the bar early because it was a slow night, strolled
into his kitchen through the
back door to find me lying on
top of a twenty-five-pound cat,
both of us covered in cherry red
paint.

I thought he would see red
(pun definitely intended because
it's always best to make light of a
potentially stressful situation).
But I have to give him credit. He
did not freak out and took it all
in stride. (Personally, I think he
may have been shell-shocked.)

As we cleaned up the mess and
washed off a growling Blueberry
in the kitchen sink, Randy just

quietly shook his head as I promised that I would make it up to him, and I would start by whipping up his favorite shrimp-and-pasta dinner the next evening, praying I had not worn out my welcome.

On the bright side, Randy did love the paint job—so, hopefully, I bought myself a few more nights! Oh, and I found the scissors right where I had left them: in the living room, on the end table, next to my giant pile of coupons. Oops.

The following night, true to my word, I prepared my shrimp pasta dish. Lucky for me, given our goal this month to make meals on a budget, I bought the frozen shrimp on sale and with a two-for-one coupon! All was forgiven!

We also both had a big craving for cherries that night, which neither of us could explain, so I trotted out my reliable cherry screwdriver recipe for our predinner cocktail!

Cherry Screwdriver

<u>Ingredients</u>
1½ ounces cherry vodka
Orange juice
Splash of grenadine
Cherry

Fill a Collins glass with ice and pour in your vodka, then fill with orange juice and a splash of grenadine. Stir and top off with a cherry.

Garlic Shrimp and Peas, with Linguine

<u>Ingredients</u>
8 ounces linguine
10-ounce package of frozen peas, thawed
12-ounce package uncooked shrimp with tails on, thawed
¼ cup butter, divided
2 to 3 cloves garlic, minced
Pinch of salt
½ cup white wine (you can use chicken broth if you prefer)
¼ cup lemon juice
1 teaspoon lemon zest
¼ cup fresh chopped parsley

Cook your pasta according to the directions, adding the peas during the last five minutes of cooking, then drain pasta and peas.

Meanwhile, in a large skillet, melt 1 tablespoon butter over medium-high heat. Add the shrimp and pinch of salt, cook and stir shrimp just until they are light pink, about 5 minutes, adding the wine during the last minute of cooking.

Stir in lemon juice, zest, and remaining butter. Then add your pasta and peas, stirring until heated through. Remove from heat; stir in parsley. Serve and eat immediately!

Chapter 16

After e-mailing Monday's column to Sal, Hayley decided to spend the rest of her Sunday relaxing and forgetting all about Candace Culpepper's murder. Randy was at the bar working, so she had the whole house to herself. Except there was Leroy, who at the present was upstairs still hiding under a bed, hoping to avoid any more confrontations with the devil cat, Blueberry.

And, of course, there was Blueberry, perched in front of a roaring fire in the living room, eyes fixed on Hayley, who was sitting on the couch, cradling her laptop. Blueberry's eyes narrowed; a low, guttural growl erupted every time Hayley made the slightest move. The flickering flames from the fire served as an appropriate backdrop, painting a picture of the angry, vicious animal as *literally* the cat from hell.

Hayley's cell phone buzzed from inside her bag. She fished it out and checked the caller ID.

It was Mona.

"Don't tell me. Your kids are driving you crazy and you need a quick escape. Well, come on over," Hayley said.

"Hayley, you need to haul ass down here to the police station before I get myself into even bigger trouble," Mona wailed.

"Mona, calm down. What's going on?"

"Well, that dumber-than-a-post Officer Donnie showed up at my door tonight and wanted to drag my butt down to the police station to ask me a bunch of stupid questions. I told him to get lost because I was serving my kids dinner and would come down when it was convenient for me."

Mona had a quick temper.

Plus she was almost twice the size of beanpole Donnie.

Hayley instinctively knew this was not going to end well.

"Mona, please tell me you didn't hurt him."

"Of course I didn't hurt him. I just roughed him up a little. Now don't worry. His nose isn't broken."

"You hit him?"

"I didn't plan to. But when I refused to go with him, he pulled out a pair of handcuffs. Can you believe that? That rat-faced, pimply bastard thought he could subdue me, so I gently popped him in the nose with my fist. I guess I hit him a little too hard, because blood spurted everywhere and got all over my new lime green sweatshirt I bought at Walmart last week."

"That's assault, Mona."

"Next thing I know, he's swinging a rubber baton at me like he's friggin' Luke Skywalker with a lightsaber. I just laughed in his face at that. That's when he dropped the baton and maced me."

"He maced you?"

"Right on my front lawn. Right in front of my kids. They were drawn by the commotion and came to the door and were chanting, 'Fight, fight, fight' and cheering me on, because, well, they're my kids. Of course they're going to root for me clobbering that sniveling son of a bitch."

"Brawling with a police officer is not the best example to set for your kids, Mona. I'm just saying."

"I know that, but I was blinded by Mace. And it really pissed me off because it hurt like hell, and I had Donnie in a headlock. . . ."

"Oh, dear God . . ."

"Yeah, my oldest said Donnie's eyes were bulging out of his head and he was wagging his tongue as I choked him. I wasn't going to kill him or anything. I was just going to teach him a lesson. That's when he stomped on my foot and I let him go, and that pathetic little wimp ran back to his squad car and locked himself inside, because he was so scared, and he called for backup. My kids led me back inside, because I couldn't see a damn thing, so I could scoop out some ice cream for their dessert. That's when two cop cars came screeching down my street, sirens blaring, lights flashing, like they were cornering the friggin' Unabomber! They completely overreacted!"

"You hit a cop, Mona! When is that going to sink in?"

"Right about now, Hayley. I'm sitting here, freezing my butt off, in this rinky-dink jail cell, and I only got one call, and my husband is too ticked off at me right now to even answer the phone. Plus I sure as hell wasn't going to call Liddy, so guess who was next on the list? And do you know that Officer Donnie, that little shit, is talking about pressing charges? I donated a fortune in lobsters to his parents' thirtieth wedding anniversary last summer. Talk about an ingrate."

"I'll be right down. Maybe I can calm Donnie down. You just sit tight, Mona, and please promise me you'll keep your mouth shut until I can get there."

"Don't worry. There's nobody around to talk to. Donnie's hiding in the chief's office right now, crying about his bloody nose."

Hayley hung up and scribbled a note to Randy; then she pulled on her boots and threw on her coat and trudged the half mile from Randy's seaside home to the police station, which was right in the center of town across from the village green, which served as the town square.

Donnie's sometimes patrol partner, Officer Earl, who was as rotund as Donnie was skinny, and a foot and a half shorter—but just as slow-witted—was sitting at the reception desk as Hayley blew through the front door.

"Evening, Hayley."

"Hi, Earl. I hear it's been pretty exciting around here tonight."

"Mrs. Barnes is back there in the cell and she's madder than a wet hen! She just stopped yelling a few minutes ago, but I think it's just because she lost her voice."

"Can I speak with Donnie?"

"Sure. He's in Chief Alvares's office. He's pretty embarrassed about getting beat up by a woman."

"Well, don't make it worse by teasing him."

"Too late," Earl said, grinning from ear to ear.

Hayley made her way down the hall to the chief's office and knocked on the door.

"Go away," Donnie said from inside, his voice cracking.

"Donnie, it's Hayley Powell. I just want to talk to you," she said, trying the door handle.

It was locked.

"I'm not releasing her, Hayley. She assaulted an officer."

"I know, Donnie. You have every right to charge her. And you can testify in court how you lost control of the situation and got clobbered by an unarmed mother of seven children and how you locked yourself in the squad car until help arrived. And I promise you, I will write the story for the paper myself. I bet Mona's oldest even recorded the whole thing on his phone and will post it online so all the evidence is out there."

There was a *click* as Donnie unlocked the door and opened it a crack.

"You don't think her kid got what happened on his phone, do you?"

"Who knows? Her kids are always posting things on YouTube and Facebook. But the important thing is we bring Mona to justice by getting the truth out there for everyone to see."

"Now hold on, I said I'm not releasing her. Just yet. I haven't decided about charges, but she needs to learn a lesson. The chief's not here, and I don't want him worrying about something like this, so I'm leaning toward forgetting the whole thing and sending her home in the morning, as long as she promises not to hit me again."

"Mona's a reasonable woman. I'm sure . . ."

Donnie raised an eyebrow.

"I'll talk to her."

"And I want an apology."

"Absolutely. Can I go back and see her?"

Donnie nodded as he stuffed some more tissue up his nostril to soak up the blood.

Hayley hurried down the hallway to the jail cell. Mona was pacing back and forth, muttering to herself. She stopped when she spotted Hayley standing outside the bars.

"Thank Christ you're here. Did you talk to Officer Doofus?"

"Keep your voice down. I think I got him to agree to let you go in the morning."

"In the morning? What the hell? I got my kids' lunches to make for school tomorrow and I'm doing the car pool, since I don't trust the school buses on these icy roads this time of year."

"I can handle all that if you let me borrow your car. You just concentrate on not causing any more scenes, being a good girl, and you may get out of this mess with no charges filed against you."

Mona finally realized Hayley had successfully defused the situation, and her attitude shifted. She was much more quiet and compliant.

"Now promise me you won't engage that poor kid anymore. His nose is still bleeding."

Mona nodded.

"I'll have Randy pick me up here and drop me off at your house. I'll make sure everything's fine and I'll get a cold breakfast on the table before I head home. Just relax. I'll take care of everything."

Mona's eyes welled up with tears.

Hayley was struck by the emotion on her friend's face, because, frankly, Mona rarely showed any.

"Everything's going to be fine, Mona. You don't have to worry."

"It's not that. I'm royally screwed, Hayley. I don't have an alibi."

"What are you talking about?"

"For Candace's murder. Donnie told she was killed around nine o'clock. I wasn't home then!"

"Where were you?"

"Dennis and I had a fight and I needed to get some fresh air and clear my head, so I took a drive around the island. I was all alone and the roads were empty and I parked over in Seal Harbor and just stared at the ocean and played some Kenny Chesney on the car radio. I must've been there two hours and nobody saw me."

"Did you tell Donnie this?"

"No. I didn't get the chance to, obviously. But he's not going to believe me. Those people heard me joking about killing Candace, and now everybody's going to think I did it. You gotta help me, Hayley. I'm drowning here."

Hayley reached through the bars and clasped Mona's hand. She was more determined than ever to find out who stabbed Candace Culpepper.

Her best friend's life could depend on it.

Chapter 17

Hayley was released from her duties of transporting Mona home from jail early the following morning. Instead, Mona's husband, Dennis, would no doubt take the opportunity during the ten-minute truck drive home to lecture his wife about her short temper. Hayley was able to relax a bit, shower, and have some coffee before she trekked to the office. The freezing weather had finally given way to some warmer temperatures, so walking to work wasn't going to be as harsh on this Monday morning as it had been when the thermometer hovered below zero.

As she strolled down Main Street toward the *Island Times* office, Hayley noticed the snow melting on a few of the landscaped lawns out in front of some local businesses.

She checked her watch: 7:45 A.M.

She had fifteen minutes before she was due at the office, so she decided to veer up Hancock

Street to make sure Mrs. Tubbs's house was locked up tight and undisturbed, since she was still in the hospital.

As Hayley approached the house, she saw that the police had removed the yellow tape from around the crime scene on Candace Culpepper's lawn. She walked by Candace's house and enough snow had melted in front of Mrs. Tubbs's house that the cement walkway to her front door was clear.

Hayley jiggled the knob. The door was locked. She peeked inside. Nothing seemed out of the ordinary. She would stop by the hospital on her lunch hour and let Mrs. Tubbs know everything was safe and secure at home.

As Hayley turned and started walking back toward Main Street, passing Candace's house again, her eye caught a flash of color in the squishy brown mud that was mixed with what little snow was left. She stopped and looked closer. Whatever it was had specks of green, red, and yellow. She knelt down and cleared away some of the mud with her hand. It was a piece of paper. The color was the image of a can of Del Monte Green Lima Beans.

It was a coupon.

Hayley gently picked it up and inspected it.

Sure enough, a two-for-one coupon.

Had Candace dropped it when her assailant stabbed her in the back?

Hayley suddenly gasped. This could not have belonged to Candace, because she made it very clear in the hospital cafeteria that she detested lima beans—all beans, in fact—so it wouldn't make sense that she would have a coupon for lima beans on her person at the time of the murder.

Perhaps the killer dropped the coupon.

That would make more sense. Clearly, whoever had it out for Candace collected coupons as well.

Which didn't look good for Mona, who was her chief rival trying to get picked to appear on the *Wild and Crazy Couponing* show.

Could the coupon belong to Drew Nickerson? The two were having an affair. Hayley had yet to report that fact to Officer Donnie. Frankly, she didn't trust him to handle it right. One wrong move and he might scare Nickerson, who could blow town.

And if there was one thing she could count on, it was Donnie making a wrong move.

No. She would investigate further on her own before she brought the acting chief up to speed.

But Drew Nickerson raked in thousands of dollars for every appearance he made on *Wild and Crazy Couponing*. Why would someone like that need to collect coupons and save money on groceries?

Her gut told her this coupon belonged to someone else.

Hayley slipped the paper into her pocket and

headed to the office, when a pickup truck pulled up alongside her and splashed her leg with some dirty brown slush from the side of the road.

"Want a ride to the office?" she heard Lex say as he rolled down his window.

"No. The office is just a few minutes away. But you can give me a lift to the dry cleaner later and pay the bill to clean my pants," Hayley said with a smile.

Lex leaned out and saw the muddy mess on the leg of her pants.

"Sorry about that. Can I make it up to you later? Have dinner with me," Lex said.

"You think one dinner's going to cover it?"

"I'll try to think of more ways after dinner," he said, winking.

"Let me call you this afternoon. It's going to be a crazy week, and despite all the chaos surrounding Candace Culpepper's murder, I have to think about how I'm going to win the grand prize on this coupon-clipping show."

"They're still going ahead with that after all that's happened?"

Hayley nodded, feeling guilty for even thinking about how relieved she was that in this case the old saying was true: "The show must go on."

"What are you doing on this side of town? You have the morning off?" Hayley asked.

"No. I'm heading to the estate now. I had to stop by the hospital."

"Why? Has there been a change in Edgar's condition?"

"No change. But in case there is, and they eventually send him home, Edgar's nephew, Clark, has put me in charge of hiring a new nurse. I just offered Tilly McVety the job."

"Wait. Are you saying Candace was working for . . . ?"

"Yeah, she was moonlighting in her spare time, looking after Edgar. Just a few days a week. The hospital had cut back on her shifts and she needed some extra cash, so Edgar was willing to pay her a nice sum when she wasn't at the hospital."

"Why didn't you tell me this before?"

"I didn't think it was that big a deal. Besides, I haven't seen you. Clark's been a real taskmaster. He's been working me nonstop, twenty-four/seven. I finally have a night off tonight and I want to make the most of it."

Hayley's mind raced. Candace had been working as a nurse for frozen-seafood magnate Edgar Hollingsworth. Edgar was worth billions, and it was no secret he had stepped on a lot of people over the decades to get into that elusive 1 percent. If Candace had spent as much time with Edgar as Lex said, there was the possibility that someone might have wanted Edgar dead. Perhaps, Candace found out about the murder plot and had to be eliminated before she could tell someone. Hayley admitted to herself that her imagination was truly at work from reading too many detective novels. It certainly seemed to be in the realm of possibility, given just how much money was involved.

But who could it be?

And did this person have a taste for Del Monte Green Lima Beans?

Chapter 18

The last thing Hayley wanted to do was accept a ride to the grocery store from Bruce Linney. She hadn't spoken to him since he besmirched Mona's good name by implying she was the one who had stabbed Candace Culpepper in the back. But since Hayley's car was out of commission and Sal left work early, she had little choice but to nod her head when Bruce asked if he could drop her off somewhere.

She quietly mumbled, "The Shop 'n Save."

"Going to practice your couponing skills before the big day?"

"Just because you're giving me a ride doesn't mean we need to engage in conversation, Bruce."

Bruce threw up his hands and then held the office door open as she marched out. He followed her to his parked black Audi and unlocked the doors with his remote. Hayley got in the passenger side as Bruce crossed in front of the car to slip into the driver's seat. They both slammed their doors at the same time. There was absolute silence in the car, except for the sound of Bruce rubbing his hands together to warm up before inserting the key in the ignition and starting the car.

As he pulled away, Hayley folded her arms and kept her eyes fixed forward on the road. Bruce cranked up the heater full blast, and it finally dissipated the visible wafts of their frosty breath.

"So, just how long are you going to give me the silent treatment?" Bruce asked, frustrated, hands gripping the wheel.

He glanced over to see Hayley shrug.

"You know, if the police had another suspect, I wouldn't be writing about Mona in my column," Bruce said, a defensive tone in his voice.

"How do you know there aren't any other suspects?"

"Because Officer Donnie told me so, just this morning. I'm not targeting your friend, Hayley. It's just that right now she's the closest thing the cops have to a person of interest."

"What kind of reporter relies on a nervous rookie to tell him everything there is to know about a murder case?"

"A reporter relies on the information he's given."

"A true reporter should dig deeper."

Bruce eyed her warily. "Why? What do you

know? If you know something, Hayley, you have to tell me."

"No, I don't."

"Yes, you do. Out of professional courtesy. I'm the crime reporter for the *Times*. It's *my* job to gather all the facts related to any police investigation."

"What could I possibly know? I'm just a silly food-and-cocktails columnist. Like you said, I should just focus on my recipe file and not worry my pretty little head about someone who may have been intimately involved with the victim."

Bruce turned the wheel and the Audi pulled into the parking lot of the Shop 'n Save. He nearly sideswiped a truck because he was so rattled by what Hayley had just said. "You know someone who was having an affair with Candace?"

"I'm going to make Randy a nice chicken-and-stuffing casserole tonight. My mother used to make it for us when we were kids, on these cold winter nights."

She whipped open the door and was out of the car just as Bruce leaned over to grab her coat but missed.

"Hayley! Come back here!"

"Thanks for the ride, Bruce."

She slammed the door shut. She could see his mouth moving, yelling something at her, but she ignored it and bounded into the supermarket. Pulling a metal cart from the stack, she steered down to the poultry section. She half expected

Bruce to chase her down and demand she tell him what she knew, but he didn't. Bruce was desperate to crack the case, but he was even more desperate not to embarrass himself by causing a scene for the whole town to see. He didn't want to give anyone the impression that Hayley Powell made him lose his cool.

Hayley quickly maneuvered through the aisles, tossing a package of organic skinless boneless chicken, some bread crumbs for stuffing, and a can of mushroom soup into her cart. She was ticking off the items in her head as she made her way back up to the front of the store. After work was the worst time to do grocery shopping; half the population of Bar Harbor seemed to be packing the aisles. Miraculously, though, she saw an express lane wide open, with no customers, so she made a mad dash for it.

Just as she reached the magazine rack, another cart came out of nowhere and crashed into hers—just as Candace had done during that couponing dry run right before she was murdered.

But this obviously wasn't Candace.

No. This was a man. A fidgety, nervous-looking man who was wearing thick glasses, which only seemed to enlarge his coal black eyes.

Tilly McVety breezed by Hayley and the man with her own cart and waved. "Hi, Hayley. Hi, Mr. Hollingsworth."

Hayley smiled and waved back to Tilly, who was gone in a flash.

Hollingsworth.

This was Clark Hollingsworth.

Edgar's nephew and Lex's current boss at the estate.

Without apologizing, Clark turned his back to Hayley as he blocked her cart with his body while shoving his own cart ahead of her and up to the cashier.

He then bent over and began systematically unloading items from his cart, completely ignoring the seething rage he had to feel emanating from behind him.

Hayley took a deep breath.

Do not, repeat, do not give this uptight, entitled bastard the satisfaction of calling him out on his rude behavior.

If she picked a fight with him, and he realized she was Lex's girlfriend, she could very well jeopardize Lex's job, especially with Edgar being so seriously ill.

There was no one to stand up to Clark and the unilateral decisions he was making.

Clark continued slamming cans and bottles down on the conveyor belt. His cart was fully loaded. At least seventy-five items. This was the express lane, with a fifteen-item limit. The teenage checkout girl was too intimidated by Clark's dead stare and angry demeanor to protest, so Hayley just waited calmly with her seven items until the checker finished ringing up his total.

Clark reached into his pocket and pulled out a stack of coupons and began placing them on top of all the items.

Hayley couldn't believe it.

He was doling them out with such precision and know-how, she wondered why he hadn't applied to be a contestant on *Wild and Crazy Couponing*. But it did beg the question: why would a man of Clark's enormous wealth, an heir to a billion-dollar frozen-seafood fortune, be a rabid coupon clipper?

In fact, it was downright strange.

She had never seen any rich person so meticulous about his coupons. Not an item went through that he didn't make sure got a discount. The process was painstaking. He checked and rechecked every coupon. She was going to be here all night.

Hayley made eye contact with the checkout girl, who smiled sympathetically, knowing this was going to take a while.

Suddenly Clark was frantically fanning through his stack of coupons just as the girl scanned a can of Planters Mixed Nuts.

"Wait! Stop! I have a coupon for that!"

The girl snatched the can of nuts back from the bag boy, who was about to drop it into one of Clark's reusable bags, and waited patiently.

Clark kept thumbing through his coupons. "I

know I brought it. I had it in my hand when I was in the snacks aisle."

Clark began to sweat. He knew he was holding everything up, but he was not about to forgo the chance to use every last coupon. He finished examining them all in his hand and then began sorting through them again.

Hayley couldn't take it anymore. She flipped through her own stack of coupons and pulled out one for Planters Mixed Nuts. She tapped Clark on the right shoulder. He spun around as if someone was assaulting him, but he froze at the sight of the correct coupon.

"Here. Take mine," Hayley said sweetly.

Clark's icy demeanor didn't thaw much, but he accepted the coupon and nodded curtly to Hayley, mumbling a quick thank-you before turning back around and handing it to the checkout girl.

It was going to take some more time for the girl to ring up the rest of the items and apply the discounts from the coupons, so Hayley knew she had a few minutes. She coughed and cleared her throat. Clark twisted his head around, a distasteful look on his face, afraid he might catch a winter cold. Hayley seized on the momentary eye contact.

"It's terrible about what happened to your uncle's nurse," Hayley said, shaking her head, showing just how upset she was.

"Yes, I know, terrible," Clark said brusquely, without a hint of emotion.

"Did you know her well?"

She heard a groan escape from his lips, one he didn't intend to be heard, but he couldn't help it. The last thing he wanted was to be caught up in a conversation with a local yokel.

Especially if the conversation involved a dead employee.

"No, I did not," Clark said, squirming, looking back at the checkout girl and pleading with his eyes to hurry up.

"I suppose she was already hired by the time you arrived in town," Hayley said casually.

"Yes, she was. I had very little contact with her."

"I can't imagine who would want Candace dead. There hasn't been a random murder in this town in, like, I think, forever. Most homicides are done by people who know the victim. Angry spouses, duplicitous so-called friends, disgruntled employees . . . or, even in some cases, employers. Finding out something illegal the boss was up to and paying the price for it."

Clark bristled. His back stiffened and he slowly turned around and glared at Hayley. "Just what are you getting at?"

"Nothing. Just thinking out loud. I didn't mean to imply anything. Really," Hayley said without an ounce of sincerity.

"Let's get something straight, Ms. Powell. Yes, I know who you are. If you're poking a stick at me right now so I lose my temper and perhaps say something I shouldn't, to somehow inadvertently confess to a murder I had nothing to do with, then I'm afraid you are going to be sorely disappointed."

"I am so sorry. I never meant to offend you," Hayley said, trying not to smile.

"The night Ms. Culpepper was savagely stabbed to death, I was at the Porter House enjoying a steak, medium rare, some cheddar mashed potatoes, a side of garlic spinach, and my favorite bottle of Pinot Noir. And I would appreciate it if you would check with the restaurant so they can assure you that I am not making any of this up. Will you do that for me, Ms. Powell?"

"Of course, Mr. Hollingsworth, I'd be happy to."

The checkout girl said in a mousy voice, "Um, that'll be a hundred and fifty seven dollars, please."

Clark whipped his head back to the cashier. "*With* the coupons?"

The checkout girl nodded. "Yes, sir."

Clark furiously slapped a gold credit card down on the conveyor belt and once again turned his back toward Hayley,

This time for good.

After walking down the street with her bag of groceries to Drinks Like A Fish, where Randy was about to put his best bartender, Michelle, who had just arrived home from her honeymoon, in charge for the rest of the night, Hayley called the Porter House and talked to the manager.

He confirmed that Clark Hollingsworth had indeed come into the restaurant at seven-thirty and stayed until after ten, knowing full well the staff was tired and anxious to go home, but in no hurry to accommodate anyone but himself.

If Candace was stabbed at nine o'clock and died instantly, as Sabrina had determined in her autopsy, then that meant Clark was in the clear.

Hayley knew what she had to do next. Whip up her mother's famous chicken-and-stuffing casserole for Randy and confront the one suspect who was clearly hiding his relationship with the victim: Drew Nickerson, the oily, repulsive host of *Wild and Crazy Couponing*.

Chapter 19

After she served Randy dinner, Hayley borrowed his car to drive over to the Captain's Arms, where Drew was staying. Parking out front, she took a deep breath and told herself she could get through this. Drew wasn't stupid enough to make another pass at her.

Not after the last time.

Or was he?

Hayley thought perhaps in hindsight she should've swung by Mona's and borrowed her shotgun. But she was here now, so she might as well roll with it.

When Hayley walked through the front door, the heat from the fireplace made her face sweat. She peeled off her layers, hanging her coat on a wooden coatrack by the front door, and looked around. She instantly spotted Drew. He was clad in a gray wool knit sweater and khaki pants and very expensive-looking black polished boots. He was sitting in an overstuffed chair by the fire, reading his

Kindle. It was hard to miss him. He was apparently
the only customer in the entire place. The only
other living being around was Clarence Renault,
the chipper, roly-poly bartender who, growing up,
had been in Randy's class. Clarence was stuffed
into an ill-fitting black vest and was washing glasses
behind a very small mahogany bar. Before approaching Drew, Hayley thought it best to order a
cocktail.

"Evening, Hayley," Clarence said, brightening.
He was undoubtedly happy to see a friendly face on
this cold Maine winter night. He probably didn't
count a persnickety guest reading in front of the
fireplace. "Please tell me you want a cocktail. I
haven't had anything to do for the last hour."

"I'll take an espresso martini, Clarence," Hayley
said, smiling.

The caffeine from the espresso would keep her
alert and the vodka would help her deal with
having to talk to Nickerson again.

Clarence gratefully grabbed a martini glass and
began making the drink. Hayley stood by the bar,
her back to Drew, whose slurping caused her to
pivot around just in time to see his thick mustache
catch a dollop of whipped cream from the top of
his mug of Irish coffee.

Drew spotted her and broke into a wide smile.
"Intrepid reporter Hayley Powell, what a nice surprise on this chilly, lonely night. Are you here to
see me?"

"Y-yes," Hayley said, stammering, certainly not wanting to give him a false impression.

Too late.

"Well, color me surprised. I didn't think you were interested, especially after your last visit. I'm still nursing a sore tongue."

Drew dramatically rolled his tongue around in his mouth for effect and then finished downing his Irish coffee. "It seems alcohol helps deaden the pain."

Clarence put Hayley's cocktail on top of the bar. "Here's your espresso martini, Hayley. I coated the rim with chocolate because I know you've got a sweet tooth."

"Thank you, Clarence," Hayley said, picking up the martini glass and casually strolling over to Drew by the fireplace. "So, what are you reading on your Kindle?"

"Biography of the late, great Dick Clark. My hero. Not just a simple game show host. An innovator. An entrepreneur. I'm trying to model my career after him. This coupon-clipping piece of crap is just the gateway to my future opportunities. But I'm sure a small-town little girl such as yourself isn't curious about all that."

God, Hayley despised this guy.

She wanted to tell him off.

Or at least give his tongue another working over.

But she couldn't.

Not just yet.

"So, what can I do for you, honey?" Drew asked in the most condescending voice he could muster.

Hayley couldn't take the whipped cream dripping from his overgrown mustache. She raised a finger to her upper lip, trying to signal him to wipe his face. Unfortunately, he wasn't too sharp at hand signals.

"You want a kiss already? Shouldn't we engage in a little saucy banter first before I make my move?"

Yuck.

"You've got whipped cream in your mustache!" Hayley bellowed.

This startled him. Drew Nickerson wasn't used to *not* being the picture of perfection. He quickly lifted the mug from the small coffee table in front of him and grabbed the cocktail napkin it was resting on. He dabbed it against his face until all of the whipped cream was gone.

Hayley kept going. "I have a couple of questions for you."

"I'm eight and a half inches, you minx."

"Seriously? Are you for real? Can you please talk normal?"

"I have to do something to entertain myself in this idiotic and boring nowhere town," he spit out defensively. "Fine. Go ahead. Ask away."

"Do you know Candace Culpepper?"

"The woman I read about who was stabbed to death in her front yard? No. I didn't know her."

"Well, that's funny, because I happen to have

proof that you more than just knew her," Hayley said, taking a sip of her martini.

Clarence made strong drinks.

She was already feeling light-headed.

She had to keep it together.

"Well, you're wrong. I never met the woman. What proof are you talking about?"

Hayley reached into her coat pocket and pulled out the DVD that she took from Candace's house. She waved it in front of Drew.

"What's that?" Drew said, completely non-plussed, raising his arm to get Clarence's attention. "Excuse me, if you're not too busy tending to the other guests—wait, there are no other guests—could you please make me another Irish coffee? Maybe before breakfast?"

Clarence simmered behind the bar, nodding to Drew, not wanting to risk getting fired by talking back to one of the guests, possibly the only guest.

Drew turned his attention back to Hayley. "So you brought a movie for us to watch? Shall I pop us some popcorn? Is Charlize Theron in it? I love Charlize Theron. She's my pretend girlfriend when I'm feeling lonely."

"I don't think you'll be so glib once you've seen it."

"Well, I'm intrigued now. Let's go to my room and pop it in the DVD player."

"The last thing I plan on doing is going to your room with you."

"So you want to cuddle up next to the fireplace

and watch it here? Fine with me," Drew said as Clarence came out from behind the bar and delivered his Irish coffee. "What's your name again?"

"Clarence," he said softly, not wanting to be involved in this conversation at all.

"Hayley's brought us a movie to watch. I see you have a TV above the bar. You like Charlize Theron, Clarence?"

"This film doesn't star Charlize Theron," Hayley said. "It stars you . . . and Candace Culpepper. And it is intended for mature audiences only."

This stopped Drew cold.

He turned and fixed his gaze on Hayley.

Clarence froze in place, not sure whether he should stay or leave.

"You're bluffing," Drew said, eyes narrowing.

Hayley spun the DVD around her middle finger like it was a mini Hula-hoop. "Try me."

Drew studied her hard. Not sure which way to play this.

It was like a cowboy standoff on the edge of a dusty ghost town.

Guns in the holsters.

Hands on the triggers.

Waiting for the other to make the first move.

Drew finally turned to Clarence. "Go ahead. Play it."

Hayley stopped spinning the DVD and handed it to Clarence, who looked at both of them tentatively before retreating behind the bar and sliding it into the DVD player, which was hooked up to the TV hanging on the wall behind him.

The tension was palpable.

The wait was interminable.

They heard the whirring of the player coming to life and the screen went black as the DVD loaded.

And then, Drew Nickerson's mouth dropped open at the sight of himself in all his naked glory lying on a bed with Candace Culpepper straddling him.

Hayley could tell Clarence wanted to close his eyes.

But he couldn't tear them away from the jaw-dropping scene. It was like being drawn to some horrible car wreck on Route 3 on the way to Bangor.

At that exact moment the front door to the bed-and-breakfast swung open and a gust of wind sent the flames from the fireplace flickering in all directions. Reverend Staples and his wife, Edie, marched inside, stomping their boots to get rid of the clinging snow. Hayley opened her mouth to warn them not to come any farther, but it was too late. The reverend crossed the room toward Clarence.

"Our pipes froze, Clarence, and the missus and I have no water. So we thought if you have a room available, we would stay here tonight."

Clarence opened his mouth to speak, but no words came out.

And that's when Reverend Staples heard grunts and moaning coming from above him. He glanced up, just in time to see Candace Culpepper going down on Drew Nickerson. At first, he thought his eyes must be playing tricks on him, because he chuckled amiably at what he thought he was seeing. But then, as his wife, Edie, stepped into the room and gasped, moments away from needing smelling salts, that's when the good reverend came to the disturbing conclusion that this particular Bar Harbor B and B routinely played porn for its guests.

Clarence tried in vain to explain. "Reverend Staples, please, this is not what you think. . . ."

The reverend waved his hand in front of Clarence's stricken face. "No need for explanations, son. I understand this time of year people get bored being cooped up because of the harsh weather and sometimes *American Idol* just doesn't cut it as entertainment."

Edie gripped her husband's coat and squeezed hard, desperate to make a quick escape.

"Edie's cousin lives just down School Street. We'll try there. Don't worry about us. We'll find a place to stay. Joseph and Mary didn't get lodging on their first try either," Reverend Staples said, turning his wife's head away from the television and ushering her out the door.

On his way out he glanced over and saw Hayley sitting next to Drew, smiling weakly.

"Hayley Powell. Why am I not surprised to see you here?" he said, shuffling out the door and slamming it shut behind him.

Yes, the Reverend Staples had been shaking his head in judgment of Hayley since she was in the seventh grade and performed Madonna's "Like a Prayer" song for the church fund-raiser, complete with Randy, in a long brown wig and fake beard, wearing nothing but a white towel playing the role of a sexy Jesus. People still talked about that. Except Hayley's mother. Sheila made the decision that very day to move to Florida when both kids were out of high school.

"Turn it off!" Drew screamed, finally snapping out of his state of shock. "Are you trying to ruin me? I'm a married man! What if that gets out?"

"It won't. Clarence won't talk, as long as you tip him well when you leave tonight. And I'm not interested in hurting your wife, though I'd probably be doing her a favor. I just want you to come clean."

"Okay, fine. Yes. We had a brief affair. But it was nothing serious."

"Isn't that a conflict of interest, given the fact Candace was going to appear as a contestant on your show?"

"Of course not," Drew said, scoffing. "I never play favorites. In fact, I sleep with all the female contestants, so it's a completely level playing field."

"Not me," Hayley said emphatically.

Drew put a hand on her knee, which then crept up toward her inner thigh. "The night is young."

Hayley grabbed Drew's fingers and bent them back far enough that they almost touched his wrist. Drew howled in pain and wrenched his hand away. He was seconds away from crying like a baby; but with Clarence still in the room, he couldn't risk compromising his macho reputation. Instead, he choked back the tears and jumped to his feet.

"I could never hurt Candace!" Drew yelled, rubbing his hands.

"I tend to agree with you," Hayley said. "You're too much of a wuss to hurt anyone. I've seen Candace on a soccer field. If you went at her with a knife, she'd have taken you down faster than a UFC champ."

"I'm done talking to you," Drew said, beating a hasty retreat down the hall to his corner room.

Hayley turned to Clarence, who was still watching the TV, where Drew and Candace were humping. "Would you please turn that off, Clarence?"

"Huh? Oh, right. Sorry," he said, reaching under the bar and pressing a button. Mercifully, the graphic image finally disappeared.

Hayley took one last sip of her espresso martini. "So tell me. The night of Candace's murder, do you remember Drew Nickerson being here?"

"Yeah, he was here. Hanging around the bar drinking and hitting on the housekeeper, until around eight-thirty. Then he went to his room."

"And he was there all night?"

"I think so. But I went on my break shortly after that and didn't come back until nine-thirty."

"So he could've left and come back without you seeing him."

Clarence nodded.

Drew Nickerson was a whiny wuss, but he was also sleeping with the victim.

And his alibi was pretty shaky.

He could've slipped out of the B and B, stabbed Candace, and gotten back before Clarence returned to the bar to see him come through the door.

Which meant Drew was still a suspect.

Hayley put out her hand.

"You want another espresso martini?" Clarence asked.

"No, Clarence, the DVD."

"Oh, right."

He ejected it from the player. Before handing it back to her, however, he said, "You mind if I burn myself a copy? I had no friggin' idea Ms. Culpepper had such a smoking body."

"I'll pretend I didn't hear you just say that," Hayley said, snatching the DVD out of his hand and heading out the door.

Chapter 20

When Hayley arrived at the office the following morning, she didn't waste any time before sitting down and attacking her in-box. She had let things pile up the past few days, and was determined to catch up this morning before Sal arrived and began shouting orders and asking why Hayley's tasks were not getting done. She knew she had some extra time because it was snowing again, and the weather forecast was predicting six inches. That kind of rough weather always slowed Sal down.

Hayley shuffled through the papers, prioritizing what needed to be accomplished first. There were the subscription requests, the real estate listings, the local movie-theater schedule. Not to mention her column. She hadn't even started writing it yet, since most of her free time was being taken up by Candace's murder investigation. One crumpled-up piece of paper tumbled out of the stack and landed on her desk. She picked it up and was about to toss it in the trash, but a little voice inside her head told her to stop. At least take two seconds to make sure she wasn't throwing out an important document.

Hayley unfurled the crumpled paper. There was a message written in red crayon, like a child's scribbling, and it said, *I know who killed Candace Culpepper.*

Hayley sat there, in a complete state of utter disbelief. Questions were swirling about in her head: *Who could have written this? When did he or she slip it into my in-box? And, most important, who did kill Candace Culpepper?*

Hayley had been the last to leave the office yesterday and had locked the front door behind her. The door was unlocked when she arrived this morning, so someone else on staff had to be in the building.

Right on cue she heard a familiar cough and a disgusting phlegmy clearing of the throat.

Bruce was already at his desk.

"Bruce, is that you back there?"

"Yeah. Coffee ready yet?"

Of course he didn't think to make it himself.

"When did you get here?" Hayley said, flipping on the coffeemaker.

"About seven-thirty. Why?"

"Did you hear anyone come in the office?"

"Yeah, about fifteen minutes ago. I thought it was you, but then I thought to myself, 'Wait, Bruce. It's only seven forty-five. When has Hayley ever been early? What is this, an alternate universe?' So

I just went back to Words With Friends. They finally repaired my computer."

"You didn't come out to see who it was?"

"No."

Why even ask? That would involve Bruce actually getting up from his desk and having to walk the few feet to the front office.

Hayley couldn't take her eyes off the note left in her in-box. Either a kid with sloppy penmanship wrote the note or someone was trying to disguise his or her handwriting.

The door opened and a petite blond woman, with a curvaceous figure and a million-dollar smile, bounced in. She was wearing skintight pink ski pants and a baby blue down coat. Matching earmuffs kept her head warm, and blond curls were piled high above her head. She also sported a very expensive-looking white cashmere Hermès scarf. She was stunningly gorgeous; and if Bruce had any idea what this babe looked like, he'd get his butt out of his chair and into the front office.

"May I help you?" Hayley asked, folding the note up and stuffing it in the front pocket of her pants.

"Yes, I'm here to renew my subscription," the sexpot said. "I usually do it online, but I had to come up here anyway."

"What a time to come to Maine," Hayley said, opening her drawer and rummaging through it for the paper's subscription forms.

"Well, I didn't have much of a choice. Family

emergency," she said, never wiping off her big, toothy smile. "Are you Hayley Powell?"

"Yes, I am."

"You're the only reason I get this paper. I'm not much of a reader, except for those *Fifty Shades of Whatever Color* it is, because I love a lot of sex in my books, but I absolutely adore your column! I never miss it!"

"Are you an amateur chef like me?"

"Oh, honey, I don't cook. Hell, if I even tried boiling water, they'd probably have to call the fire department. But I *am* a drinker. And I have tried every one of your delicious cocktail recipes. Talk about taking off the edge!"

"Well, I'm glad you like them," Hayley said, tearing a form off the pad and handing it to the woman. "Just fill out your name and address. We accept checks and credit cards and, of course, cash."

The woman sighed, frowned for a split second at the prospect of having to write anything down, but then dutifully began scratching out her name on the top of the paper.

"So you mentioned a family emergency? Did you grow up here?"

"Oh, yes, I spent my whole childhood here. Went to the local high school. But I got out of here the day I turned eighteen. Bummed around Florida for a while, waitressing in a bunch of dive bars, before finally landing a decent job in Charlotte, waiting tables at T.G.I. Friday's."

A waitress at T.G.I. Friday's who can afford a Hermès scarf? Someone was definitely living beyond her means.

"I've lived here my whole life. I'm surprised you don't look familiar."

"Well, that's because I'm so much younger than you. I was probably something like seven years old when you graduated from MDI High School," she said, cackling.

Hayley suddenly liked her a lot less.

The woman unzipped her baby blue down jacket. "See? I've got boobs now!"

She finished jotting down her information and handed the subscription form to Hayley, who took one look at the name and gasped.

"Cassidy Culpepper? You're Candace's sister?"

"Yes, much younger sister. Did you know Candace?"

"Of course. She was in my class."

"Really? Wow. I pegged you for much older."

Now Hayley actively hated this woman.

But she kept her cool.

Cassidy was writing out a check for the subscription renewal.

"So, are you here for the funeral, Cassidy?"

"Yeah, I guess. They haven't really nailed down a day yet, and I don't really want to hang around here and freeze my ass off, so I'm pushing for just going with a memorial. Then we can just store the body on ice and worry about the burial when the ground thaws next spring."

What a loving, caring sister.

Not.

"I see," Hayley said as Cassidy tore the check out of her checkbook and handed it to her. "You must be pretty upset, given the circumstances of her death. That's pretty tough to deal with."

"What circumstances? Oh, you mean the fact somebody stabbed her? Yeah, freaky, right? Glad I wasn't up here visiting her at the time. It could've been me. But we weren't exactly on speaking terms, so the odds of that happening were pretty slim. Thank you, Jesus!"

"So you're heading back down South soon?" Hayley asked, just going through the motions now of carrying on a conversation.

"That depends on how fast the lawyers can settle the estate," Cassidy said, zipping up her down jacket.

"'Lawyers'? You mean it's going to take more than one?"

"Well, yes, everybody knows just how loaded Candace was."

"'Loaded'? Candace had money?"

"Uh . . . duh . . . at least a couple of million. I thought you said you knew her."

"We weren't that close."

"We had a rich uncle who died about three years ago. He was a boring-ass playwright who wrote some piece of crap that made a mint on Broadway. I met him, like, twice, when I was a kid. He'd talk about the theater and these actors I never heard of. I

mean, come on, it's not like he was palling around
with Justin Timberlake! He took to Candace,
though, and when he died, he left her part of his
fortune. I raised holy hell! How dare he stiff *me*?
He actually wrote in his will that I wasn't responsible enough to be in charge of that kind of money.
Can you believe that?"

Yes. Hayley could believe that.

But she kept her mouth shut.

"Well, of course, as Candace's only living relative,
I'm in *her* will. So that artsy-fartsy dead uncle of
mine is probably rolling over in his grave, now that
I am finally going to get my hands on his precious
money."

Cassidy laughed heartily, but then she let it fade
as it dawned on her that she was probably talking
too much. "Anyway, I have to go pick out a casket.
I'm sure the funeral director is going to pressure
me into buying one with all the bells and whistles—
dark mahogany, brass rails, and all that crap—but
if there's a pine box I can get my hands on, I'm
going with that!"

"I'm just so surprised Candace was wealthy. I
mean, she worked double shifts at the hospital
and then was making extra cash as a private nurse
for Edgar Hollingsworth," Hayley said. "I actually
thought she was having financial troubles."

"Hell no! She didn't do the nursing thing for
the money," Cassidy said. "That's just what she told
people so they wouldn't come by her house, begging her for a loan. She was one of those annoying

'bleeding hearts' who just liked helping people to heal."

She put "bleeding hearts" in finger quotes.

"Utter waste of time, if you ask me," Cassidy said, shaking her head. Then that million-dollar smile came back. "Can't wait to try your jalapeno margarita!"

And with that, Cassidy Culpepper breezed out the door, leaving a slack-jawed Hayley sitting at her desk with a crumpled-up note in her pocket from someone claiming to know who killed Cassidy's sister, Candace.

Island Food & Spirits
by
Hayley Powell

I have a long-standing tradition of monthly girl outings with my two BFFs, Liddy and Mona. It's a wonderful way to stay connected when our lies get too busy. We rotate choosing an activity, and the one rule is the other two can't complain, even if it's something like ice fishing. Mona actually picked that this past January: a full day starting at the crack of dawn, drilling holes in the frozen Eagle Lake, where Mona had an ice tent in order to get in some good early-morning fishing. I was game. Liddy was another story. First of all, she never got up before ten, so she made it very clear she would call us on her cell phone from the landing so one of us could swing by on Mona's four-wheeler and pick her up.

Part of the fun of ice fishing is riding around the lake, visiting other people outside their tents, and grabbing a quick cocktail and a bit of gossip. Mona and I arrived at the lake and unloaded the four-wheeler from the back of her truck down a ramp, and then attached the sled to it so we could haul all our food and fishing gear out to her ice tent. Mona grumbled about how we had enough food to feed her large family for a week, even though we were only going to be on the lake for five or six hours. I didn't care, because I have never been one to skimp on food. Better to have too much than not enough! As a rule, I keep snacks in my car, even for a quick twenty-minute trip to Ellsworth, just in case I get stuck in summer traffic.

Mona wasted no time after we arrived at the tent in the middle of the lake, grabbing the ice auger off the front of the four-wheeler, drilling holes through the ice, and baiting and setting the tip-ups of the fishing lines. I was in charge of unloading the gear and starting the fire in the woodstove, to take the chill out of the tent. Then I started preparing our breakfast sandwiches by placing a cast-iron pan on top of the woodstove so I could get the bacon sizzling in the pan. I grabbed a couple of eggs and slices of cheese, and buttered a couple of English muffins to toast in the pan. By the time Mona finished drilling, I had a nice, hot breakfast ready, with two steaming mugs of coffee from the thermos. Mona ran into the tent excited, because the first tip-up she set already had a flag and a nice-size trout on it, so we already had a head start on that evening's dinner.

As we chowed down on our sandwiches and commented on how quiet it was on the lake, suddenly out of the blue we heard a howling noise, like some wild animal. We dropped our half-eaten breakfast sandwiches on the floor and jumped up to look out the window of the ice tent.

"Oh, my God, what the hell is that?" Mona yelled.

Running across the ice was what looked like a large, possibly rabid wild animal, with dark, shaggy fur. At first, we thought it was an injured coyote; but as it got closer, we began to fear it might be one very mean and hungry Maine black bear drawn to our ice tent by the smell of the cooked bacon!

Mona ran and got her hand-gun and started loading it.

"What are you doing with a gun? Were you planning on shooting the fish?" I screamed.

But, secretly, I was relieved Mona was a proud card-carrying member of the NRA, because a gun was just what we needed at this moment to defend ourselves.

Mona was out the door of the tent in a flash. I just stood there with my mouth hanging open, which is always how I look when someone snaps a picture of me with his camera.

Mona was bellowing at the top of her lungs as she raced straight toward the shaggy beast and then fired her pistol in the air, once, as a warning. All of a sudden the monster stopped dead in its tracks and raised its hands, or paws, in the air.

I heard Mona yell, "You damn fool!" just as I raced out of the tent in time to see Liddy, arms in the air, wearing the thickest fur coat I had ever seen in my life. She was shaking in her boots from fright. Once Mona put her gun down, Liddy started screaming about how Mona had almost killed her, and Mona was yelling that Liddy shouldn't dress up like a wild animal. That really upset Liddy because she had spent a fortune on that very expensive fancy coat during one of her New York shopping sprees.

Liddy explained that she had tried calling me for a ride. However, because of the cell phone's spotty reception in the middle of Eagle Lake, her call went straight to my voicemail. She decided to start walking across the ice. Then, halfway to the tent, she received a distressing call from one of her clients, who wanted to back out of a pending escrow. She was shouting because of the bad phone connection and the gusty wind. That's when she realized someone was shooting at her!

Luckily, Liddy brought some of her famous bourbon cocktails, which Mona loves, so all was ultimately forgiven. And we caught enough fish to head over to Liddy's house at the end of the day for an evening of cocktails, a tasty trout dinner, as well as some BFF quality time, a winning combination in the cold, dark days of winter.

The best part of this week's budget-friendly recipe is that we caught the fish, which didn't cost us a dime, and foraged through Liddy's cupboards and fridge for the ingredients so this one was a win-win! But before you sit down for dinner, you have to start with one of Liddy's Bourbon Chai Toddies! They are to die for, which Liddy almost did today!

Bourbon Chai Toddy

<u>Ingredients</u>
1 ounce Maker's Mark
½ ounce Cointreau
1 ounce freshly prepared hot
    chai tea
Splash of bitter
Honey, to taste

Prepare your hot chai tea according to directions and mea-
sure one ounce in a tall glass.
Add the remaining ingredients
and stir well. If you like, garnish
with an orange twist. Yum!

Easy and Delicious
Lake Trout Recipe

<u>Ingredients</u>
1 fillet lake trout
3 tablespoons olive oil
1 lemon
2 to 3 shallots, minced
Fresh ground pepper, to taste
2 teaspoons kosher salt
1 sprig of dill

Preheat your oven to 400
degrees. Line a baking pan with
parchment paper. Wash and pat

your fillet dry. Finely mince shallots. Slice the lemon. Pour olive oil over both sides of the fillet. Place lemon slices on parchment paper. Place your fillet on top of the lemon slices, then top the fillet with the shallots, herbs, and fresh ground pepper. Bake for 20 minutes and then dig in!

Chapter 21

By the time Hayley left the office, it was still snowing, already pitch-dark outside, and only four o'clock in the afternoon. She hated winters because the sun was only out for half the day, retreating behind Cadillac Mountain and plunging the entire town into blackness before most kids were even home from school. Hayley left the office an hour earlier than usual because she had filed her column and had emptied her in-box, plus Sal was in a giving mood mostly because she had bought him a Danish during her lunch break.

Her mind was still preoccupied with who had left her the scribbled note claiming to know the identity of Candace's murderer. Who even knew she was investigating the stabbing on her own? It wasn't like she had made some grand announcement alerting the whole town to her mission of finding the killer. Given her history, however, there may be one or two people in town who would assume she might take it upon herself to clear her best friend Mona's good name.

Maybe one of Mona's kids? It did look like a child wrote the note, but that was a stretch. The young ones were more focused on *SpongeBob SquarePants,* and the older ones were too busy tweeting and playing hookey from school.

As Hayley walked toward Randy's house, she slowed her pace as she noticed there were no lights on in the house. For a moment she assumed there was some kind of local power outage; but then glancing about at the neighboring houses, she saw all of them were completely lit up. There was a gnawing feeling in her gut as she slowly approached. Randy had called to say he was on his way home around three. He should have been here by now. And if he went out to the store or to run an errand, he most certainly would have left the lights on, knowing Hayley would be home soon.

Something was definitely wrong.

As she got closer, raising her mittens and blowing into them to warm up her face, she spotted a mysterious blue glow emanating from the living-room windows.

If Hayley were less of a realist, she might have thought that the house was being invaded by aliens. She had seen that Mel Gibson movie where the space visitors spelled out messages with the farm crops and then started popping up in closets in poor Mel's house, scaring the bejesus out of him, but that was just a movie and this was simply a weird light in an otherwise dark house.

Still, she couldn't resist glancing around to see if any aliens might have drawn messages in the caked white snow.

Hayley cautiously walked up the steps to the front porch and slowly made her way to the picture window, which looked out from the living room. As she peered in, her heart nearly stopped. The whole room was bathed in blue light and there were stains illuminated in white everywhere. She had seen enough detective shows to know the CSI unit used these kinds of ultraviolet lights to identify bloodstains at a crime scene. There was blood on the floor! On the walls! Blood on every last piece of furniture!

Hayley screamed at the top of her lungs.

What was going on?

Where was Randy?

Dear God, who had perpetrated this bloody massacre?

Hayley backed away so fast from the horrific sight that she tripped and fell over the porch railing, landing flat on her back in the snow and knocking the wind out of her.

She sat up, trying to catch her breath, hoping she had no broken bones, when suddenly the lights snapped on in the house and the blue light and white stains instantly disappeared.

By the time she crawled to her feet and was trying to climb back over the porch railing, she saw

Randy running down the stairs to see who was outside his house screaming. His face didn't register much surprise when he spotted Hayley.

Sliding open the glass door, he ran out to assist his sister in hauling her big butt back over the railing and onto the porch.

"What the hell are you doing out here yelling at the top of your lungs?" Randy said, leading her inside.

Hayley didn't answer him. She pushed past him and looked around. "What happened to all the bloodstains?"

"That wasn't blood. I went to PetSmart in Bangor today and bought a Whisker City Stink Free UV Urine Detector Light to see just how much damage that possessed devil cat we've been stuck with has left all over my house."

"Oh," Hayley said, feeling silly.

Randy marched over to the wall and flicked off the lights. Once again the blue light and white stains appeared. "As you can see, Blueberry is leaving his mark everywhere. My Oriental rug from Istanbul might as well be a kitty litter box. That seems to be his favorite dumping ground. And you haven't even seen the upstairs yet."

"I'm so sorry," Hayley said meekly, not sure how she was going to fix this. "Where's Leroy?"

"Where else? Hiding underneath my bed, whimpering softly, wondering when this nightmare is finally going to be over."

"I'm on my way to the hospital now to check on

Mrs. Tubbs. I'm sure it's only going to be a couple more days."

"That's too long, Hayley," Randy said, flipping the light switch again, unable to look at the repulsive stains any longer. "I think we should put the cat in a shelter until Mrs. Tubbs is out of the hospital and is capable of caring for him."

"Animal shelter? We can't throw him into an animal shelter. I'm sure we can board him at the vet's or the groomer's until Mrs. Tubbs can pick him up."

"I've already called both! The vet said there was no space available, but I could tell he was lying, and the groomer just laughed on the other end of the phone and said she was not going to be suckered into taking that monster off my hands. So, clearly, Blueberry has a reputation in town, which makes it difficult for us to get rid of him except by dropping him off at the animal shelter. They can't refuse us!"

"All right. Point taken," Hayley said. "I'll talk to Mrs. Tubbs. Where is Blueberry now?"

"Just go to the room with no cat piss stains and I'm sure you'll find him christening it," Randy said, grabbing his coat and heading for the door. "I'm going to the bar. Can I drop you off at the hospital?"

Hayley nodded. She felt terrible for bringing Blueberry into her brother's house. He was such a neat freak, and it had to be killing him that this cat was causing such a mess. If she hadn't been forced out of her own home, things would have been easier.

Except for poor Leroy, who would still be a jittery bundle of nerves.

They barely spoke as Randy drove her to the hospital and let her out. He was fuming. And she didn't blame him. She promised to make another big batch of her garlic shrimp pasta; but even though he cracked a slight smile, she knew that wouldn't begin to mend the fences Mrs. Tubbs's cat had torn down.

Mrs. Tubbs was watching Fox News on her television when Hayley rapped lightly on the door and sashayed in, with a big smile on her face.

Better to ease her into it.

"How are you feeling, Mrs. Tubbs?"

Mrs. Tubbs had the bedcovers pulled up to her neck, and her frail bony arms dotted with age spots were stretched out at her sides. Her mouth was turned down into a sad frown, and her eyes were blank as she stared at the news crawl at the bottom of the screen.

Hayley tried to break the ice. "Fox News, huh? I'm not big on Bill O'Reilly. Too full of himself. And what's his name, Sean Hannity? Cute, but he needs to calm down and get his facts straight. I used to like watching Greta Van Susteren. But then her crooked mouth started bothering me, so I gave up altogether and now I just stick to Diane Sawyer."

Nothing.

It was like playing to an empty house.

Hayley reached over and lightly touched Mrs. Tubbs's arm. "Mrs. Tubbs, Nurse Evelyn told me on my way in here you're doing much better, so why do you look so distraught?"

Finally Mrs. Tubbs moved her head slightly so she could look at Hayley. Tears ran down her wrinkled cheeks and she sniffled softly. "They're suing me, Hayley."

"Who?"

"Mark and Mary Garber. I just got a call from my lawyer."

"Well, even if they do, you have liability insurance, right?"

"Not according to Gretchen Maxwell, at the insurance company."

Poor Gretchen was delivering a lot of bad news to her policyholders lately.

"My husband handled all the bills," Mrs. Tubbs said, sighing. "When he died a few years ago, I just got so overwhelmed with everything that I had to take over, and, well, I suppose I let things pile up on the desk and I forgot to send in the check to pay the premium. How could I be so stupid?"

"You're not stupid, Mrs. Tubbs. A lot of smart people forget to mail in their checks. Life just gets in the way sometimes."

And then you wind up having no way to repair your car when your garage roof caves in and crushes it, Hayley reprimanded herself.

"What am I going to do, Hayley? Am I going to lose my house? Where will Blueberry and I live if we lose the house?"

Blueberry.

She had almost forgotten why she was here.

There was no way she was going to be responsible for worsening Mrs. Tubbs's condition by announcing her beloved pet was about to be incarcerated at the local animal shelter. No, she would somehow convince Randy to allow the cat to stay for at least another day or two, until she could come up with an alternate plan.

In the meantime, she would drop by Mark and Mary Garber's house and have a little chat. There was nothing to lose in trying to appeal to their sympathetic nature. After all, Mrs. Tubbs was a kind, sweet elderly woman who didn't mean anyone any harm and who would be physically and emotionally devastated by a long, drawn-out lawsuit.

Yes, Hayley was confident the Garbers would see things her way.

Chapter 22

"That old bat deserves to lose everything after what she did to our Range Rover," Mary Garber slurred, swishing the ice cubes around in her gin and tonic to punctuate her point.

So much for the Garbers seeing things Hayley's way.

She had found the young couple where they always were after work. They were sitting on their front porch, even now in the dead of winter, enjoying what they called "deck chat," where they would invite friends over, mix their favorite cocktails, and everyone would gossip about who and what pissed them off that particular day. It was a reliable way to blow off some much needed steam.

The Garbers were relatively new to Bar Harbor. They had moved to the island full-time after visiting from Rhode Island one summer. They had fallen in love with the natural beauty of Acadia National Park, made fast friends with a few of the locals, and decided they were much happier living in a small town rather than in the bustling city of Providence.

Hayley shivered as she took a sip of her Jack Daniel's and Coke, which Mark had mixed for her. The fumes of the alcohol shot out through her nose because the drink was so strong. She didn't dare ask if he had forgotten to add the Coke.

Hayley couldn't believe the Garbers were happily sitting outside in this freezing February weather, but they didn't seem to notice the subzero temperatures at all. In fact, they relished the harsh winter as a challenge, announcing they were not going to postpone deck chat just because it was a little cold outside. Of course that meant all their friends refused to show up to participate during the winter, so it was just the two of them partaking on this blustery February evening.

And add on Hayley, of course, who was fearing frostbite at this moment.

Thankfully, it had at least stopped snowing.

"I can understand how upset you must be over the accident," Hayley said, treading lightly. "It's very traumatic for all parties involved."

"Especially for the unsuspecting couple who innocently stopped at the Big Apple for some Diet 7UP and a pack of Camel Wides and then got blindsided by Angela Lansbury driving on the wrong side of the road," Mary said, lighting up after reminding herself she liked Camel Wides.

"Let me refreshen your drink, Hayley," Mark said,

snatching the glass out of Hayley's green mittens and dashing inside. Mark was in his early thirties, with a receding blond hairline, wire-rimmed thin glasses, a handsome face, and a lanky build.

His pretty wife, Mary, had dark, wavy hair and ageless lily-white skin, which was at the moment being threatened by her obsessive need to be puffing on a cigarette every five minutes. "I'm so happy you dropped by for deck chat, Hayley. Mark and I were just saying how much we miss all our friends. They can't take a little chill in the air—what a bunch of wimps!"

"Well, to be honest, Mary, I'm one of those wimps," Hayley said, shivering.

Mary laughed. She actually thought Hayley was joking.

Hayley plowed on, hoping to make a little headway. "Anyway, I stopped by the hospital to visit Mrs. Tubbs earlier and she was very upset over your plans to sue her."

"She should be. We're taking that old biddy down," Mary said, almost gleefully.

"Isn't that a little harsh, Mary?" Hayley said softly, not wanting to raise Mary's ire.

Mary was a much better friend than an enemy.

"I don't think so. In fact, I see this as a public-safety issue. By keeping 'Grandma Leadfoot' off the road permanently, we're making the streets much safer for all drivers. This is our way of performing a public service. It's not like we're doing any of this for the money."

Mark swung open the screen door and emerged with Hayley's cocktail. It was running down the sides of the glass because it was so full. After he handed it to her, Hayley sipped enough to get the drink below the rim of the glass. She also nearly choked on the whiskey. Mark still hadn't thought to add any Coca-Cola.

In Mark's other hand was a brochure. He knelt down and showed Hayley.

It was a car brochure.

Mark unfolded it in front of her, his face beaming.

"Take a look, Hayley. Mercedes-Benz E550. Alarm system, rear-window defroster, black leather interior, GPS, satellite radio, and rearview camera for easy backing up. Isn't she a beauty? We'll have enough for the down payment, once we get the settlement. Right, Mary?"

Mary glared at her husband, but she kept her cool. "It's something we're considering down the road. Once we're through with our public duty to protect the residents of Bar Harbor."

"'Considering'? We filled out the loan application today. The lawyer says the insurance company will probably want to settle within weeks."

Mary downed her gin and tonic and nearly threw her glass at her husband. "Mark, shut your trap and go make me another drink."

Mark retreated inside, slumped over like a misbehaving dog swatted on the rear end with a rolled-up newspaper.

"The problem is, Mary, Imogen Tubbs isn't covered by insurance. She forgot to pay her premium," Hayley said.

"What? What kind of idiot forgets to pay her premium?" Mary wailed, thoughts of her dream car fading.

"Well, sometimes life gets in the way . . . ," Hayley said, a tad defensively.

"You pay your insurance so when the unthinkable happens, you're prepared! That's the whole point! What imbecile doesn't know that?"

"Mrs. Tubbs has never been the same since her husband died. She's a sad, confused old woman who is just in a little over her head when it comes to taking care of details," Hayley said.

That was Mrs. Tubbs's excuse.

Now what was Hayley's?

"Okay, so we're looking at bupkus from the insurance company. That changes everything," Mary said, grinding the butt of her cigarette against the wide arm of the brown wooden deck chair where she was sitting.

"Good. I'm glad that's settled," Hayley said, relieved.

"You think that house of hers is paid off? Because that place is at least worth a couple hundred grand."

"Mary, you're not thinking of taking Mrs. Tubbs's house, are you? That's crazy!"

"Of course not, Hayley! I would never live in an ugly little house like that! It's only got one bathroom!"

"Well, I'm happy to hear that."

"I'm going to sell it and buy Candace Culpepper's house next door. Now that she's pushing up daisies, I'm sure the family will want to unload it. That's a house we can work with. Three bedrooms, full dining room, two-and-a-half baths. But I'll have to turn one of the bedrooms into an office, because I don't want Mark's crazy mother thinking she can come up from Atlanta and visit us anytime she wants!"

The screen door creaked open and Mark quietly returned to the porch, armed with a new cocktail for his adoring wife. He gingerly handed it to her, gauging her face to see if her mood had improved.

He seemed to exhale when he saw her smiling.

"Mark, forget the Mercedes. We're getting out of this money trap and moving into a new house!"

Mark broke into a wide smile, relieved to be out of the doghouse.

"But, Mary, won't it feel weird living in a house where a woman was murdered on the front lawn?" Hayley asked, her mind racing, desperate to stop this madness.

"Please! It'll be a great ice breaker at all the fabulous cocktail parties we can throw there. The spot where she was stabbed to death will be the first stop when we give tours of the house!"

"That's a little cold, isn't it?" Hayley asked, revolted.

Mary leaned in, lighting up another cigarette. "Not if you know the history we had with that bitch—excuse my French. Right, Mark?"

Mark nodded, stepping away, not anxious to get into it. But Mary was buzzed enough from her six gin and tonics, and there was no stopping her now.

And, honestly, Hayley was dying to hear the gossip.

This is what deck chat was all about.

"When we first got to town, Candace put the moves on Mark when we dressed up in period costumes and went to the Way Back Ball. She showed up in her nineteenth-century *Pride and Prejudice* getup, complete with hoopskirt. She basically lifted it up and trapped poor Mark inside it when he bent over to tie his shoe. I don't know what she was expecting him to do under there! Well, I do have some idea—but every time I try to picture it, I get sick to my stomach."

"Are you sure she was making a pass? It might have just been a bad joke," Hayley said, looking to Mark to back her up.

But Mark just looked away.

"She had been eyeing my husband ever since we set foot on this island, and I was ready to snap. I will tell you this, Hayley. I applaud whoever it was who finally did her in, because I was *this* close to doing the job myself. If we weren't at the police station filling out the paperwork from the accident for Officers Donnie and Earl, we probably wouldn't have an alibi and my ass would be in jail right now," Mary said.

"What time did you arrive at the station?"

"Around eight-thirty that night," Mark said, calculating in his mind.

"Officer Earl didn't know what the hell he was doing," Mary scoffed. "So we didn't get out of there until right before ten."

If they were telling the truth, and Hayley could easily confirm it with Officer Earl, then despite their thorny relationship with Candace, they were definitely innocent of her murder.

Hayley emptied her lethal cocktail into the snow off the deck when Mark and Mary weren't looking. Then she thanked them for allowing her to intrude on their deck chat and walked back to Randy's house. She passed by the hospital and was grateful that visiting hours were over. Because she just didn't have the heart to break it to Mrs. Tubbs that the Garbers had big plans that included Imogen becoming homeless.

Chapter 23

Lex's face lit up when he opened his front door to find Hayley standing there; she was holding a covered green Tupperware container.

"I brought you dinner," she said, handing it to him. "And I made enough for two."

Lex reached down and kissed Hayley on the cheek; then he ushered her inside. "You just made my night. Come in."

After extricating herself from Mark and Mary Garber's bone-chilling deck chat, Hayley returned to Randy's house, where she opened the refrigerator and saw enough shrimp left over, thanks to her two-for-one coupon, to whip up some more of her garlic shrimp pasta dish. She had been feeling guilty for basically ignoring Lex lately, so why not prepare him a home-cooked meal and deliver it to him in person? The Hollingsworth estate was walking distance from Randy's house. So after checking her watch, she knew she would have enough time to prepare it and then rush over to Lex's caretaker house before he had a chance to slap some baloney between a couple slices of Wonder bread, lather on some mayonnaise, pop open a Bud Light, and call it a night.

She knew Clark Hollingsworth was working Lex's fingers to the bone ever since he blew into town, and Lex wasn't getting home from all his estate duties until well after eight every night.

Lex went upstairs to take a quick shower, having just walked through the door seconds before Hayley showed up. She went about setting two places at the kitchen table, lighting some candles for ambience, and heating up her dish in the oven. It felt good having a meal with Lex, relaxing with some cheap red wine, and just catching up.

She was still contemplating her feelings. They had been in a holding pattern for some time now, not sure whether either was ready to take it to the next level. So it was nice, finally, to spend a little quality time together.

Lex wolfed down his meal gratefully, downed two glasses of wine, and then checked his watch.

"What could Clark possibly want you to do this late at night?" Hayley asked.

"It's not Clark, babe. We got six inches of snow today and I promised a few friends I'd come by tonight and plow their driveways."

"Do you have to do it tonight?"

"Afraid so. Clark's got a list of chores in the morning and I have to be up and out the door by four-thirty."

"What a slave driver," Hayley said, shaking her head. "I really can't stand that guy."

"You and me both. I'm going to be done by noon, though, and could sneak away for a few hours. Why don't we take some time and do something fun, like go cross-country skiing in the park or something?"

"Oh, that's right. I forget you're 'Action Man,' someone who considers grueling physical exercise as fun."

"Damn straight. I wouldn't mind doing something physical right now," he said, throwing his napkin down on the table and standing up. "But duty calls. So, how about tomorrow?"

"Tempting. But can I have a rain check? I'm working tomorrow," she said with a sigh.

"Come on, take a personal day. You must have a dozen or so stockpiled. You're always at that office."

It was true. She had plenty of free days coming to her, but she didn't want to admit to herself that she was also demurring because she didn't want to waste time skiing in the park when she could be following up on leads connected to Candace Culpepper's murder. She couldn't admit that to Lex; he would most certainly take it personally.

"Let me think about it," Hayley said. "In the meantime, you go be the town's sexiest snowplow driver and make sure everyone can back their cars out of their driveways in time for work tomorrow. I will clean up here and load the dishwasher and call you tomorrow. Deal?"

"Deal," Lex said, leaning in again and kissing her. He cupped his hand around her neck and pulled her closer this time. Her lips pressed against his, and her first thoughts were wondering if she put too much garlic in the pasta and if he could smell it on her breath. But then she realized he had eaten twice as much as she did, so it didn't really matter.

She grabbed his neck too and pressed his lips tighter against hers.

Lex reluctantly threw on his coat and a hat and headed out the door, winking at her as he left. Hayley blew him a kiss and then took their dirty dishes to the sink and began rinsing them off with water as she watched the headlights of his truck come to life before he drove off the property toward town. She dropped the dishes and wineglasses and empty Tupperware container into the dishwasher, added in a little detergent, locked it up tight, and pressed a button to begin the cycle. She stood at the window for a moment, soaping up her hands, when she noticed something going on inside the main house on the estate.

She could see through the windows to the living room, where Clark Hollingsworth was waving his hands and yelling like a crazy man. He was having some kind of argument with someone, and it looked as if he was losing his cool big-time.

Hayley kept telling herself over and over again *not* to get involved. Just ignore it and go home. She put on her coat and zipped it up and walked out the door, closing it behind her. But deep down she knew there was no way she would not trot down and peek in the window to see what was happening, and that's exactly how events unfolded from that point.

Hayley crunched through the snow as quietly as she could. Her eyes were fixed on the living-room window, where Clark was pacing back and forth, still yelling. She was close enough now to see his face and it was beet red, and his head was twitching as if he was experiencing some kind of seizure.

She stepped over the hedges and ducked down underneath the windowsill to stay out of sight. Slowly raising her head, Hayley peered through the window in time to see Clark angrily swat at his own head with his hand, like some disturbed child trying to injure himself. That's when she realized there was no one else in the room with him. He wasn't having an argument with anyone. He was just yelling and screaming to himself.

It sent a shiver up her spine.

This guy was whacked out of his mind.

Suddenly a dog barked.

Hayley swiveled her head around to see where it was coming from. The barking was faint, from the direction of a neighboring seaside estate, off in the distance. The wind was carrying the barking sound and it soon began to fade away. Hayley turned her head back around to look inside, only to see the living room empty.

Clark was gone.

She took this as a sign to beat it and started to stumble through the hedges to get back on the plowed path, which would take her back up to the main road and home.

She was about halfway there when a stern voice called out from behind her, "What are you doing here?"

She spun around. It was Clark. Glaring at her. Not at all happy to see her on private property. "I, uh, brought Lex some dinner. He's been working so hard and not eating right, so I wanted to make sure he had at least one proper meal that didn't involve a Snickers bar this week."

"Where is he?" Clark asked, stone-faced.

"Well, we finished dinner and he went to plow some driveways around town."

"He works full-time here. He shouldn't be moon-lighting for extra cash. We pay him very well."

"He's not doing it for the money. He's just a very kind and generous man who likes helping people out."

Something rich 1-percenter Clark Hollingsworth would never understand.

But she wasn't about to say that.

"Why were you looking in my windows?" he asked, not moving, staring her down.

"Well, as I was leaving, I saw you in the house and you looked upset and I wanted to make sure you were all right," Hayley said, clearing her throat, not wanting to set him off.

"As you can see, I'm fine," he said, folding his arms. "Did you check out my alibi at the Porter House?"

"Uh, yes, I d-did," Hayley stammered.

"And?"

"And you were right. You were there most of the night."

"So I couldn't have stabbed my uncle's nurse. Now that we've settled that, are you going to leave me alone?"

"Yes, of course."

"Okay. When are you planning to start? To leave me alone."

"Right now."

"Good. That works for me too."

"Clark, I think we may have gotten off on the wrong foot and I would hate for you to think ill of me because I remember we were quite friendly when we were kids."

Clark bristled, clearly not wanting to go anywhere near the past.

Hayley was very perceptive when it came to body language.

But, of course, she kept going anyway.

"I remember when you were around ten years old and would come up here for the summer, and your uncle Edgar gave you that big, goofy Great Dane and you would walk him around town, or, I should say, *he* walked *you* around town."

Hayley laughed at the memory.

Clark didn't crack a smile.

"He was such a sweet dog. What was his name?"

Clark's eye twitched and his face started turning red again; he clutched his fists tightly.

There was a long, agonizing pause, until finally Hayley couldn't take the tension anymore. "Amos! That was his name, right?"

"Yes. Amos," Clark said quietly.

"You would bring him into the ice-cream shop where I worked during the summers and you would always order the same double scoop, peanut butter cup and chocolate chip mint."

"Yeah."

"And Amos would stand in the doorway, watching me like a hawk, waiting for me to spill some so he could swoop in and lap it up."

Still, no smile from Clark at the childhood memory.

"No, wait. My friend Liddy's favorite was chocolate chip mint. Yours was cherry vanilla," Hayley said.

"I guess so. Yeah, cherry vanilla," he said, resisting the urge to grab his face to stop his eye from twitching.

"We went to the same summer camp one year, remember?"

Clark folded his arms and nodded.

"I think that was the last time I saw you, until I ran into you at the supermarket," Hayley said. "I remember that summer we both signed up for the drama production of *West Side Story*. You were a Jet and I was a Shark, because I had spent most of the summer at the beach tanning, so I looked at least a tiny bit Spanish."

Finally he spoke. "Yes. I remember. I was a Jet. Who the hell cares? I didn't have a very happy childhood like you, apparently. I don't remember it so fondly. And I'd really like it if you left my property now."

His property?

Edgar wasn't dead yet.

This guy was definitely planning ahead.

"Okay, Clark, I'll go," Hayley said. "But just for the record, the drama production was *Hello, Dolly!* and I played Minnie, the hatmaker, and you were Ambrose Kemper, the artist. So your long-term memory really sucks."

Hayley turned and began walking away.

"I was in a car accident in my twenties," Clark called after her. "Messed me up pretty good. Did a number on my brain and affected my memory, and a lot of other things. It's not something I really like to talk about. It's very painful."

This took Hayley by surprise. "I'm sorry."

She then turned and walked backward, staring at him one last time, raising a mitten to give him a quick wave. He just stood in the snow, watching her go. His eye was twitching so rapidly now that his whole face was contorting.

Hayley could have bought his story about the car accident. It would explain why he barely remembered his summers in Bar Harbor. But a little voice inside her told her something else was going on here.

And she was determined to find out what.

Chapter 24

The headlights blinded Hayley and she stumbled back, tripping over her own boots, trying to get out of the way. The car slammed into a mailbox just a few feet from her, sending the letter box hurtling up in the air. Hayley knew she was about to be mowed down, so she hurled herself to the right, praying she wouldn't be hit. The front end of the car whooshed past her as she landed facedown in a snowbank. She heard the tires squealing as it spun into a hairpin turn, finally coming to a stop on the sidewalk.

And then there was silence.

Hayley sat up slowly and rubbed her knee. She banged it against the concrete sidewalk when she jumped out of the way and it hurt like hell.

She couldn't believe she was almost hit by a car. She was just walking home from the Hollingsworth estate, minding her own business, going over her bizarre conversation with the mysterious and creepy

Clark, when all of a sudden the car appeared out of nowhere and sped directly toward her. Was someone intentionally trying to take her out by breaking every bone in her body with a four-thousand-pound automobile?

She heard the door open and someone struggling to get out, huffing and puffing, unable to stand up. The person stopped, sighed loudly, and tried again. This time, though, the driver managed to climb out, but had trouble maintaining balance and grabbed the door for support.

"Hayley, is that you?" a woman's voice slurred.

She recognized the voice immediately.

It was Cassidy Culpepper, Candace's sister.

And she was stinking drunk.

"I want to talk to you," she bellowed, pointing a finger at Hayley, or trying to, since she was pointing nowhere near where Hayley was standing.

"I'm over here, Cassidy," Hayley said. "I hope you realize you just nearly killed me."

"Oh, don't be so dramatic," Cassidy sneered, stepping into the light from a streetlamp, her eyes half closed, her body swaying from side to side.

"Please don't tell me you've been at my brother's bar all night."

"Yes, I was, as a matter of fact, 'Miss Know-It-All,'" Cassidy said, nearly slipping on the icy sidewalk as she made her way toward Hayley's voice. "But he cut me off hours ago. Said he didn't want me drinking and driving, and tried calling me a cab, but nobody bosses me around! So I left and went to the store and bought my own bottle. I am not a child. I am a grown-up, who can make my own decisions about how much I can drink before it affects my ability to operate a motor vehicle."

Clearly, she was in no condition to make any decisions—let alone be driving. Hayley noticed the car keys jangling in Cassidy's hand. Hayley waited until she was close enough and then snatched them away from Cassidy.

"What are you doing? Are you trying to steal my car? Well, joke's on you. It's a rental. It's not even mine. So go ahead. Take it."

"I'm not stealing your car, Cassidy. I just don't want you driving anymore tonight."

"I don't like you," Cassidy hissed.

"I'm sorry to hear that," Hayley said.

"I don't like nosy people, who butt into everybody else's lives and stir up trouble and mess everything up."

"I'm not sure I know what you're referring to, Cassidy."

"Yes, you do. I've heard the rumors. I overheard your brother talking to some of your friends at the bar tonight, Middy and Lona!"

"You mean Liddy and Mona."

"Whatever! Who cares? I heard all about how you've been running around town asking questions about my sister. Well, I don't appreciate you sticking your nose into a private family matter."

"Private family matter? Your sister was stabbed to

death with a pair of scissors! Aren't you the least bit curious about who did it and why?"

"It's none of your business! Just stay out of it!"

"Why wouldn't Candace's own sister want to find out the truth about what happened? Unless you already know."

Cassidy's head nodded forward and she slumped over in a desperate attempt to look mean and threatening.

But, really, she just looked drunk.

"I don't like what you're implying. Why on earth would I ever harm my this-ter . . . sister?"

"Well, you said yourself, now that she's gone, you're coming into some much needed cash, which will feed your obvious shopping addiction."

"You think you're so smart, don't you, Doctor Phil . . . *Phyllis*? Well, I am warning you. Don't keep digging up stuff that has nothing to do with you. It slows everything down, and makes it harder for me to get what's coming to me, so I can finally get the hell out of this freaking lame-ass town."

Cassidy was now right in front of Hayley and trying to focus on her. She thrust her hand out at an invisible person next to Hayley. "Now give me back my car keys so I can go."

"No," Hayley said firmly. "I will walk you back to wherever you're staying or call you a cab, but I will not hand these keys back to you. And if you're seeing double of me, you're looking at the wrong one."

Cassidy snorted and turned her gaze to the real Hayley. She reached out and touched Hayley's coat, just to make sure.

"Oh. Okay. Keys, please . . . ," Cassidy said, tugging at Hayley's coat, forcing a smile. "Let's not take this to the next level. I don't want to have to hurt you."

"I'm not giving you the keys, Cassidy," Hayley said, speaking a bit louder.

"You're a bitch!" Cassidy screamed, stepping back, clenching her fists.

Hayley knew what was coming. Cassidy was going to try and punch her. As she reared back, Hayley ducked to the left, anticipating her move. The only problem was, Cassidy didn't raise her right arm. She was left-handed; and when she took the swing, Hayley leaned right into it.

Cassidy's fist caught Hayley in the jaw, a direct hit, and Hayley crumpled to the sidewalk.

Cassidy loomed over her and stuck out her hand again.

"I said keys, please!"

Hayley threw the keys into the darkness, like a Red Sox starting pitcher, so Cassidy could not get her hands on them.

At least not tonight.

She was way too drunk to ever find them in the snow.

Hayley then rubbed her jaw to make sure it wasn't broken.

Finally, giving up, Cassidy stumbled off down the

street, still swaying from side to side and muttering to herself.

Hayley climbed to her feet, to continue her walk home. She may have gotten clobbered, but at least she probably saved a life tonight.

Even if it was Cassidy Culpepper's.

Chapter 25

Hayley was still nursing a bruised jaw when she got up the following morning to make Randy breakfast. He didn't get home until two-thirty because he was busy balancing the books at the bar, so Hayley decided to surprise him with strawberry pancakes, his childhood favorites. By the time he ambled into the kitchen, yawning, dressed in a ratty t-shirt and gray sweatpants, she was already pouring syrup on his pancakes and setting them down on the table, along with a cup of piping-hot coffee and a copy of the *Island Times*.

"You're too good to me, sis," Randy said, giving her a peck on the cheek before sitting down. "I'm suddenly back in the fifth grade, late for the bus, and looking for my book bag."

"Well, I'm glad I could bring you back to a happy time in your life."

"Actually, I was late for the bus on purpose. I was trying to avoid that big bully, Jason Simmons, who used to tease me and call me 'precious' and steal my lunch money."

"Oops. Never mind."

Randy smiled and dug into his pancakes. "He's in prison now, so karma wins out again."

Hayley watched as Randy devoured the pancakes, stopping only once to close his eyes and savor the fruity taste. "Oh, man, I love these. Sergio never lets us have anything decadent like this. It's always fresh fruit only and maybe cereal, but it has to be multigrain and with almond milk. Yuck. And then, to make things worse, he's always saying things like, 'You know, if we got up an hour earlier, we would both have time to go to the gym.' Sometimes I wonder why we're together."

"You know what they say, 'Opposites attract,'" Hayley said. She stopped. The pain in her jaw was excruciating, and she turned away from Randy to touch it again and make sure it hadn't cracked. She didn't want him worrying, so she had no intention of filling him in on her confrontation with Cassidy Culpepper on her way home last night.

Randy opened the paper and perused the front page. "Officer Donnie claims to be making headway in the Candace Culpepper murder, but I don't believe him. Part of me thinks I should call Sergio and let him know what's going on before Donnie blows the whole case."

"Don't drag him back from Brazil. He hasn't seen his family in two years. Let them enjoy their time together. I'm sure Donnie has people helping him investigate," Hayley said.

"Yeah, and I know just who Santa's secret helper is too," Randy said with a grin. "Liddy, Mona, and I talked about that last night at the bar."

Hayley really didn't want to inform Randy that his little gossip session almost resulted in her untimely death in a hit-and-run accident.

Lucky for her, she only ended up with a sore jaw.

There was a knock at the door. Lex stood outside, waving.

"It's open," Randy called out, turning the page of the paper.

Lex strolled in, putting his arm around Hayley and giving her a squeeze. He tried kissing her, but she didn't want anyone getting near her throbbing jaw, so she turned away at the last minute.

"You all right?" Lex asked, a little hurt.

"Oh, yes. Fine. Just late for work."

"That's why I'm here," Lex said. "I have to talk fast. Clark likes to time my coffee breaks now. But I'm done at noon today and I want to go cross-country skiing."

"You should definitely go. You deserve an afternoon off," Hayley said.

"I want to go with *you*," Lex said.

"Lex, I can't. I have to work today."

"Come on, Hayley. We went through this last night. You have plenty of personal days coming to you."

"He's right, sis," Randy said, stuffing another forkful of strawberry pancakes into his mouth. "It's also a great way to work off this huge breakfast you made."

"I'm not the one eating it," Hayley said, rolling her eyes, before turning back to Lex. "I have a column due."

"You can write it when you get home, before you go to bed. I'm working late again tonight. You'll have the whole place to yourself," Randy said. "You'll whip something out in an hour and be done by the time *NCIS* starts. Then you can drool over Mark Harmon," Randy said before catching himself. He looked up at Lex. "She only likes Mark Harmon because he reminds her of you."

"Nice save," Lex said, smiling. He then looked Hayley in the eyes. "What do you say?"

She was tempted. That was for sure. And one afternoon skiing in the park was not going to make that much of a difference at work or in finding answers to Candace Culpepper's murder.

"Do it," Randy said, folding up the sports section and handing it to Lex. "Here. You can have this. I never read it."

"Okay, fine. I'll call Sal and let him know," Hayley said. "But I have to be back by five so I have plenty of time to write my column."

Hayley knew allowing Lex to have his way for once was the smart decision. Because if in the future an argument ever arose over how they always had to do what *she* wanted, she could trot out this prime example, which would clearly illustrate why he was dead wrong and was being completely unreasonable.

Yes, relationships were sometimes very hard work.

Lex returned to Randy's house a few minutes past twelve o'clock. After loading the skis in the back of Lex's truck and driving into the heart of Acadia National Park, Hayley began to question what she was doing. Cross-country skiing was far more arduous than downhill skiing. And she hadn't done it in a year, ever since her last skiing excursion ended in disaster. But that was another story.

She was also hopelessly out of shape. She was afraid she would force Lex, a natural athlete, to lag behind to the point where he wasn't having any fun. So she instructed Lex to choose a snowy path she knew well so he could ski ahead of her if she felt she was slowing him down, and then she could move at her own pace.

Lex, on the other hand, didn't care at all about how fast he skied the trail. He just wanted to spend the afternoon with Hayley. As they set off, Hayley was feeling winded and out of breath within minutes. Although the path was relatively flat, the snow was heavy and sticky, so it took a lot of effort to propel the skis forward. Lex showed no frustration with Hayley, who was obviously struggling, but she immediately started feeling bad.

"Why don't you go on ahead, Lex, and just let me catch up."

"It's a beautiful day. Sun's shining. Temperature's not too bad. I'm in no hurry."

"Okay," Hayley wheezed, digging her ski poles into the compacted snow and pulling herself forward a few inches more.

This was much worse than that yoga class.

Lex rambled on about how he was no longer happy working at the Hollingsworth estate, how Edgar's illness and Clark's unexpected appearance had changed everything. His crew's morale had sunk to a new low and he was no longer happy living in the caretaker's house because Clark was constantly around, reminding him how unsatisfied he was with the work Lex was doing. It was getting to the point where it just wasn't worth it.

Lex asked Hayley's advice.

Should he stay and hope Edgar recovered?

Or should he be looking around for different opportunities?

The only trouble with that was that in the dead of winter in Maine, those opportunities were few and far between.

Hayley wanted to tell him to follow his gut. Lex was well liked in town. He would find something else, given a little time. However, she couldn't get the words out. No matter how hard she tried, she couldn't speak. She was out of breath and ready to collapse. She actually would prefer the StairMaster at the gym at this point.

They had reached an incline—or in Hayley's mind, a steep hill—and she was having trouble climbing it with her skis. Every step forward she clumsily took with the skis, she slid back four more.

Lex extended his gloved hand to help her, but she waved him off.

"No, Lex, I need to do this on my own," Hayley said, determined. "But please keep going. I don't want to hold you up."

"You're not holding me up," Lex said.

"I have some advice for you, about what you should do, but I can't talk right now. In fact, I can't breathe. But once I reach the top of this godforsaken hill and take a little break, I'll tell you everything I think."

"You sure are stubborn, Hayley, but, okay, if you want me to ski on ahead, I will. I'll meet you at the top. I brought us a thermos of hot cider, spiked with rum, so that should give you a little incentive to get your cute butt up there," he said, winking.

Then, like an Olympian, he glided forward, without a hint of effort, up and up, until he was over the crest and gone.

Hayley gripped her poles and kept moving, inch by inch, making little progress, but at least going in the right direction.

She was about halfway up when she heard a

noise. Like an engine. It couldn't be a car. They were too far away from the road.

At least she wasn't worried about Cassidy Culpepper coming for her again. That poor girl was probably in bed nursing a killer hangover right about now.

The engine noise got louder and Hayley managed to twist her body around, keeping her feet planted in the skis to see a snowmobile approaching.

It was barreling up the trail behind her. She couldn't tell if it was a man or woman straddling it, because the driver was bundled up in a bulky black winter coat, jeans, black boots, hat, and goggles.

Still, her guess was it was a man.

Hayley smiled and waved, but she couldn't tell if the driver was smiling back. He just kept revving the engine and speeding toward her. Hayley lifted her left leg up and awkwardly moved her ski close to the edge of the path, followed by the other leg, to give the snowmobile enough room to get past her.

That's when she noticed the snowmobile veer in her direction.

She couldn't believe it.

Last night a drunken Cassidy Culpepper in her rental car, and now a renegade snowmobile. She knew there was no way to outrun him. Her only option was to fall off to the side and hope the snowmobile missed her.

She tumbled over, crashing through a low-lying branch and landing on her left hip, as the snow-mobile sped past her and up toward the top of the hill.

Although Cassidy was drunk and may not have in-tentionally been trying to run down Hayley, this snowmobile was a completely different story. The driver spun the snowmobile around and came flying back down the hill, taking direct aim at Hayley, who was lying just a few feet off the path.

There was no way she could get out of the way this time—not while wearing a pair of bulky skis. Hayley frantically reached over and unbuckled her boots from the skis, freeing herself. Then she crawled to her feet and ran as fast as she could. Deep into the woods. Finally hiding behind some trees out of sight.

The snowmobile slowed to a stop next to her abandoned skis.

Hayley poked her head around the tree to see the driver standing up on the running board and looking around trying to catch sight of her.

She ducked back behind the tree and hid there, until she heard the driver finally give up and drive off, back in the direction from which he came.

By the time Hayley trudged back over to her skis and was clicking her boots into place, Lex came gliding back down the trail to find her.

"Hey, what happened to you? I thought you were trying to ditch me."

Hayley was about to tell him what had just happened.

But then, something stopped her.

Lex would call the police and then Officer Donnie and everyone would make a big deal about someone trying to run down Hayley Powell with a snowmobile in the park.

All the focus would be on her.

She couldn't let that happen.

Not yet.

Not until she got a few more answers.

Chapter 26

After Lex dropped Hayley off at Randy's house, at around five in the evening, she shuffled inside slowly, nursing an aching hip from her fall on the trail. She was also still rubbing her throbbing jaw from the night before, when Cassidy Culpepper decked her with that unexpected left hook. The injuries were piling up and she still didn't have any concrete answers to the murder.

She slowly sat down on Randy's couch, cradling her laptop, ready to write her next column, when she felt a dampness underneath her. Her pants absorbed a sticky wetness just as the smell of urine wafted up into her nostrils.

Hayley groaned as she shot back up to her feet, forgetting about her hip and howling as a sharp pain shot through her side.

That damn cat.

She glanced around, spotting the big blue ball

of fur underneath an end table across the room, glaring at Hayley with his narrow yellow eyes and emitting a low growl.

"You are on very thin ice, mister. So help me God, if you don't shape up soon, I'm going to take you to the vet myself and have him stick a needle in your side and put you to sleep so you can never terrorize anybody ever again! Is that what you want? Is it?"

Was she really threatening a cat?

Had it come to this?

And did she seriously expect Blueberry to answer her?

Blueberry didn't seem to take her threats too seriously. He just flapped his tail up and down, making the point that he was not at all impressed with her angry tone.

Hayley looked up and saw Leroy at the top of the stairs, quietly approaching the edge, eyes wide open, his whole body slightly shaking. He glanced down to make sure the coast was clear before he descended to the kitchen to eat his dinner. But the second his paw hit the landing, Blueberry shot out from underneath the end table as fast as his fat body could manage, hissing and clawing his way toward Leroy. Leroy yelped and darted back up the stairs toward Randy's bedroom.

Hayley wanted to help her poor little frightened dog, but she knew he would find a safe spot out of Blueberry's reach and just ride it out.

Right now, she needed to find something to clean the stain on the couch with before Randy discovered it. She couldn't let him find more evidence that Blueberry was destroying his entire house. Randy just might poach the needle from the vet and put the cat down himself.

As she searched the shelves in the pantry, her cell phone buzzed in her back pocket. She pulled it out and checked the caller ID.

It was Gemma.

Finally something to brighten her day.

A call from her daughter.

Hayley answered the call. "Gemma?"

"Hi, Mom," Gemma sighed, sounding like your average put-out teenager.

"You guys having fun?"

"Have you forgotten we're in Des Moines? In the winter? If Dad's Wi-Fi goes out—and there's a pretty good chance it will—because he's having money problems again and can't pay all his bills, I will literally kill myself."

"You've only got a few more days to go, so hang in there."

Hayley made a mental note of her ex's financial difficulties. That might mean he would miss next month's child support payment, and that would be a disaster for Hayley. But no need to deal with that now.

"Dad's working all the time, and his girlfriend, Becky, won't leave me alone. She's trying to be my best friend, just because she's only a few years older than me. But we have nothing in common. She belongs to a knitting club, Mom. Yes, a knitting club. I'm being totally serious."

Hayley thought about joining one of those in town, too, hoping it might calm her mind down by giving her something to focus on when life got too complicated.

Right now, for instance.

She had been spending all her time chasing clues to a local homicide and trying to figure out how to fix a busted furnace before her kids came home from their dad's—and before they were all forced to bunk with Uncle Randy and Uncle Sergio until spring. Hayley was already wearing out her welcome, and her rambunctious, independent-minded kids showing up at the door would pretty much hit the fast-forward button on Randy's limit of generosity.

"Wait," Hayley said, finally registering Gemma's last few words. "Just how old is your father's new girlfriend?"

"Twenty-two," Gemma said. "But she tries to act all mature when Dad's around, because she wants him to think she's old enough for him to marry."

"Wow, twenty-two. That's really . . . young."

There was little comfort in knowing her ex-husband hadn't changed much. He always liked them young. He met Hayley when she was young. And the day she turned thirty, that's when their marriage troubles began.

Coincidence?

"Yeah, so she knits and cooks and acts like some 1950s housewife. But then when Dad's at work, she's bopping to Justin Bieber and begging me to let her streak my hair purple. It's kind of gross. I am *so* ready to come home!"

"Well, have you at least been able to spend time with your father?"

"Oh yeah. Tomorrow night we're going to the Olive Garden. Oooh, rubbery pasta and bottomless salad. Does life get any better than that?"

"You're so sarcastic. Where did you get that from?"

"You, Mom."

She knew Gemma was right.

So she decided to drop the subject.

"How's your brother?"

"He's right here. Hold on," Gemma said, passing the phone. "It's Mom."

There was some muffled discussion before Dustin spoke into the phone. She could hear the rat-a-tat-tat of machine-gun fire and the *ka-boom* of explosions in the background. He was obviously playing a high-stakes video game.

"Hey," he said, distracted. It was pretty clear he didn't want to risk a bad score by having to talk to his mother.

"I miss you. I'm so looking forward to you coming home," Hayley said.

And she meant it.

It was tough not having her kids around.

She would make a lot of noise about how she

relished the idea of a break from them; but when they were gone, she always quickly realized how much they worked as a unit and how much she loved them.

"Uh-huh. Did Spanky come by to see you?" Dustin asked.

"Spanky?"

Spanky was a friend of Dustin's since kindergarten. The two had grown up playing James Bond in the backyard and still hung out, even though their social circles had widened since starting freshman year of high school. Spanky also worked after school and on weekends at the Shop 'n Save as a bag boy.

"No, Dustin, why would Spanky need to see me?"

"Beats me," Dustin said; then in a surge of excitement, he screamed, "Yes!"

"Dustin, stop playing the video game and talk to me, would you, please?"

"Sorry," Dustin said, the gunfire and explosions suddenly gone. "I got a Facebook message from Spanky the other day asking me what time you go to work in the morning. He said he wanted to drop something by your office on his way to school."

"Well, he never came to the office. Do you have any idea what he was going to bring me?"

"Nope."

"Well, weren't you the least bit curious?"

"Nope. Should I be?"

Gemma may have gotten her sarcasm from Hayley, but Dustin certainly didn't get his mother's curious nature. Which was probably a good thing. She didn't want him running around town trying to solve murders after school, like his mother did after work.

It suddenly hit Hayley: the note in her in-box.

Could Spanky have written it and dropped it off before she arrived at the office for work, around eight in the morning? And if Spanky did sneak into the office and leave the note, then did that mean he really did know who killed Candace Culpepper?

She checked the clock on the wall.

It was late.

But she had to talk to the kid.

Once she wrapped up the call with Gemma and Dustin, Hayley looked up Carla McFarland's phone number.

"Hello?" a woman's rushed voice said.

"Carla, it's me, Hayley."

Carla McFarland was Spanky's mom and a fellow PTA member. She was in a perpetual state of frenzy and always answered the phone out of breath and annoyed she had to take time out of her personal chaos to talk.

"Hayley, you wouldn't believe the day I had."

And she was off and running. Ten minutes of how awful the winter had been, how she hated her job, how her husband was traveling too much and never around, how her youngest child, Spanky, was constantly getting himself into trouble, and how she didn't know how much more of this she could possibly take.

Hayley indulged her, letting her prattle on, knowing that at some point she would get tired and finally stop talking. Just when it felt like Carla was about to wind down, she said abruptly, "Hayley, it's been great talking to you, but I really have to go—"

"Carla, wait! I was hoping I could speak with Spanky."

"Why do you need to talk to Spanky?" she said, finally allowing the conversation to move off her.

"Well, as you know, Dustin is at his dad's in Iowa, and I just wanted to make sure there wasn't any homework he was missing."

"But the kids are on winter break."

"Yes, but Dustin missed the last few days before school recessed, and I'm afraid he won't be up to speed when he gets back and starts classes next week."

She seemed to buy it.

"Okay, hold on, Hayley. I'll get him. Nice talking to you and catching up and hearing what's going on in your life."

Hayley hadn't said one word about her life at any point during the ten-minute call.

"Spanky! Pick up the phone! It's Mrs. Powell. She wants to talk to you!"

She heard muffled yelling as Carla covered the mouthpiece with her hand. Hayley could still make out enough words to know Spanky did not want to take the call. But Carla was insisting. Finally, after almost a minute of back-and-forth yelling, Hayley heard a *click* as Spanky picked up the other extension.

"Hi, Mrs. Powell," he said shyly.

"I'm hanging up now, Hayley," Carla said. "Let's have coffee soon. Be polite, Spanky. Mrs. Powell will tell me if you cop an attitude. You hear me?"

"Yeah, okay, Mom."

Click.

"We're on winter break, so there's no homework. My mother already told you that," Spanky said, immediately copping an attitude.

"No homework at all? Not even penmanship?"

"Penmanship? Mrs. Powell, we haven't had that class since the second grade."

"Well, a little refresher course wouldn't hurt you, Spanky. You have plenty of room for improvement. Or did you just scribble that note like a child to hide the fact it was you if anyone, like the police, decided to check the handwriting?"

There was a long pause on the other end of the line.

"You didn't think Dustin would mention to me that you were asking when I arrive at the office in the morning? How did you know I wouldn't be there? I might have shown up at the office early that day and caught you?"

"Because Dustin is always saying how you can never get your act together and be on time for anything, especially work."

Note to self. Ask kids not to spread the word they have a disorganized and tardy mother.

"It was you, wasn't it, Spanky?"

Another long pause.

"Not answering my questions isn't very polite, Spanky. Should we get your mother back on the line?"

"No! Please! Okay, okay. Yes, I left the note."

"Why would you write that you know who killed Candace Culpepper?"

"Because I *do* know."

"I'm listening."

"You have to promise me that you won't say I told you. I'm getting my driver's license next summer and I'm saving for a moped, so I can't risk getting fired from my job at the supermarket."

"You have my word, Spanky. I didn't hear this from you. Now tell me."

She could hear Spanky take a deep breath. Then he spoke softly, almost too softly. She had to strain to hear what he was saying.

"The day someone stabbed Mrs. Culpepper, I was doing a price check in the household cleaners aisle for Bethany, the cashier. It was near closing time and Mrs. Alley was checking out, and she is always tearing the price tag off everything and then insisting things are on sale, when they're not. So I always have to go and get another bottle of something or other to prove to her we're charging her the right price. It gets so annoying—"

"Spanky, please get to the point."

"So, anyway, as I was going to find the price of some Windex, I saw Ms. Culpepper by the mops and brooms and she was having a really big fight with Ron."

Ron Hopkins. The owner of the Shop 'n Save.

"What were they fighting about?"

"I don't know. But Ms. Culpepper was laughing at Ron and then he told her that he was going to kill her. That made her stop laughing, and it was kind of quiet for a second, and then Ron looked up and saw me. And then his eyes were really scary and he screamed at me to get back up front, so I dropped the bottle of Windex and hightailed it out of there. And then the next morning, I heard from my mother that someone had stabbed Ms. Culpepper in the back."

"So, why did you just write me a mysterious note and not bother to tell me what you knew?"

"I didn't get the chance to finish. The door to your office was open and I was writing you that note because I know how you're always sticking your nose into creepy stuff like murder that's really none of your business. . . ."

"Spanky . . ."

"Oh, I didn't say that. My mother said that."

Note to self. Be less friendly with Carla McFarland.

"Anyway, as I was writing you the note, I heard someone coughing in the back and I got nervous and afraid he'd come out and catch me, so I didn't get the chance to finish what I was writing. I just got as far as saying I know who killed Candace Culpepper, and I was writing really fast so that's why it was kind of messy. I actually have very good penmanship."

"I'm sure you do, Spanky."

"Anyway, when I got home, I decided to just stay out of it. Until you called."

"Thank you, Spanky. I'm glad you finally spoke up. You've been very helpful."

"No problem. You want to talk to my mom again?"

"No, thank you, Spanky."

Not in this lifetime.

Island Food & Spirits
by
Hayley Powell

The other day after a rather extreme-sports-style cross-country skiing trek in the park, I was reminded of another skiing adventure I had last winter, which ended in disaster. Most of the town heard about it over breakfast at Jordan's Restaurant, so any hopes I had of maintaining a shred of dignity were quickly dashed. It all started when I went down to the cellar to look for a few sweaters I kept stored there, as we were experiencing a particularly bone-chilling cold spell. February in Maine. Big shock, right?

I was a bit depressed because my best friends, Liddy and Mona, were in Cabo San Lucas, Mexico, drinking pomegranate margaritas, poolside, at their fancy all-inclusive resort. They had invited me to join them, but I was too cash-strapped to go. Story of my life. Plus I didn't want to leave my kids, because I would miss them too much. That, and I knew if I left them unattended, they would seize the opportunity to throw a blowout party with all their friends at my house.

Anyway, while I was rummaging around for my sweaters, I happened to notice my cross-country skis standing up against the cellar wall and I realized I hadn't had them out all year. I decided the way to cheer myself up for not being able to go to Mexico was to clear my head with a little exercise. Yes, I was going to get up at five in the morning and go skiing and watch the morning light crest over Cadillac Mountain. What a refreshing and peaceful way to start my day before work.

Well, true to form, I overslept.

It was six in the morning and I was tempted to pull the covers back over my head. No, I was going to do this. I dragged myself out of bed and peeked out the window to check on the weather conditions. It was sunny and the ground was covered with a fresh coating of snow. Perfect! I quickly threw on my long underwear, pullover shirt, and pants. I topped that off with a sweater, ski pants, and a down vest. Then I got my ski boots on, grabbed my gloves, hat, skis, and poles. Because I overslept, and it was now going on six-thirty, I didn't have time to drive to the park, so I decided to stick close to town. I let Leroy back inside after he finished his morning business. For once, he had no interest in accompanying me and just trotted back up the stairs to my still-warm bed.

I skiied on some back roads, which took me to the shore path trail, and I huffed and puffed my way along the snow-covered route to the town pier. There wasn't another soul in sight, not like in the summertime when thousands of cruise ship passengers and tourists clog the scenic path.

I was merrily coasting along, when I rounded the corner in front of the majestic Bar Harbor Inn, which stood high on its hill above the town pier. I pictured myself skiing down the big slope that ran from the inn to the path. Why not? No one was around. A little downhill skiing instead of the rather monotonous, slugging-along cross-country version. It would be fun!

Sidestepping with my skis up the hill to the top, I took a deep breath and shoved off down the hill. My plan was to fall down to my side so I wouldn't overshoot the path and hit the rocks and water below. I laughed and screamed at the top of my lungs all the way down. Why not? It wasn't like anybody else was around.

Wrong again. Bobby Spear, who was chugging out in his lobster boat, which he had rigged for winter shrimping, saw me waving my poles in the air and screaming. Bobby assumed I was headed straight for disaster. He radioed the police station, claiming some damn fool was trying to commit suicide by skiing off the town pier and straight into the ocean. The police called the fire department for rescue assistance. (Since they share the same building, they probably yelled across the room.) The fire department, in turn, brought along the ambulance with paramedics.

In the meantime, after safely falling over in the snow, I decided to ski down the hill just one more time before heading home. That's when I heard loud sirens and truck horns honking. I hoped Bruce, my colleague and the paper's crime reporter, was home listening to his police scanner because he would finally have something to write about instead of bothering me.

I began to push off for my final descent, when suddenly, from out of nowhere, I felt arms grabbing me around my waist. I was lifted straight up into the air and my boots snapped right off my skis. As I tumbled, I found myself staring into Wilbur White's eyes. As you know, Wilbur is one of our big, burly, handsome firefighters. When we came to an abrupt stop, Wilbur was lying on his back. His giant arms were wrapped around me, our noses touching. He just stared at me in shock.

You know, I never noticed what nice brown eyes Wilbur has. I can't believe he's still single. Anyway, as we stood up and brushed the snow off ourselves, Wilbur explained about the frantic call he got from Bobby Spear. I was completely mortified, having to explain that I was just skiing down the slope for fun and was not attempting to take my own life. By now, word of my ill-fated escapade was all over the police scanner. Locals were showing up at the scene, hoping for a little excitement. Most of them had looks that said, "Oh, it's Haley Powell. Now we understand."

I was so embarrassed and didn't want to make eye contact

with anyone, so I looked out at the ocean, noticing how the islands dotting the bay resembled giant marshmallows. I'm not a morning drinker, but after this humiliating episode, I went straight home and prepared a big mug of Irish coffee, which I like to call the Snowman because of the three scoops of Marshmallow Fluff I put on top.

The Snowman

<u>Ingredients</u>
1 coffee mug
1 ounce Baileys Irish Cream
1 ounce Irish whiskey
3 dollops of Marshmallow Fluff,
   or whatever you prefer, but,
   honestly, who doesn't love
   Marshmallow Fluff?

Into a coffee mug pour the Baileys and Irish whiskey and fill with hot coffee, leaving enough room on top to add your desired amount of fluff. Then sit back and relax and let the stress of the day be washed away.

After work I went to the grocery store with my two-dollars-off coupon for a rotisserie chicken. I completely scored; because on top of using the coupon, they had just reduced the prices for the evening. I decided at that moment if I couldn't go to Mexico with Liddy and Mona, I would bring Mexico home to me. So it was going to be chicken tostadas for dinner! Simple, quick, and yummy! Olé!

Easy Chicken Tostadas

Ingredients

1 rotisserie chicken, skinned, boned, and shredded

4 large 10-inch flour tortillas (or 8 six-inch tortillas, depending on people)

2 tablespoons vegetable oil (more as needed)

2 cups shredded cheese or more, to taste

Shredded lettuce, diced tomatoes, salsa, sour cream and guacamole—optional

To assemble or to let those who are eating assemble their own. Place your chicken and other ingredients in bowls.

Heat a large frying pan to medium-high heat and brown tortilla on both sides until golden brown. Be careful not to burn. You can always turn down the heat a bit. Place tortilla on a plate and add the ingredients you desire. Oh-so-simple and mouthwatering.

Chapter 27

Hayley knew she couldn't just march into the Shop 'n Save and start hurling accusations at Ron Hopkins. That would be bad form and pretty stupid. No, she had to be more subtle in her approach. And she knew just how to do it.

She had heard through the grapevine that Ron Hopkins's wife, Lenora, had recently taken a second job moonlighting as a cashier at Bark Harbor, the local pet store.

She checked her watch.

It was ten minutes to nine.

She was pretty sure the pet shop closed promptly at nine. If she hurried, she just might catch Lenora before she locked up and went home for the night. The store was close to Randy's bar, but she didn't have a car to get there. So she threw on her boots and ran like the wind.

Her hip was still shooting pain. Her whole body was exhausted from all the cross-country skiing she had done earlier that day. As she trudged through the snow at lightning speed—okay, she trudged through the snow at a reasonable pace—but not fast enough to make it in time, because by the time she was standing outside the shop, the door was locked.

But the lights were still on.

She pressed her nose up against the window and saw Lenora counting one-dollar bills and slipping them into a bank envelope as she cashed out for the day.

Lenora was a petite woman, much smaller than Hayley. She had thin arms and legs, and her fine brown hair was pulled into a ponytail. She wore wire-rimmed glasses and a blue smock, which wasn't very flattering. Working in a pet store, she wasn't out to impress anybody. She used to look a lot prettier years ago, before she married Ron and settled into supposed domestic bliss.

Hayley rapped on the door and it startled Lenora, who thought someone was about to bust down the door and rob her.

A ridiculous thought.

There was very little crime in Bar Harbor.

Other than the fact someone had recently stabbed a local woman in the back with a pair of scissors.

Maybe Bar Harbor wasn't as safe as people assumed.

Hayley gave Lenora the biggest smile she could muster. Lenora zipped up the money bag and set it down on the counter as she came around and walked over to the door.

"I'm sorry, Hayley, we're closed."

"But it's an emergency! Please, Lenora, let me in."

"Can't it wait until tomorrow?"

"No, Lenora, it can't! Please! I need your help!"

Lenora didn't own the store, so she wasn't comfortable ignoring protocol. No customers were allowed inside after closing, especially while she was cashing out. But Hayley didn't seem threatening—or, at least, Lenora hoped not. Hayley was pleading with her eyes, making them as big and pathetic as humanly possible. Lenora finally shook her head, slightly annoyed, and unlocked the door.

Hayley tried to step inside, but Lenora blocked the door with her body.

Hayley took a step back and smiled. "I'm taking care of Mrs. Tubbs's cat, Blueberry, while she's recovering in the hospital."

"I heard. I'm surprised you're still alive to talk about it. You didn't hear about that maniacal beast's reputation before you agreed to take him in?"

"Apparently, I'm the only one in town who hasn't. Anyway, he's been peeing all over my brother's house, where I'm staying temporarily, and he just did a number on his couch. I'm trying to get it cleaned before Randy comes home from the bar later, so I need an industrial-strength stain-and-odor remover, pronto!"

Lenora nodded. "I have just the product. Anti-Icky-Poo. Works miracles. Come on in, Hayley. Just don't tell Doris I let you in after hours."

"I promise," Hayley said, crossing her heart.

Lenora stepped aside and allowed Hayley to enter. Lenora crossed to the back and started searching the shelves.

"I thought we had some right here," Lenora said, eyes scanning up and down the shelves.

"I didn't know you loved animals," Hayley said, leaning on the front counter as Lenora searched for the bottle.

"I don't. I hate mangy dogs and I'm allergic to cats, but I desperately needed a second job, and this was the only one that worked with my teaching schedule. We all know how poorly middle-school teachers are paid, and I have triplets who are almost college age. So I have to bank as much as I can, so I'm not caught flat-footed when those tuition bills start pouring in."

"Well, I know Ron's looking forward to doing some traveling, once the kids are finally off to college."

"Oh, is that what Ronnie told you? He wants to see the world? Isn't that special? What big exciting plans."

"Well, I'm sure you're looking forward to taking some time—"

"Oh, you don't understand, Hayley. Ron doesn't want me going with him. No, he knows I hate traveling, I'm afraid to fly, and I don't even have a passport. No, whenever I get the travel bug, I turn on Nat Geo and watch *Locked Up Abroad*, and that pretty much scratches my itch to get out and see this dangerous, crazy world. There's no way I'm risking someone slipping forty kilos of heroin into my suitcase! Then I wind up eating cockroaches for protein, while I'm spending the rest of my life in some prison in the Philippines. No, let him go without me."

"Won't you miss him?"

"Miss him?" Lenora laughed derisively. "No, Hayley, I won't miss him."

"Are you two having problems?"

"You might say that," Lenora said, returning from the shelves empty-handed. She pointed to a stack of papers on the counter next to the register. "Just going over his lawyer's latest offer. Of course he's lowballing me, that cheap son of a—"

"You and Ron are divorcing?"

"It's not public yet, but yes. We were going to wait until the triplets were out of the house, but we're only hurting them by staying together. We tried putting on a brave front the last few years, but it's hopeless. We just hold everything in, and then one of us inevitably explodes and the knock-down, drag-out fights start all over again. There's no point in trying to keep up a facade anymore. Might as well just get it done with, so we can both finally find some peace."

"Lenora, I'm so sorry. . . ."

"Don't be, Hayley. The last few years have been hell. Ron's not the man I married. He's angry and sometimes his temper, well, it can be rather intense."

"He hasn't hit you, has he?"

"No, but there were times when he'd go off

about something, when the kids were gone, and
he'd just yell at me and scream these awful threats.
I would get so scared that I'd run upstairs and lock
myself in the closet until he calmed down. It's been
that brutal."

Hayley was shocked.

Was Ron really as unstable as Lenora claimed?

Spanky did see him verbally threaten Candace.

Maybe it wasn't so far-fetched to believe Ron
Hopkins was unhinged enough to be capable of
murder.

"I heard a rumor, Lenora, that Ron had an argument with Candace Culpepper on the day she was
killed."

"Honestly, Hayley, I know nothing about that.
But I will tell you, if some evidence surfaced suggesting Ron had something to do with it, I wouldn't
be the least bit surprised."

Hayley stood there, staring at Lenora, flabber-
gasted. She was basically saying that her husband
from whom she was about to be divorced could be
a murderer.

Lenora put her hands on her hips. "I'm certain
we have some of that stain remover. Let me check
out back. Hang on a second."

Lenora marched past a curtain into the stockroom. Hayley couldn't resist picking up the divorce
papers and leafing through them while Lenora was
preoccupied.

Interestingly, Ron's lawyer had counteroffered a
generous alimony payment, plus child support,

until the kids were of legal age. But Lenora had written expletives all over it. She was clearly expecting more—a lot more. As Hayley got to the last page, she saw that in the upper-right corner, Lenora had written, *Half the business or we see you in court!*

So Lenora had her own motives for badmouthing Ron and suggesting he was unpredictable and possibly dangerous. Maybe she was even coaxing Hayley into drawing the same conclusions about Ron so she could haul her into court and have her testify against him in a divorce trial at some later date. Lenora was nothing if not smart. She was tiny but formidable; and like Mary Garber, she was another woman in town a person did not want to cross.

But even if it was Lenora's master plan to cement Ron's reputation as a bad husband with a vicious streak, in order to achieve her own personal goals, Hayley couldn't ignore the fact that Spanky McFarland was pretty much claiming the same thing, having witnessed Ron's red-hot temper firsthand.

And that made Ron Hopkins the number one suspect in Candace's murder.

Chapter 28

Hayley made a beeline from Bark Harbor, carrying the brown paper bag with the pet stain remover she had bought from Lenora, to Drinks Like A Fish, which was just a few doors down the street. She was hoping to hitch a ride with Randy back to the house after he left his trusty bartender Michelle in charge for the rest of the night. There were very few customers there when Hayley blew through the door: a couple of fishermen, playing darts in the back, and Liddy, sitting atop her usual bar stool, sipping a Manhattan and chattering to Randy, who looked tired. Michelle washed glasses at the other end of the bar.

Randy looked up and smiled, relieved to see her, probably in need of a break from Liddy. "Hey, sis, didn't expect to see you here tonight. Can I get you something?"

"No, thanks. I just had to go talk to Lenora

Hopkins at Bark Harbor and was wondering if you might be heading home a little early, so I wouldn't have to walk back to your place. It's too cold out."

Not having a car was really starting to become a major pain.

Much like her hip and jaw at the moment.

"Sure. Give me a few minutes to finish up some paperwork in the back and then we can go," Randy said.

"What's in the bag?" Liddy asked, swallowing the rest of her Manhattan.

Hayley had forgotten she was even carrying a bag. She didn't want Randy to know she had bought super-industrial stain remover, because it would raise his suspicions about another direct attack from Blueberry on his furniture.

"Just some treats for Leroy. Poor little guy has been so abused lately. I thought he deserved a reward for putting up with Blueberry."

It disturbed her that she was getting so good at lying.

Randy nodded and headed into the back. Hayley slid up on the stool next to Liddy, who signaled to Michelle that she was ready for another cocktail.

Hayley leaned into Liddy and whispered, "Did you know Ron and Lenora Hopkins are getting a divorce?"

Liddy spun around on her stool to face Hayley, her eyes nearly popping out of her head. "No, I did not! And how did you find out something that juicy before me? I pride myself on getting all the best gossip before anyone else! It's like my thing. It's what I'm known for!"

"She just told me. And apparently it's getting pretty ugly. There are lawyers involved and she's looking to get her hands on at least half of the grocery business."

"Well, she should take what she can get now and just walk away and forget all about the Shop 'n Save. That place is struggling financially and is very close to going under."

"How can that be? It's the only major supermarket in town."

"Well, I was up at the Bangor Mall doing a little shopping last week. For the record, I wasn't there shopping for clothes, because we all know their selections are, like, two decades behind. I mean, seriously, their idea of a fashion show is just opening the Sears catalogue and pointing. Anyway, I was only buying some facial products, just a few creams and cleansers—"

"Liddy . . ."

"I know, I know, I just need to clarify what I was there for. If word gets out I was actually buying a dress at the Bangor Mall, my reputation as a clothes horse is kaput."

"So you *were* buying a dress?"

"I've been very busy juggling three escrows this month and have not had a moment to get on a plane to New York to do some real shopping—so, yes, I needed an outfit for a fund-raiser on the fifth. You've busted me, Detective Powell! Another mystery solved. But—so help me, God—if you breathe a word to anyone . . ."

"My lips are sealed."

"Thank you. Anyway, I was coming out of—God, I can't even say it—JC Penney, when I ran into Sissy Rivers. I had to stuff the bag with the dress I had just bought into a garbage can before she spotted it. Luckily, Sissy is *finally* talking to me again after she caught me peeking into her windows a while back when I was personally investigating Karen Applebaum's poisoning. . . ."

"Yes, Liddy. I was there, remember?"

"Oh, right. I always think I was the one who solved that murder, but I guess you were around to help, too, as I recall."

"Yes, I had a little something to do with finding the killer," Hayley said impatiently, knowing she was the one who put all the clues together and finally unmasked the murderer. Liddy had a habit of bolstering her supporting-player status into a leading role. Which was why when she played one of Ophelia's ladies-in-waiting in a high-school production of *Hamlet,* she went around acting as if the play had been renamed *The Story of Ophelia's Best Friend* by William Shakespeare.

"Well, Sissy was complaining because her husband, Ted, the big-time attorney, has been working overtime lately. It seems the bank has retained him to represent them in a lawsuit against Ron Hopkins."

"The bank is suing Ron? Why?"

"The cost of the renovations to his store were spiraling out of control, and Ron needed to take out a huge loan to complete the job. The bank agreed because Ron played with the numbers and gave a rosy picture of how well his business has been doing. But it wasn't doing well at all. The store has been steadily losing money and he's in the hole for hundreds of thousands of dollars and he's already defaulted on the loan. So now the bank is initiating plans to take it over."

"So the coupon-clipping show taping at Ron's store is some kind of a last-ditch effort to bring attention to the Shop 'n Save and hopefully save it from bankruptcy," Hayley said.

Michelle brought Liddy her Manhattan.

"Thanks, Michelle, you're a doll," Liddy said, then swiveled back to Hayley. "Yes. They're paying him enough cash at least to keep the bank at bay until he can figure something else out. But he's playing a losing game. He's drowning in way too much debt."

"If that's true, then why would he jeopardize the game show by stabbing one of the contestants? He knew Candace had been selected to appear on the show. Ron would've wanted everything to go smoothly. It doesn't make sense for him to kill her."

"You think Ron Hopkins was the one who offed Candace?"

"It's a theory. He had a huge argument with her the day she was murdered."

"Hayley, I've known Ron since we were little kids.

When we were in the fifth grade, there was a spider crawling on his desk and he cupped it in his hand and gently went to carry it outside to let it go free."

"That's sweet."

"Yeah, it was, until he accidentally bumped into me as I was coming into the classroom and dropped it on my sweater. I screamed and brushed it off me and then stomped on it four times with my penny loafers."

"So, basically, you don't think Ron has it in him to kill someone?"

"Absolutely not. He's always had a bit of a temper, but he's really a pussycat. Sorry. I know you don't like thinking about cats right now."

"Lenora told me she was scared of Ron."

"Lenora also used to go around saying she was a distant relative of Princess Diana, until it came out Lenora was actually Lithuanian. She'll say anything to make herself look good. And if she's trying to take Ron to the cleaners in a divorce settlement, then I wouldn't put it past her to play the battered-wife card, which is despicable. Once it's out there, people in town are going to believe it—whether it's true or not."

"Ron was under a lot of pressure. Sometimes desperate circumstances cause people to do desperate things. They were fighting. Ron was already at his tipping point. Maybe things blew up between him and Candace and he just temporarily lost it."

"And stabbed her three times? That's someone with a real ax to grind."

"I need to find out what they were fighting about," Hayley said.

A part of her didn't want to know.

Because she was afraid she wouldn't like the answer.

Island Food & Spirits
by
Hayley Powell

While standing in front of the open refrigerator last night, contemplating what to make for dinner, I noticed one of the left-over chickens I had purchased tucked in the back, so I decided I would make a hearty chicken noodle soup. As I started pulling out the ingredients from the refrigerator, I reminisced back to a dark, cold night last winter when my days of making chicken soup nearly came to a grinding halt.

A friend of mine had dropped by my house and gifted me with a very large roasting chicken that she had won at the Congregational Church Christmas Bazaar. Since she had already bought a roasting chicken earlier that day for her Christmas dinner, and knew how much I love chicken, she chose me as the lucky recipient of her prize.

I immediately knew what I was going to do with it. Dig out an old family chicken soup recipe I hadn't used in a while and invite a few friends over to share my bounty. Well, they all jumped at the chance to come over the following evening for cocktails, conversation, and some good old-fashioned chicken soup.

Don't ever let anyone tell you cocktails and chicken soup don't go well together. Trust me, they do!

Luckily, I had three mason quart jars of a hearty, rich chicken stock already in the fridge from some experimenting I had recently done with another recipe. I placed the chicken in the pot, poured the two quarts of chicken stock over it, followed by a quart of water, and brought the whole thing to a boil before simmering until the chicken was ready to fall off the bones. Then I removed the chicken and cut it up into pieces, placed it in a plastic container, and set it aside to add to the soup tomorrow. Finally I added my secret seasoning ingredient to the stock. A little cayenne pepper always gives my soup an added kick and really warms everyone up. I placed the stockpot in the fridge to sit overnight so all of the flavors would blend together, because that's the way my grandmother had always done it, God rest her soul.

The next evening six girlfriends showed up—all of them commenting on how heavenly the soup simmering in the kitchen smelled. And I attributed it to my secret spice.

My famous pitchers of sage sangrias were flowing and we were having a wonderful time telling stories.

Have you ever noticed when you're with your friends and having cocktails, everyone tends to tell the same stories they've already told a hundred times? I swear, the more sangria we drank, the funnier the stories got, like we were hearing them for the

very first time. My sides were
hurting from laughing so hard.

I stood up to add the egg
noodles to the soup so they
could cook while I warmed some
loaves of crusty French bread in
the oven. When everything was
done, we all grabbed our glasses
and headed to the table and I
ladled out big bowls of the hot
chicken noodle soup for everyone to enjoy with the bread.

We were still laughing and
joking and I began to tell one
of my stories that everyone had
already heard. I knew it was a
corker and worked every time;
but as I got to the funniest part,
I suddenly noticed everyone getting a little quieter and reaching
for their glasses of sangria more
often than usual. Pretty soon
after that, one by one, they all
dropped their spoons and gulped
their drinks down like they were
stranded in the desert and dehy-
drated.

When I brought in a fresh
pitcher of sage sangria, everyone
began fighting over it. Liddy got

hold of it first, so the rest of them stampeded into the kitchen to get some water. Several ransacked the cupboards for glasses. Mona didn't waste time finding a glass; she just stuck her head underneath the faucet and let the water pour into her mouth.

Liddy, teary-eyed, dabbing at her face with a napkin, her voice hoarse as if it were burning, finally managed to ask, "Hayley, what did you put in that soup? I know you like things spicy, but, good Lord, did you try it?"

Staring at all the chaos around me, I said, "I guess I was so busy trying the sage sangrias, I forgot to taste the soup."

I picked up my spoon and dug into the soup, tasting it for the first time. At first, I didn't know what all the fuss was about. I had only put a teaspoon or two of cayenne pepper in it, but as I kept spooning it in my mouth, I felt a stronger burning heat start to kick up in the back of my throat. And then, as the burning became a raging inferno, the awful realization hit me that something definitely wasn't right with this soup, and it wasn't the cayenne pepper.

I jumped up from the table and ran to the fridge, whipping open the door and sorting through my mason jars. I should add that from now on I will start labeling them instead of relying on my memory. I identified two mason jars full of chicken stock still in my fridge, but two jars of jalapeno juice, which I use for pickling, were now missing!

When I finally mustered up the courage to turn around and face my friends, who were all staring at me, only now with red faces and sweat pouring down their cheeks, I put on a big smile and said, "I've got a funny story to tell you. And, hopefully, next year, when I tell it again over cocktails, we'll all be laughing together!"

For this week's recipe of chicken soup, it might be better if you follow the recipe, and, please, if you do want to add your own touches for heaven's sake, read your labels! Or if you're like me and don't use labels, check your ingredients very carefully!

Sage Sangrias

<u>Ingredients</u>
⅓ cup honey
⅓ cup boiling water
15 sage leaves
750-milliliter bottle rosé wine
Ice
Slices of lemon, to garnish

In a heat-proof bowl, mix your honey and boiling water together until dissolved.

Add the 15 sage leaves to the syrup mixture and muddle with the back of a spoon and let cool slightly, then strain into a pitcher, pressing the leaves.

Pour your bottle of rosé into the pitcher and stir well. Serve in ice-filled wineglasses and garnish with a lemon slice. Your friends will forgive you anything!

Hearty Chicken Soup

Ingredients

1 stewing chicken (about 4 pounds), cut up

3 quarts water

2 cans chicken broth (14 ½ ounces each)

5 ribs celery, chopped and divided

5 carrots, chopped and divided

2 medium onions, quartered and divided

½ cup chopped green pepper, divided

Kosher salt and fresh ground pepper, to taste

1 bay leaf

8 ounces uncooked medium egg noodles

1 teaspoon cayenne pepper (optional)

Place your chicken in a large stockpot and add the water, broth, half of the celery, carrots, onions and green peppers, ½ teaspoons salt and pepper and the bay leaf. Bring to a boil and reduce heat; cover and simmer for 2 ½ hours or until the chicken is tender.

Remove the chicken from the broth, cool, then remove the chicken from the bone and set aside.

Strain the broth and skim the fat; return your broth back to the stockpot. Add the rest of the onion, celery, carrots, green pepper; and salt and pepper, to taste. Bring to a boil. Reduce heat; cover and simmer until veggies are almost tender, about 10 minutes. Add your noodles and cook for 10 to 15 minutes until noodles are tender. Ladle yourself a nice big bowl. It's sure to warm you up on a chilly night.

Chapter 29

It was snowing again the following morning. The forecast was bleak. At least ten more inches, with temperatures dipping below zero. Hayley brought some hot chicken noodle soup, which she made the night before at Randy's house, so she wouldn't have to leave the office for lunch and spent the entire day working on her next column. She had been so busy thinking about Candace's murder, she had completely forgotten that the *Wild and Crazy Couponing* taping had been rescheduled after the murder to Friday morning.

Tomorrow.

She hadn't even practiced since that ill-fated run-in with Candace at the Shop 'n Save shortly before her murder. Mona hadn't been doing any dry runs either. She was keeping a low profile, hiding out at home and not venturing out much after she got sprung from the local jail.

By quitting time Sal offered to drop Hayley off

at the supermarket to get one last practice in before the big show.

Sal could hardly contain himself; he was so excited. His wife was finally arriving home from her trip this evening, so his life was finally going to get back to his much revered routine.

No more frozen dinners in the microwave.

No more wrinkled shirts.

No more sleeping alone.

Now he was just worried the bad weather would delay her flight from arriving on time. After dropping Hayley off at the store, he was going to drive straight to the Bar Harbor Airport and sit there in one of those hard metal chairs near the baggage claim area, where she would eventually emerge. He was not going to move until he saw her. Even if her flight from Boston was canceled and she had to spend the night at Logan, it didn't matter. He was going to wait for as long as it took to finally bring his wife home.

Hayley was happy for Sal. His poor wife was never going to be allowed out of his sight again. But at least she loved him.

The store wasn't busy when Hayley grabbed her cart, armed with a fresh stack of coupons, and, after starting the stopwatch app on her phone, began to tick off to herself the items she needed.

She knew household cleaning supplies were her best bet, so she rushed past the aisle of spices and ethnic foods and veered down, past the laundry detergents and surface cleaners, to the mops and brooms and sponges. She grabbed a couple of bottles of Pine-Sol and Scrubbing Bubbles off the shelf and then quickly perused her coupons, finding one with a whopping two dollars off a Lysol Toilet Bowl Cleaner Value Pack. She reached down to grab it, when she noticed that a big bottle of Clorox Concentrated Regular-Bleach had been stuffed in the wrong place behind a stack of Mop & Glo Multi-Surface Floor Cleaners.

Hayley knew Clorox was on her list, so this happy accident would save her valuable time in trying to find it in the aisle.

As she lifted it up, she noticed the white bottle was smeared with a red streak.

Upon closer inspection Hayley's heart nearly stopped.

The red mark wasn't ink.

It looked like dried blood.

Spanky McFarland had told her Ron and Candace were arguing in the household cleaning supplies aisle. He also said it was close to closing time when he saw them, so the place was probably close to being empty. Once Ron shooed Spanky away, he could have grabbed the scissors Candace was undoubtedly carrying, being the consummate couponer, and could've stabbed Candace. Then, perhaps, he dragged her lifeless body into the stockroom, which was just a few feet away from where they were standing, and hid the body until his staff working the night shift—Bethany, the cashier, and Spanky, the bag boy—clocked out and went home.

He could have dragged the body to his car and then stuffed it in his trunk. Driving over to Candace's house, he might have dumped the body facedown in the snow on the front lawn to make it look like she was attacked outside her home. Then he could have conceivably returned to the store and used the Clorox to clean up any bloodstains that might have splattered in the aisle. In his frantic attempts to scrub the crime scene clean, a speck of blood got smeared on the bottle. When he was finished, he stuffed the bottle behind the mops, and just forgot about it.

It made perfect sense.

But it was a wild theory.

And it depended on Ron Hopkins being a cold-blooded killer.

Hayley went to put the bottle of Clorox in her cart. She could have the police test the red mark to see if it was, in fact, Candace Culpepper's blood.

Suddenly a hand shot out and grabbed her wrist.

Hayley spun around and found herself, face-to-face, with a very agitated-looking Ron Hopkins.

"You don't want that bottle, Hayley. It's only half full. I use that one to clean up messes in the aisle. Kids dropping cartons of milk. That sort of thing."

"It's okay, Ron. I'll take it anyway," Hayley said, wrenching her wrist free.

"Why would you want a used product?"

That's when he noticed the speck of red on the side of the Clorox bottle.

His eyes narrowed as he focused on it.

He made a grab for it.

Hayley anticipated the move and pulled the bottle closer to her breast, as if she were a mother protecting a child.

"I can't let you take that, Hayley," Ron said, an urgency overtaking him. "There's plenty of bottles at the other end of the aisle."

"I'm taking this one, Ron."

He kept his eyes fixed on the red smear.

"What is that, Ron? What are you looking at?"

"It looks like . . ."

"Blood?"

Ron moved his eyes from the bottle to Hayley. "I'm not sure what you're trying to say. . . ."

"Is it Candace's blood?"

Ron stared at her for a moment before a flash of anger hit him and he lashed out, punching a fist into a display of Mrs. Meyer's Clean Day Limited Edition Gingerbread Dish Soap, sending a dozen bottles clattering to the floor.

"Give me that bottle, Hayley. You don't know what you're talking about."

Hayley backed away from him, still clutching the Clorox, suddenly believing Lenora wasn't making it up when she told Hayley about her husband's ferocious temper.

He moved closer to her.

Spanky McFarland, alerted by the crashing

soaps, rounded the corner, got one glimpse of Hayley's showdown with Ron, and scooted back up front, pretending he hadn't seen anything.

"Do you think I killed her?" Ron asked.

Hayley shook her head. "No, Ron. Honestly, I don't. But what happened here that night? What were you two fighting about?"

Hayley put a hand up, making the point she didn't want him invading her space by getting any closer.

Ron immediately got the message and backed off. He shook his head solemnly.

"I couldn't stand that woman and she knew it. She was always in here with her coupons, using them for everything, leaving with hundreds of dollars of free groceries. My business was already in trouble, Hayley. I was losing money by the hour and she knew it, and she took a perverse pleasure in bleeding me dry with her obsessive couponing."

"You clashed over coupons?"

Ron nodded, embarrassed.

"Okay, so if I take this bottle to the police and have it tested, then it will turn out that this speck right here is not blood?"

"No, it's definitely blood."

"But you can assure me it's not Candace's blood?"

"No . . . it's Candace's blood."

"Ron . . ."

"Look, that night I came out of the stockroom and saw her cleaning out this whole aisle. She was going to get everything here for something like a buck-fifty. I couldn't take it anymore, so I yelled at her to stop. I guess my voice startled her, because she had her scissors out and was clipping a coupon out of a flyer and accidentally cut herself. She was holding her hand and it was bleeding, and some of it must have gotten on the Clorox bottle. She was cursing me out, and that's when we really got into it. I told her I was no longer going to accept any coupons from her, and she just laughed at me and threatened to sue me, and that's when I totally lost it."

"Did you strike her, Ron?"

"No, Hayley. I did scream at her and, yes, I did threaten her. But I could never hit a woman, despite what Lenora might tell you."

"How did it end?"

"We both calmed down after a while and I apologized to her."

"Did she accept your apology?"

"Yes. And believe it or not, she actually said she was sorry, too, and asked if we could forget the whole thing. She told me that when she came into the store, she was already upset about something that had just happened, and me yelling at her just caused her to snap."

"Did you ask why she was upset?"

"Yeah, but she said she didn't want to talk about it. I saw tears in her eyes and she had a hard time keeping it together. When I reached out and touched her arm and asked if there was anything I could do to help, she just left her cart and ran out of the store without buying anything."

Hayley believed Ron.

Liddy was right.

He couldn't hurt a fly.

Or spider.

The question now was why was Candace Culpepper so distressed when she arrived at the Shop 'n Save with her coupons on the day she was murdered?

And who was responsible for making her feel that way?

Chapter 30

"Donnie, what the hell are you doing?" Hayley screamed, startling Officer Donnie, who flapped his arms frantically to keep himself from tipping over in his chair.

He had been sitting in Sergio's office, feet up on the desk, casually cutting a picture out of an old *Rolling Stone* magazine, when Hayley appeared in the doorway.

"Nothing! Sergio said I could use his office while he was in Brazil, so I'm not doing anything wrong," Officer Donnie whined, a bit too defensively, planting his feet on the floor and sitting upright in the chair.

Hayley marched inside and over to the desk. "Using Sergio's office is *not* the hot-button issue here."

"Oh. Okay," Donnie said, relieved. He thought for a moment and then looked up at Hayley with a crinkled brow and a curious look on his face. "What's the hot-button issue?"

Hayley pointed at the scissors in his hand. "What are you doing?"

"This? It's Mila Kunis," he said, holding up the picture from the magazine and showing Hayley. "She's an actress I grew up watching on this sitcom called *That '70s Show*, but now she's this, like, serious actress and she's in all these big, important movies, and she's getting nominated for Academy Awards and stuff like that. But she's even hotter now that she's gotten older, but she still seems really nice, and I've always had this, like, big crush on her. . . . She's so beautiful and she inspires me, you know. She's the kind of girl I'd like to settle down with someday—"

"Donnie . . ."

"And Sergio said it was okay to hang pictures in our lockers, here at the station, and I thought to myself, 'Whose beautiful, smiling face do I want to see every day when I show up for my shift?'—"

"Donnie . . ."

"And that's when I thought . . . 'Mila Kunis!' So I dug through some magazines and found this old *Rolling Stone* article that called her the sexiest actress in Hollywood, or something like that, so I decided to cut it out and—"

"I'm not talking about Mila Kunis, Donnie! I know who Mila Kunis is! I'm talking about those! What are those?" Hayley yelled, pointing at the scissors in Donnie's hand.

"Um, they're scissors, Hayley," Officer Donnie said, snorting and shaking his head at Hayley's stupidity. He demonstrated how to use them, before saying under his breath, "Like, duh . . ."

"I know what scissors look like, Donnie. But those particular scissors look exactly like the ones I found sticking out of Candace Culpepper's back!"

Donnie's face froze for a few seconds. When he opened his mouth to speak, his words came out in a tiny squeak. "Well, they're not the same ones."

Hayley folded her arms and stared at him. "You're lying."

"Am not," Officer Donnie said in a tiny whisper.

Hayley waited him out.

She knew he would crack.

Eventually.

Officer Donnie carefully set the scissors down on the desk and sat back in his chair. He looked like a child caught red-handed trying to pilfer a Nutter Butter from the cookie jar and ready for his scolding.

There was an unbearable silence.

Finally Donnie spoke. "What if they are the same scissors?"

"Then you've just used a murder weapon to cut out pictures for the collage in your damn locker! That's called 'contaminating evidence,' Donnie!"

"Well, I couldn't find any scissors in Sergio's desk, and then I went hunting in the office supply closet for another pair, but we didn't have any. So that's when I remembered logging these in as evidence, and I didn't think it would do any harm just to cut out one picture. I was going to put them right back."

"Your fingerprints are all over them now, Donnie!"

"That docsn't make me guilty!"

"I know," Hayley said.

Only guilty of being an idiot.

But saying that out loud was not going to help matters.

"I suggest you take those scissors and go put them back in the plastic bag you found them in and return them to the evidence room. Then you need to write a full report informing Sergio what you've done."

"Why do I have to tell him? It's only going to make him mad!"

"Because if you try to bury the fact you've accidentally tampered with the evidence, it's only going to make the department look bad, and when I find the killer and he goes on trial—"

"When *you* find the killer?"

Hayley stopped.

She didn't blink.

She just kept going.

"I mean, when you, the police, find the killer and he goes on trial, a screwup like this is bad enough. A cover-up is immediate grounds for an appeal."

She had seen enough *Law & Order* episodes to know Donnie's stalker-like fixation on Mila Kunis

and his obsessive need to have her image near him
at all times was a potential disaster for the case.

"Okay, fine. I'll type up the report. I wish I never
touched these scissors. They're broken anyway."

"What do you mean? They look fine to me."

"They don't work right."

For a moment Hayley studied the scissors lying
next to the copy of *Rolling Stone* on the desk and
then she gasped.

"Are you all right, Hayley?"

"Yes, I'm great. There's nothing wrong with
those scissors. You're right-handed, aren't you,
Donnie?"

"Yeah. Why?"

"Those scissors are made for a left-handed
person."

"Oh, that explains why I had a hell of a time cutting out the picture."

The significance of this discovery was totally lost
on Donnie.

And Hayley was not about to bring him up to
speed. He had botched things enough for one day,
and she didn't need him to know that she had just
zeroed in on a major suspect.

Hayley rubbed her jaw.

It still throbbed from her run-in with Candace's
mouthy, trashy sister, Cassidy Culpepper. As Hayley
replayed their big confrontation scene from the
other night over and over in her mind, she remembered assuming Cassidy was right-handed when
Cassidy reared back to take a swing at her.

That's why she leaned into the punch and took a direct hit.

Because Cassidy came at her with a left hook.

She was left-handed.

And a left-handed person would most certainly own a left-handed pair of scissors.

Chapter 31

After she left the police station, Hayley grabbed her cell phone and started making calls. Cassidy had said she was Candace's only living relative, so that meant she couldn't be staying with an aunt or cousin while she was in town. She had exited town the minute she was old enough, so it was also unlikely she kept in touch with any friends she could crash with while she was handling funeral arrangements. And after nearly mowing down Hayley and crashing her car, she stumbled back to wherever she was staying on foot. That meant she had to be checked in at one of the three hotels open for the winter and within walking distance of Main Street, where her drunken confrontation with Hayley had taken place.

Hayley knocked off the first two in less than a minute by calling and asking for Cassidy Culpepper's room and being quickly told there was no guest by that name registered.

That left the only bed-and-breakfast on the list. The Captain's Arms.

When she called the number, Clarence answered the phone.

"Hi, Clarence, it's me, Hayley Powell."

"Hey, there. It's kind of slow around here. Want to bring a movie over that we can watch together?" the bartender asked, chuckling.

"I'm going to forget you said that. I was wondering if you could tell me if a woman is staying there. A brassy blonde with big—"

"Oh yeah, Ms. Culpepper. Who could miss those . . . ? I mean, yes, she's a guest here."

"Is she there now?"

"I think so. She called the front desk to complain a few minutes ago that she didn't have enough fresh towels in her room. As you can see, I'm kind of a jack-of-all-trades around here. Bartender. Phone receptionist. Housekeeper. They got me doing everything because they're so short-staffed during the winter."

"Thanks, Clarence. I'm on my way over."

It was just a five-minute walk and Hayley picked up her pace. She didn't want to miss Cassidy running out to her lawyer's office.

When she arrived at the bed-and-breakfast, Clarence was behind the reception desk; there was a warm fire crackling in the fireplace.

Hayley approached Clarence, who was reading a copy of *Car and Driver* magazine. He looked up and smiled.

"Hey, Hayley, take a look at this 2013 Hyundai Veloster Turbo I'm saving to buy next summer. That's why I'm working so many shifts here, trying to come up with the down payment. I've calculated in my mind that by April I'll have—"

Hayley quickly glanced at the magazine photo Clarence was holding up in front of her and cut him off, "She's a beauty, Clarence. Cassidy didn't leave, did she?"

"Nope. But I haven't seen her since dropping off the towels, so I assume she's still in her room. Let me call her and tell her you're here."

He reached for the phone, but Hayley shot a hand out and stopped him from picking up the receiver. "No, don't tell her I'm here. I want to surprise her. Just tell me what room she's in."

Clarence eyed her suspiciously. "I'm not supposed to give out a guest's room number. House rules."

"Oh, come on, Clarence. It's me."

"Sorry, Hayley. I can't."

"Gee, Clarence, that's too bad. But I understand. Good luck saving for that car," Hayley said. "I just hope the bosses don't find out what kind of movies you play in the bar when they're not here."

"That was *your* DVD, Hayley! I didn't bring it in here!"

"I know that. But you were the one who put it in

the machine and had it playing in all its HD glory when Reverend and Mrs. Staples came in," Hayley said, feeling bad for having to resort to blackmail.

"You wouldn't," Clarence wailed.

"Of course not. But you know me. Sometimes after a few cocktails at my brother's bar, I'm such a jabberjaw, yammering on about this and that, and sometimes slipping and saying something I shouldn't. . . ."

"Room 4, down the hall to the left. And you didn't hear it from me."

"Thank you, Clarence. I can't wait for you to take me joyriding in that fancy new car of yours this summer!"

Hayley dashed off down the hall, leaving a very nervous-looking Clarence watching after her.

She reached the door to room 4 and tapped on it lightly.

No answer.

She pressed her ear to the door to see if she could hear any movement inside.

Hayley tried the handle. It was unlocked. She opened it slowly.

She poked her head inside and looked around.

The room looked as if a bomb had exploded: Clothes strewn everywhere. Empty liquor bottles on the floor. Makeup dumped out all over the bed. The bathroom door was wide open. There was a stack of fresh towels on the basin and some used wet ones on the floor.

No sign of Cassidy.

Hayley glanced around to make sure no one was there and stepped inside the room, quietly closing the door behind her. She poked around to see what she could find. She crossed to Cassidy's open pink suitcase on the floor in the corner and knelt down and began rummaging through it. Just a lot of twisted candy wrappers, old fashion magazines, and wrinkled clothing. She was about to move on, when she noticed something protruding from the lining of the suitcase. She unzipped it and a stack of file folders and paperwork fell out.

Hayley began poring over everything. Most of it was overdue bills and threats from department stores to turn Cassidy's accounts over to a collection agency. It was very clear Cassidy Culpepper was in deep financial trouble. There was a plane ticket stub that was dated the day before Candace was murdered. Which meant Cassidy lied. She told Hayley at the office that she came to Bar Harbor specifically for her sister's funeral. But according to the plane ticket, Candace was very much alive when Cassidy arrived in Maine.

Hayley was on a roll now, sifting through all the papers for more evidence she could use to nail Cassidy for the murder.

And that's when she found the smoking gun.

On one of the last files in the stack, Cassidy had scribbled the word "will" on the tab. When Hayley flipped it open, she found a very simple legal document signed and notarized by Candace that basically stated she was cutting her estranged sister off from receiving any of her money in the event of her death.

This had to be it.

Cassidy must have gotten her hands on a copy of this latest will, which was dated just two weeks prior to Candace's murder. Candace may have mailed a copy to her, just to rub it in that she was not going to get a dime of her money. Desperate, Cassidy probably flew to Maine to try and talk some sense into her sister, with the hope of changing her mind. When Hayley first spoke to Cassidy at the *Island Times* office, Cassidy was quite confident she was going to inherit her sister's entire fortune as her last living relative. That would mean Candace probably had not filed the new will yet and Cassidy knew it. Cassidy went to Candace's house to try and convince her not to file the new will, but Candace refused. They argued on the front lawn. Things got out of hand. Candace probably tried to walk away, and Cassidy stabbed her in the back with the left-handed scissors, knowing the original will, which gave her everything, was still on file in the lawyer's office. Officer Donnie was botching the case big-time, so Cassidy probably felt good about getting away with it. That is, until she heard Randy talking at the bar about Hayley independently investigating the case. She got nervous that Hayley might uncover something she shouldn't, like a copy of the new will, and that's why Cassidy nearly ran her down with her car and threatened her if she continued sticking her nose where it didn't belong. And perhaps she tailed her and tried to scare her off by chasing her down on a snowmobile in the park.

It all made perfect sense.

Hayley folded up the copy of the will and the flight stub and stuffed it in her coat pocket.

She stood up to leave, when she heard a noise.

It sounded like a woman moaning.

As if she was injured.

And then it was muffled.

Suddenly there was a loud banging against the wall.

Hayley jumped.

Was it an earthquake?

Bang. Bang. Bang.

More muffled moaning.

Dear God.

It was the headboard of a bed hitting against the wall.

Two people were having sex next door.

There was some girlish giggling.

A man's voice shushing her.

More banging.

Hayley instantly recognized the woman's voice.

It was Cassidy Culpepper.

And from her first visit to the Captain's Arms, Hayley knew exactly who was staying in the next room: Drew Nickerson, the host of *Wild and Crazy Couponing*. No wonder Cassidy's room was unlocked.

She had just slipped next door for a late-afternoon slap-and-tickle session with Drew.

Hayley marched out of room 4 and knocked on the door to room 3. At first, they didn't hear her, because the banging was too loud, so Hayley pounded on the door with her fist.

The banging stopped and she heard some faint, frantic whispering.

Finally a man's voice demanded, "Who is it?"

"Room service," Hayley said.

"Go away. I didn't order anything," Drew barked.

"Maybe Ms. Culpepper did. Why don't you ask her, Mr. Nickerson?"

There was a long pause.

The door flew open and Drew was standing there, wearing a pair of blue silk boxer shorts and nothing else. He frowned. "I should've known it was you."

Hayley pushed the door open wider to reveal Cassidy sitting up in bed; the comforter was pulled up enough to cover her ample breasts. She gasped at the sight of Hayley.

"What the hell are you doing here?" she screamed.

Hayley pulled the copy of the will out of her coat pocket and unfolded it, holding it up for Cassidy to see.

"Where did you get that? Did you break into my room?"

"I'm sure even Officer Donnie is smart enough

to put two and two together when I give him this, Cassidy. I'm sorry to say, you may be spending a lot more time in Maine than you ever intended. In the state prison," Hayley said.

"No! It's not what you think!" Cassidy screamed, grabbing a plush white robe draped over an end table and throwing it on as she leapt out of the bed.

Drew turned and looked at Cassidy. "What the hell is she talking about?"

"She thinks I murdered my own sister," Cassidy said.

"I have proof you were already in town the day of the murder, despite what you told me at my office," Hayley said.

"Yes, I was here. I came to ask Candace for a loan. I'm having some money issues right now and Candace had so much. She wouldn't even miss the amount I needed to pay off my debts. She kept dodging my calls when I tried to get in touch with her, so I flew up here to beg her in person. I figured she'd have a harder time saying no if I was standing right in front of her. But I was wrong. She actually took joy in refusing me, and then she sent over a copy of the new will she had just made up, completely cutting me out. I was devastated. I didn't know what I was going to do," Cassidy said, eyes brimming with tears and sniffling pathetically.

Drew sighed impatiently, annoyed to be sucked into this family drama that had nothing to do with him.

Hayley continued. "So you stabbed her, knowing

if she hadn't yet filed the new will, you'd still be the primary beneficiary. And then you lied about arriving in Bar Harbor after she was killed."

"Yes, I lied. I panicked. I knew if the police found out I was in town at the time of the murder, I'd be the number one suspect and I just couldn't handle that. Not now, when I'm in so much other trouble," Cassidy cried. "But I didn't kill her, Hayley. I swear I didn't."

"I'm sorry, Cassidy. The evidence suggests otherwise."

"She didn't murder her sister," Drew said.

"How do *you* know?" Hayley asked, keeping her distance from the slimy game show host with the nice pecs.

"Because she was here with me that night."

"But you were in the lobby alone, drinking," Hayley said.

"Yes, I was. Until around eight-thirty. And then I went to my room because Cassidy and I had previously arranged a little playdate. We had met the day before when she was checking in."

"I couldn't believe I was staying at the same bed-and-breakfast with a famous celebrity," Cassidy cooed, before catching herself and crying again.

"So you never saw Candace the night she was murdered?"

Drew and Cassidy exchanged nervous glances.

Hayley stepped forward. "You did see her, didn't you?"

"Yes," Cassidy said. "She showed up here, looking

for Drew. I had no idea he had been seeing her too. I guess we didn't hear her knocking, because the next thing we knew, she was standing in the door-way watching us and seething. I never saw her so mad. She told me she'd burn every last dollar before she let me get my dirty hands on any of her money. Can you believe she would say that to her *own* sister?"

Yes. Hayley could. If the sister was Cassidy Cul-pepper. But she decided not to make matters worse.

She turned to Drew. "And what did you do?"

Drew shrugged. "I invited her to join us. I've always had this sister-threesome fantasy, so I thought why not take advantage of a perfect opportunity?"

This guy made Hayley want to throw up.

Hayley went over the facts in her mind. Unfortu-nately, the pieces did fit together. Candace could have shown up at the bed-and-breakfast around eight-thirty. Clarence previously stated he was on his break, so he would have missed seeing her arrive or leave after her confrontation with Cassidy and Drew. Then Candace went to the supermarket and had her fight with Ron. Ron told Hayley that Candace was upset about something already when they had their heated exchange. Candace had just seen her own sister in bed with the same man she was infatuated with and who was also her costar in that grainy sex tape she made as a keepsake of their fateful encounter.

"Okay, so if you are telling me the truth, how can

you prove it? You two could be in this together and lying to protect each other. You could have both left here together and intercepted Candace on her front lawn after she arrived home from the super-market."

"Do you know how much I make per episode, Hayley?" Drew scoffed. "I do not need to commit murder for some kind of payday."

"You could've been blinded by love, willing to go along with anything to make Cassidy happy," Hayley said.

"'Love'? Are you serious? I'm a married man. I love my wife!" Drew laughed.

"You're *married?*" Cassidy gasped before picking up a pillow from the bed and whacking him in the side of the head with it before turning back to Hayley. "Call the woman who works in the kitchen here at the Captain's Arms. After Candace left, Drew demanded room service. The cook had left for the night, so there was no one here to prepare him anything. Drew raised holy hell because he says sex always makes him hungry. Finally they called the poor woman at home and had her drive back over here and prepare him a turkey club sand-wich and French fries. I'm sure she will remember. How can you forget being called back into work after you've just finished a twelve-hour shift?"

"I'll be sure to talk to her," Hayley said, turning to leave.

Hayley knew the cook at the Captain's Arms. She

was an honest woman with no reason to lie. If she backed up their story, and Hayley suspected she would, then both Cassidy and Drew would be in the clear.

And Hayley would be back to square one.

Island Food & Spirits
by
Hayley Powell

Last night before I sat down to write this column, I was looking around for my cranberry-banana-oat muffin recipe to share this week with you, because it's a nifty way to use up a lot of ripe bananas before they spoil (a budget-conscious cook never throws anything out). This I know from experience because a couple of months ago someone in my house who shall remain nameless, but whom I gave birth to sixteen years ago in an excruciatingly painful delivery, which I like to remind her of when she acts up, begged me to buy bananas and strawberries because she and her friends were going on an all-fruit cleanse for two weeks. After two days of whining about how hungry she was and how desperately she needed protein, she grabbed a couple of hot dogs out of the fridge. With all the suspect ingredients in a hot dog, can you really call it protein?

Anyway, this muffin recipe is extra special to me because I've been making them ever since I was a kid. So every time I smell the muffins in the oven, a lot of high-school memories come flooding back. Some good. Some bad. One really hard to forget.

I was a junior in high school and my girlfriends and I were sitting in the cafeteria and complaining, as usual, about how boring and immature all the high-school boys were, how they hadn't really changed much since we met most of them in kindergarten, and how none of them would ever be boyfriend material. Basically, we concluded that the whole lot of us was fated to spend these critical years of our lives single and doomed to loneliness. Well, all of a sudden, the most gorgeous-looking young man, with wavy brown hair, rugged good looks, and the cheek-bones of an Abercrombie & Fitch model, strolled into the cafeteria, blinding us all with the most perfect pearly white teeth I had ever seen! And don't get me started on his mesmerizing deep brown eyes! Who was this manly god from the heavens?

When you live on an island and know pretty much everyone, a tall, dark, handsome stranger tends to stand out. And when it comes to cute boys, high-school girls are like CIA agents digging up intel. We pulled together a complete dossier on him by fifth period. His name was David Wilkins. Transfer student from San Bernardino, California. Six-two. A Leo, with Virgo rising. Star basketball player, who was arriving just in time for our upcoming season. And my new boyfriend. Although he didn't know it yet.

I wasn't aware at the time that at the next table Sabrina Merry-weather had set her sights on him, too, and was saying the exact same thing to her friends. It was only a matter of time before our competing plans to win David's heart collided. During the next couple of days, no matter how hard I tried to strike up a casual conversation with David, Sabrina was always right there, butting in and adding her own two cents. It was so annoying!

When I got up the nerve to sit next to him at lunch with a tin of my homemade chocolate chip cookies, which I had prepared especially for David, Sabrina suddenly showed up. She plopped herself down in between us and began grabbing cookies out of my tin and shoveling them into her mouth, munching and chatting to the point where I couldn't get a word in edgewise (which is a miracle in itself, so I've been told).

When Sabrina finally took a breath, David thanked me for the cookies and said he had to get to class. Well, wouldn't you know, Sabrina was heading in the same direction for English lit, and even slipped her arm through his as they strolled out of the cafeteria together. I had to do something. I was losing this war! Mona, who was sitting across the table, had an idea.

She said, "If Sabrina's going to eat your cookies uninvited, then maybe you should add a special ingredient just for her, like a little laxative. That would keep her in the girls' bathroom for the rest of the day, and you can spend time with David!"

I couldn't believe what Mona was suggesting. I could never do something so awful. What a terrible idea. If anyone ever found out, I would be expelled! And then how could David ever ask me to be his date at prom? But later that night, while I was making my favorite cranberry-banana-oat muffin recipe to take to lunch the next day to share with oh-so-hunky David, I kept thinking of Sabrina. Suddenly I found myself searching my mother's medicine cabinet for some powdered laxative and then sprinkling it liberally into some extra batter I set aside for two special muffins for Sabrina.

The next day at lunch, I was careful to hand David two of the "nontoxic" muffins. When Sabrina sashayed into the cafeteria and squeezed her way in between us again, I sweetly offered her my extra special muffins, which she accepted with a fake smile. Mona was also at the table; she instantly knew I had taken her advice, because she had never seen me being sweet to Sabrina Merryweather. It was a dead giveaway.

That's when I heard my name over the loudspeaker being called to report to the main office because I had forgotten to hand in my permission slip for an upcoming field trip to a museum. I raced down the hall to drop it off, because I didn't want to miss seeing my muffins doing their handiwork on Sabrina. But when I returned, Sabrina looked perfectly fine. She was prattling on about how she was allergic to cranberries and that's why she had given her muffins to David, because he seemed to love them so much. He was at that moment chewing and smiling. This was the biggest disaster of my life! I had poisoned my future boyfriend! I immediately faked a migraine and got excused from school for the rest of the day. Later I heard from Liddy that David did indeed get sick and spent the whole afternoon in the boys' bathroom and couldn't even play in the basketball game after school against our chief rival, Ellsworth High, and we lost the game! I would be a pariah when everyone found out the truth!

Just as I began researching boarding schools abroad, Mona showed up to let me know she had saved my butt, and I owed her big-time. When Mona realized I had spiked the muffins, she waited for David to guzzle down the three cartons of milk Sabrina bought him to wash them down with. Then she slammed down her own milk and screamed, "Don't drink the milk! It's curdled!" David made a funny face and dashed off to the toilet, believing the milk Sabrina gave him was the culprit for his sudden need to go to the bathroom. Poor Sabrina was traumatized, and I did feel bad about that, but at least my reputation as a talented baker was still intact! Nobody was dissing my muffins!

Sadly, in the end, I didn't win my man. And neither did Sabrina. That weekend Darcy James, a sophomore, who was a candy striper at the local hospital, heard David wasn't feeling good and rushed right over to be at his bedside and cater to his every need. By Monday morning they were roaming the halls, holding hands, and I was back to moaning to my girlfriends how there were no good boys to be found.

It's always nice to relax with a cocktail before taking a trip down memory lane, and there's nothing more refreshing than a crantini.

Crantini

<u>Ingredients</u>

1½ ounce vodka
½ ounce triple sec
½ ounce vermouth
2 ounces cranberry juice

Mix all ingredients in shaker with ice, then strain into a chilled cocktail glass!

Cranberry-Banana-Oat Muffins

<u>Ingredients</u>

1¼ cups all-purpose flour
1 cup oats
⅔ cup granulated sugar
1½ teaspoon baking powder
½ teaspoon salt
1 egg
2 cups mashed ripe bananas
   (about 5 or 6)
⅓ cup butter, melted
1 cup cranberries
30 milligrams of your preferred pow-
   dered laxative (just kidding!)

Combine your first six ingredients in a mixing bowl and mix well.

In a separate bowl beat together the egg, bananas and melted butter until smooth; add to dry ingredients; stir to blend.

Stir in the cranberries, just until combined.

Spoon the batter into prepared muffin pans, filling almost to top.

Bake in a preheated 375 degree oven for 20 to 25 minutes or until tops spring back when lightly touched.

Then serve to your favorite man, ladies!

Chapter 32

As Hayley left the Captain's Arms, it was starting to snow again. She hadn't checked the forecast, but the flakes were falling in droves and it looked like yet another merciless storm was about to sweep over the island.

As Hayley trudged through the slushy sidewalk back toward Randy's house, her cell phone chirped; she checked the screen to see who was calling.

The Bar Harbor Hospital.

She was almost afraid to answer. She worried it might be bad news about Edgar Hollingsworth, and how that might affect Lex. Or what if something happened to Mrs. Tubbs? She could be stuck with Blueberry forever.

Hayley took a deep breath and answered the call.

"Hi, this is Hayley."

"Hello, Hayley, this is Evelyn Tate, over at the hospital. I'm calling because I have some news for you."

"Okay, I'm ready. Go ahead."

An agonizing silence followed as Hayley heard Nurse Evelyn shuffling through some paperwork on the other end.

"We're releasing Mrs. Tubbs tonight."

Hallelujah!

She was finally getting rid of that damn cat.

Oh, and, of course, she was happy Mrs. Tubbs was healthy enough to go home.

That was cause to rejoice too.

But, more important, she was getting rid of that damn cat!

"That's wonderful news, Evelyn."

"I know. And not a moment too soon. There was a mutiny brewing at the nurses' station. Nobody wanted to be assigned to her room. Way-too-high maintenance. I had two nurses call in sick yesterday when they found out they were going to have to take Mrs. Tubbs's blood pressure and dispense her medication during their shifts. And just tonight she made poor Tilly McVety cry when she delivered her dinner of beef Stroganoff and vegetables. Mrs. Tubbs called it pig slop and threw the tray against the wall!"

"I don't have a car right now, Evelyn, but let me call my brother and see if I can borrow his. I don't think he's working tonight. Then I can drive right over and pick her up and take her home."

"Don't worry, Hayley, my shift ends in fifteen minutes. I'm going to finish the necessary paperwork for her release and then I can drive her home myself and get her settled. She's been asking about her cat, so you can just bring him over to her tomorrow morning."

"No!" Hayley screamed, much too loud. "I'm sure Mrs. Tubbs wants her beloved cat to be with her on her first night home. I'll go to Randy's house and get him and meet you over there."

"Suit yourself," Evelyn said. "See you soon."

Hayley was beyond ecstatic.

She picked up her pace, practically running through the streets to her brother's house. She found herself giggling to herself, giddy over the prospect that Leroy would no longer have to quiver in fear and hide under a bed; that no more urine stains would devalue Randy's pricey rugs and furnishings, at least not more than they already had.

When Hayley arrived, Randy's car wasn't parked in the driveway. He was probably out stocking up on food and supplies, given the fact that the storm just seemed to be getting worse with every passing minute.

She raced up the steps of the front porch and inside.

As the sun descended, there was enough light left outside that she didn't have to switch on a lamp to find Blueberry. It was hard to miss him. He was a massive ball of blue fur, with demon eyes. And at the present moment, he was on the couch, flapping his tail, after having been awakened from a deep sleep by Hayley rudely slamming into the house. And he was not amused.

"Don't move! I'll be right back," Hayley said, not the slightest bit embarrassed to be talking to an animal that couldn't talk back. She was grateful for his silence, because it was easy to assume if Blueberry could talk, there would be a lot of four-letter words and constant judgment in the conversation.

Hayley found the plastic carrier in the kitchen and unhooked the cage's metal door, airing it out a bit before lining the bottom of the carrier with a ratty dish towel she found in the pantry. The question now was, how the hell was she going to get Blueberry inside the carrier? It wasn't like he was going to just prance in there willingly. No, she had to draw him in somehow.

She had bought some catnip on the first day she agreed to look after him, but never gave it to him because he was such a bitter, angry cat. She just didn't want to be around him much and had completely forgotten about it.

The plan was simple. Put the catnip in the corner of the carrier. The smell would attract Blueberry. And once he was lured inside, she would slam the door behind him and latch it and reunite him with his owner.

Well, you know what they say about the best-laid plans.

If you don't know . . . they say they never work.

And this evening was no exception.

The second Hayley walked in with the large

carrier, Blueberry's eyes popped open in horror. He flew off the couch, landing hard on the floor, and scurried for the stairs. Hayley couldn't let him get upstairs. He'd hide under a bed or a dresser, and then she would never be able to reach him— let alone get him into the carrier.

The cat was moving at a clip, but he was also morbidly obese and not as fast as a regular cat. Hayley had a few seconds to block his escape.

Blueberry darted to the right, in the hopes of running around Hayley. She hurled herself to the floor, using her body as a barrier; the carrier clattered to the floor next to her. Blueberry didn't stop. He took a running leap over her face. Chunks of blue fur flew up her nose and into her mouth and got into her eyes. She was blinded and gagging, but she managed to grab Blueberry's tail before his paws reached the landing.

Blueberry screeched and hissed and wriggled his body around. His claws scratched Hayley's hand, drawing blood, but she was not about to let go.

This was ending right here.

Tonight.

The cat was going home.

Alerted by the commotion, Leroy cautiously deserted his hiding place and was peering down from the upstairs railing to see just how this battle of wills was going to turn out.

Hayley was on her side, still gripping Blueberry's tail, now with both hands, determined to hold on. Blueberry's screeching and hissing just got louder and more intense. Hayley knew if she let go, it would be over. Blueberry would win. And she was not about to let that happen.

The carrier was on its side. The cage's metal door was still open. She could see the catnip wrapped in the dishrag. Hayley let go of Blueberry's tail with one hand, while she squeezed the tail even more tightly with the other. She extended her arm in the opposite direction toward the carrier. She managed to stretch her fingers enough to get inside the cage. She was just about an inch from the catnip.

Meanwhile, Blueberry was scratching and biting Hayley's hand, which still gripped his tail. She was afraid if she didn't do something soon, all that would be left of her hand would be a bloody stump. Her index finger was touching the catnip sewn with felt, which was in the shape of a tiny white mouse. She could feel the fabric, but she just couldn't get a good grip on it. She was stretching her fingers so far, they were aching. She ignored the pain in her other hand from Blueberry's wild scratching and biting.

Finally her middle finger tapped the catnip mouse enough so it rolled half an inch closer. Then she got it between her two fingers and slowly extracted it from the carrier. Scooping it into her hand, she brought her arm back around and mashed it against Blueberry's wild, crazed face like it was a cloth doused in chloroform.

Blueberry fought at first, madly thumping his tail, violently jerking his fat body around to wrestle away from the catnip, but Hayley had adrenaline on her side. It had all come down to this: a fight to the finish. And she was not going to lose to this four-legged Antichrist. She kept the catnip firmly clamped over Blueberry's face until his energy began waning. She knew it was working.

The catnip didn't cause him to pass out, of course, but he became disoriented, and less aggressive, and intoxicated by the smell. He was still fighting, but he lost his bearings, his sense of purpose. This was enough for Hayley to drag him by his tail to the animal carrier, stuff him inside, and then slam the door shut, quickly latching it. Blueberry was stunned at first, not used to losing a fight. He just peered out through the cage door, not quite sure what had just happened.

Hayley was still on her back, arms stretched out on the floor. She turned her head away from the carrier and closed her eyes.

It was over.

It was finally over.

She felt something wet on her face.

Opening her eyes, Hayley saw Leroy standing next to her, happily licking her right cheek, anxious to show his love and appreciation for finally ridding his kingdom of this wicked dragon.

Hayley took a moment to savor the victory and then she sprang to her feet. She found some doggie treats in the cupboard and gave one to Leroy to celebrate. Then she picked up the carrier by the handle and marched out the door, heading straight to Mrs. Tubbs's house, wiping the snowflakes out of her face.

By the time she got there, Blueberry was sound asleep in the carrier. All the lights were on in the house, but Evelyn's car was gone. Hayley knocked on the door and tried the handle. It was unlocked. She opened it a crack and poked her head in.

"Mrs. Tubbs, guess who's come home to be with you?"

"I'm in the living room, dear. Please bring him to me."

Hayley walked in and found Mrs. Tubbs sitting on her couch, looking remarkably healthy and spry for an eighty-five-year-old woman just out of the hospital. She threw her hands to her face and began to cry.

"Oh, Blueberry, I've missed you so!"

Hayley unlatched the carrier, but Blueberry didn't come out. He was still asleep, so she up-ended the carrier, perhaps with a bit too much gusto. The big, fat, furry blue blob tumbled out onto the floor. He opened one eye, stretched, and then groggily climbed to his feet, looking around, sniffing, still completely disoriented.

"My baby, I'm so happy you're home," Mrs. Tubbs said, clapping for him to come to her.

He turned his head and stared at her; then he swayed from side to side as he stumbled over to her and rubbed the side of his body against her leg.

"Isn't he a doll?"

"Yes. He sure is."

A voodoo doll maybe.

"I can't thank you enough for looking after him, Hayley."

"My pleasure."

"I hope he wasn't too much trouble."

"He was an angel."

Why upset the woman?

"Now that you're no longer cat sitting, I'm sure you'll have more time to spend with that handsome caretaker I've seen you out and about town with. What's his name?"

"Lex Bansfield."

"That's right. Handsome fella."

"He is, but he's been awfully busy lately. Ever since Edgar's taken ill and his nephew, Clark, has arrived on the scene with his own way of doing things, Lex has been working crazy hours."

"Oh, I've heard all about that one. The nephew," Mrs. Tubbs spit out.

"What have you heard?"

Mrs. Tubbs stopped and had to think about it. "It was Candace. She was trash-talking him. And she said she had some really juicy gossip about him. What's his name again . . . Clint?"

"No. Clark. Candace Culpepper told you she had dirt on him?"

"Yes, she did. Well, actually not to me directly. She was outside on her cell phone and I was upstairs airing out my bedroom, because poor Blueberry

had just eaten some of my peach cobbler, which I
had left out to cool, and had run upstairs and was
having a severe case of the squirts, if you know what
I mean. . . ."

Hayley closed her eyes, trying desperately to get
that image out of her head.

"Anyway, I opened the window and saw Candace
down there, and she was talking to someone on her
cordless phone. She was saying how she knew
Clark's secret, and she wasn't sure if she should go
to the police. . . ."

"What kind of secret?"

"I don't know. I tried to listen, but my hearing's
not so good anymore. She was pacing back and
forth, so I was only picking up a few of the words. I
poked my head out to the side, so my good ear was
pointing in her direction, but that's when my damn
windowpane fell and almost cracked my skull open.
Well, I guess I yelped loud enough, because that's
when Candace looked up and saw me. She gave me
this rude stare and went back inside her house, like
she thought I was eavesdropping or something."

The nerve of her.

Candace knew Clark's secret.

What secret?

And was it the kind of secret that ultimately got
her killed?

Chapter 33

On her way home from Mrs. Tubbs's house, Hayley called Randy's cell. He picked up on the first ring.

"Hey, sis," Randy said, his mouth full as he chewed something.

"Where are you?"

"At home eating your chicken-and-stuffing casserole. I'm not even using a plate. I'm just eating right out of the baking dish. I hope you weren't planning on having it for your dinner."

"No, help yourself."

"Good, because I just finished it off and I'm still hungry and dying for a pizza or anything with a crust or breaded. Why did our whole family have to inherit an obsessive need to inhale carbs?"

"It's our family curse. I'm on my way home. I should be there in about ten minutes."

"You want me to come pick you up?"

"No, I can walk. Besides, with how much it's been snowing the last few hours, you may not be able to get your car out of the driveway."

"It's no problem. . . ." Randy's voice trailed off.

"Randy? Hello? Are you still there?"

"Yeah, I'm here. I think someone just pulled into the driveway."

"Who is it?"

"I don't know. I don't recognize the car. I'm hanging up now to go see who it is. See you when you get here."

"Randy . . ."

Click.

Hayley couldn't understand why her stomach was churning and this overwhelming sense of dread was washing over her. She was never a big believer in women's intuition. It struck her as decidedly sexist. But she could not ignore the sick feeling she was experiencing at the moment. She picked up her pace, power walking fast, at first, and then jogging slowly before breaking out into a run. She nearly slipped on the icy sidewalk twice, but she managed to keep her balance before rounding the corner to see the house lit up and Randy's car parked in the driveway. She noticed a double set of tire tracks in the fresh snow and surmised it was one vehicle coming and going. Whoever had arrived at the house ten minutes ago when Hayley called her brother had clearly already left.

She mounted the porch steps and reached into

her pants pocket to retrieve her key, when she suddenly noticed that the front door was wide open. She cautiously entered and looked around. Instantly she saw one of the dining-room chairs tipped over.

That was odd.

"Randy?"

She heard a faint scratching.

She moved a little farther inside the house and the scratching got louder.

Then she picked up a soft whimpering.

Leroy.

She followed the sound of the persistent scratching to the downstairs coat closet and swung open the door.

Leroy scurried out, with a frantic look in his eyes.

Hayley bent down and scooped him up in her arms and held him tightly to her chest. "Hey, there, boy, where's Uncle Randy?"

Leroy licked her face a dozen times; his tiny little body was shaking.

Blueberry was gone at last. So, why was Leroy so upset?

Unless Randy's visitor spooked him.

The sick feeling in her stomach only got stronger.

She carried Leroy into the kitchen.

The empty casserole dish Randy was eating out of when she called had fallen to the floor and was smashed to pieces.

She hugged Leroy more tightly.

What the hell happened here?

Suddenly there was a high-pitched screaming and Hayley jumped, yelping in surprise. She nearly dropped Leroy, but he clung to her winter coat, not about to let go.

They were both scared.

Hayley spun around in the direction where the screaming was coming from.

It wasn't screaming.

It was whistling from a teakettle. Steam shot out of the spout. The burner was jacked up too high and was fiery red.

Hayley crossed to the stove and shut off the burner underneath the teapot and the whistling faded.

Randy was making himself a cup of tea, but he didn't stick around long enough to drink it. She looked down at the floor and saw a box of Earl Grey tea crushed as if someone had stomped on it.

Tea bags were strewn across the floor.

Randy's favorite *The Golden Girls* mug was on its side in the corner.

Cracked in half.

Hayley didn't want to admit it to herself, but she had no choice.

It looked to her as if some kind of struggle had taken place.

She glanced out the window.

The snow was coming down harder than she could ever remember.

She was going to be stuck in this house all night. At least until Lex could come by in the morning with his plow truck.

Hayley had no idea what had just happened to her brother.

Or where he had been taken.

Chapter 34

Hayley tried Randy's cell phone three more times, and each time she got his voicemail.

She was worried and was feeling really alone and isolated now.

Part of her wanted to start scouring the town looking for him, but she knew that would just be a waste of time. Snow was blanketing the entire island, making it treacherous to drive and impossible to walk.

She wasn't going anywhere, and she knew it.

She kept trying to convince herself that she was blowing this out of proportion, but then she would glance at the tipped-over dining-room chair, *The Golden Girls* mug lying, cracked, in the corner, and the unattended teakettle.

Those clues clearly told her she wasn't blowing anything out of proportion.

Something disturbing had happened here.

And she started panicking all over again.

Her first thought was to call the police, but that would entail Officer Donnie spearheading the search. In Hayley's mind this would be a colossal waste of time. Clark Hollingsworth's name kept creeping into her mind.

Hayley fed Leroy and went back into the living room, sat down on the couch, and flipped open her laptop. She googled the name Clark Hollingsworth and started reading various articles, hoping to find some kind of clue that would indicate what kind of dirt Candace might have had on him.

Based on the material coming up in her search, it became obvious Clark was the kind of man who refused to just live off his family name and indulge in the typical hedonistic lifestyle of a spoiled heir. No, Clark Hollingsworth was trying to make a difference in the world: building toilets in Africa, working in an orphanage in Haiti. Fighting poverty was a passion in his life. It was a noble pursuit, and it didn't jibe one bit with the Clark Hollingsworth who had arrived in town after Edgar fell ill.

Hayley did a quick search for images of Clark Hollingsworth. But the only ones that came up were family photos from his childhood, surrounded by his cousins at a Hollingsworth family picnic on the island, which was covered by the local press. She instantly recognized the cherubic face she went to camp with that one summer.

But why were there no recent photos available?

She kept clicking, bringing up more articles, reading about more philanthropic deeds Clark had done all over the world. There was one photo that caught him, standing outside a new orphanage he had just helped build, surrounded by twenty beautiful, smiling Haitian children. He stood in the back, his face in the shadows, being very careful not to be seen.

Hayley leaned in for a closer look. He was about the right height as the Clark she now knew. Same build. The shape of the head hidden in the shadows was similar. But what was troubling was she just couldn't get her mind around this much beloved do-gooder being the same Clark Hollingsworth as the petty, secretive, coupon-clipping Clark Hollingsworth she had been dealing with the past couple of weeks.

Hayley went on to read about how press shy Clark was, how he didn't want his family name overshadowing the plight of the poverty-stricken he was working so hard for, how unseemly it was for anyone to make the story about him.

This was a good, kindhearted, spiritual man.

And there was no way this was the same Clark Hollingsworth as the one taking the reins at his uncle's estate and making Lex's life miserable.

Hayley had a gut feeling.

She kept researching.

Skimming more articles.

Desperate to find one clue that would back up the theory that was now taking hold in her mind.

And then she found it.

A tiny article from three weeks ago in a small Port-au-Prince newspaper. Clark Hollingsworth was hospitalized after experiencing a potentially life-threatening anaphylactic shock in response to an ingestion of peanuts. One of the orphans he was caring for brought him a chocolate bar and Clark didn't realize it was loaded with the nut, which he had been severely allergic to ever since he was a boy.

Hayley's blood ran cold.

Peanuts.

The Clark in Bar Harbor had bought peanuts at the Shop 'n Save.

Hayley had even given him a coupon so he could get a discount.

It wasn't the kind of evidence that would hold up in court.

But it was enough for her finally to be sure that the man who showed up at the Hollingsworth estate claiming to be Clark Hollingsworth was a big, fat fake. A con man who probably read about Edgar's medical condition and showed up posing as his nephew in order to pilfer as much as he could from the endless piles of Hollingsworth money.

He must have known Edgar was in a coma. And given how averse the real Clark was to photos and publicity, the locals just might buy his story.

And they did.

Hayley included.

Then there was the matter of Candace Culpepper.

When she wasn't at the hospital, she was working as a nurse tending to Edgar. She had access to his personal belongings. Maybe she saw a family photo of the real Clark Hollingsworth. So when the fake Clark showed up, she might have seen right through his insidious plot and threatened to expose him. He could not have her blowing his cover, so he had to get rid of her.

The only hitch in Hayley's mind was his alibi.

According to the entire staff at the Porter House, Clark was in plain view, shoveling down a steak and chugging a whole bottle of red wine at the time of the murder. Sabrina was adamant that Candace had died instantly, around nine o'clock, when one of the stab wounds punctured her lung. That meant Clark could not have committed the murder.

Suddenly the lights in the entire house went out and Hayley was plunged into darkness, except for the glow from her computer screen. But because of a low battery, she was about to lose that too. She used the few moments of light she had left from the computer to maneuver her way into the kitchen, where she found a candle and some matches in the pantry. She lit one just as her computer shut down and the screen went black.

She picked up the flickering candle and looked out the kitchen window. Complete darkness. Definitely a citywide blackout due to the snowstorm.

Hayley heard a noise.

Like someone jiggling a doorknob, trying to get inside the house.

Then she heard a loud *bang*.

Someone was using his shoulder to force open the front door.

Leroy jumped away from his food bowl and skidded out of the kitchen toward the front door, barking.

She held her breath.

Hayley used the candle to search the pantry for some kind of weapon. Canned fruits and vegetables just weren't going to cut it. She hadn't played softball since high school, so her throwing arm was rusty.

She held the candle up and searched the kitchen, spotting a knife block on the kitchen counter next to the stove. She rushed over and withdrew the largest knife she could find.

A butcher knife.

She gripped the handle and blew out the candle.

Leroy's barking was getting more frantic by the second.

Then she slowly walked out of the kitchen, back into the living room.

Another *bang* against the front door caused Leroy to go crazy and run in circles and bark as loudly as he could.

Hayley raised the knife, cleared her throat, and then yelled, "Who is it? Who's there?"

No answer.

Just more pounding.

Hayley moved a step closer and spoke more loudly. "I said who's there?"

"It's me. Open the door."

It was a man's voice.

One she knew well.

Hayley took a deep breath, stepped forward, and opened the door to find Lex Bansfield standing on the porch.

And he was stinking drunk.

Even more so than Cassidy Culpepper on the night she nearly ran Hayley down with her rental car.

"Lex, what are you doing out on a night like this?"

"I quit today, Hayley. I couldn't take it anymore, so I quit," Lex slurred, gripping the door to keep from falling over.

"Come in here before you freeze to death," Hayley said, pulling him inside.

"I finally told that bastard what I thought of him. Said he was a mean son of a bitch and I wasn't going to take orders from him anymore. And neither were my men, so we all walked."

"When did this happen?"

"This afternoon . . . right before happy hour . . . lucky coincidence. . . . Me and the guys have been celebrating our freedom at Drinks Like A Fish . . . since four this afternoon. . . ."

"So you haven't seen Clark since you told him

you were quitting? And that was around four this afternoon?"

"Yup . . . your brother have any whiskey on hand?" Lex took a step toward the kitchen, but then he stopped and steadied himself. "Whoa. Is it me or is the room spinning?"

Lex stumbled to the right, tripping over the upended dining-room chair and falling flat on his face.

Hayley rushed over and knelt down. "Lex, are you all right?"

She checked his skull for bleeding.

He started snoring.

It was so loud that Leroy quietly backed away, as if trying to steer clear of some kind of monster.

Lex would be fine.

But at this point she wasn't so sure about her brother, Randy.

She tried his cell phone one more time.

Voicemail.

She had to do something.

If only she knew what.

Chapter 35

Hayley reached down and tried lifting Lex by the shoulders to drag him toward the couch, but he was too heavy. She got him a few feet and then gave up, opting just to grab a pillow and gently place it underneath his head. He snorted, raised his head a few inches, opened his bloodshot eyes, and then looked around. He tried focusing on Hayley's face, a smile forming on his lips; but then he dropped his head down into the pillow and passed out.

His deafening snoring picked right up again.

Lex was going to be no help whatsoever. Hayley was just grateful he passed out in a heated house. If he had been stumbling along the sidewalk on his way here in such a drunken state, he could have toppled off the curb and twisted his ankle or fallen to the pavement and just passed out. He might have spent the whole night outside facedown in the snow.

He would have frozen to death.

The thought of that stopped Hayley.

Frozen to death.

Of course.

It all made sense.

It would explain everything.

Hayley treasured the giant white chest freezer out in her garage. Whenever choice meats and expensive seafood went on sale at the Shop 'n Save, she would buy up as much as she could afford and then store it in her freezer until she needed them. It was a great way to save money because the sales never lasted long and the food kept for months.

What if someone stabbed Candace and left her dead on the front lawn, but because of the cold temperature—it was below zero that night after all—her body froze, slowing down the decomposition of the corpse?

She remembered seeing something about that on the Discovery Channel last November.

Thank God she paid her cable bill that month.

What if Sabrina forgot to factor in the freezing temperature that night and got the time of death wrong?

What if Candace died hours earlier?

Then Clark Hollingsworth's airtight alibi would be blown wide open.

He could have stabbed Candace with the scissors and then strolled over to the Porter House for a steak and some red wine, where he hung out the rest of the night, closing the place well after ten o'clock when the murder supposedly took place.

Hayley grabbed her cell phone and looked Sabrina Merryweather up in her list of contacts. She hastily tapped the number and heard ringing.

Sabrina answered in a huff. "Yes?"

"Sabrina, it's me, Hayley Powell."

"Hey, girl. Can you believe this nasty weather? I hate it. It's nights like this I want to quit my job as county coroner and move to Hawaii. Not Florida. Why punish myself by going someplace where I'd be spitting distance from my crazy mother?"

"Listen, Sabrina—"

"Hold on a sec, Hayley, I have to yell at my deadbeat husband," she said. "Put your pants on! We're not having sex tonight! Get it through your thick skull! I've told you a dozen times already!"

Hayley didn't relish the idea of having to listen to this.

"No, I'm not in the mood! You want to get me hot and excited? Get a friggin' job!" she bellowed before returning to her usual sweet-and-fake tone. "I'm back, Hayley. Can you believe him? I work hard performing autopsies and assisting the police with complicated murder investigations, while he lounges around all day in his underwear watching Ellen DeGeneres and painting one Acadia National Park landscape a year! If I want to see this beautiful place where we live, I can just step outside. I don't need to hang a painting on my wall! Am I right?"

"Listen, the reason I'm calling—"

"I don't mean to unload on you, but I came home early today because of the storm and, shock of all shocks, he was actually at his easel working. I just about fainted dead away. But then the damn power went out and he couldn't see what he was doing, so he decided he wanted to do his other favorite pursuit. Me! Can you believe it? All I wanted was to sit on the couch with a glass of Chablis to relax and watch my TV shows I have stored on the DVR. I am so far behind on *Revenge*. Don't you just love that one, Hayley? That conniving girl sticking it to everyone who wronged her? She's like my role model. Only half my age, which is why I hate her. But I do love that Madeleine Stowe. If only I could be as bitchy and mean and hateful to my husband as she is!"

Hayley tactfully chose not to respond to that.

Instead, Hayley forged ahead. "Sabrina, I just need to know if it's possible for a dead body to decompose at a slower rate if it's out in the cold in freezing temperatures."

"Yes, of course, it's possible. Don't you watch the Discovery Channel?"

"So then it's also possible for a medical examiner to get the time of death wrong if she perhaps . . . or, um, he . . . didn't take the outside temperature into account when performing the autopsy and just focused on how much the body had decomposed?"

There was a long, stony silence.

"I'm not sure what you're getting at, Hayley," Sabrina finally said flatly.

"Well, is it possible you got the time of death wrong?"

"Absolutely not."

Hayley had known Sabrina since high school. And she knew she was lying. Hayley was right. She had forgotten to take the temperature into account. But she also knew Sabrina was never going to admit it.

"Do you have any idea the reputation I have built in this state, Hayley? I will not have you running around tearing me down by suggesting I got a very important detail wrong in my autopsy report. I thought we were friends. I thought you had changed since high school."

Changed? Me?

Sabrina was the ultimate mean girl, who had made Hayley's life miserable when they were fifteen. The idea that Sabrina believed Hayley was the one who was somehow . . .

Hayley stopped herself.

She couldn't get caught up in these memories now.

She had just identified Candace's killer.

And she still had to find Randy.

"You're right, Sabrina. I don't know what I was thinking."

"We all make mistakes, Hayley. You're forgiven," she said, taking a dramatic pause. "This time."

"Thank you. Sorry to bother you," Hayley said.

She knew she had to keep the county coroner on

her good side if she was going to keep jumping into the middle of murder investigations in between writing her food-and-cocktails column.

"You have a good night. Oh, great. My husband just walked by, eating a candy bar. The sugar rush is just going to make him hornier! I hate my life!"

She hung up.

Hayley's mind was racing. If Clark was indeed the killer, then he had to be the one who had tried to run her down with the snowmobile. And what if he had come back to finish the job, only to find Hayley not here.

But Randy was.

The thought of that sent a chill through her bones.

Chapter 36

"I don't know what you expect me to do," Officer Donnie whined on the other end of the phone.

"You're acting chief, Donnie. What you need to do is get yourself a search warrant from the judge—who, I'm sure, is home because of the storm—and get over to the Hollingsworth estate!"

Calling Donnie at the police station for help was Hayley's best option at the moment.

And that scared the hell out of her.

"Can't it wait until morning, Hayley? I mean, have you looked outside? It's going to take me at least an hour to shovel enough snow so I can back the squad car out of the driveway."

"Donnie, my brother is missing and I have reason to believe Clark Hollingsworth had something to do with it."

"Well, how long has he been gone?"

"I don't know. Maybe an hour."

"I hate to break it to you, Hayley, but you're not

supposed to file a missing persons report for at least forty-eight hours."

"Twenty-four."

"Yeah, I loved that show. Kiefer Sutherland kicked ass!"

"I'm not talking about the TV show, Donnie. It's twenty-four hours, not forty-eight. You only have to wait twenty-four hours before filing a missing persons report."

"Seriously? I could've sworn it was forty-eight."

"It doesn't matter, Donnie! That's not the point!"

"It kind of is, if you ask me, Hayley. You said your brother's only been missing an hour or so. That doesn't exactly add up to twenty-four."

Hayley wanted to reach through the phone and strangle his scrawny, little neck.

But she took a deep breath and tried again.

"Listen to me carefully, Donnie. Sabrina Merryweather got the time of Candace Culpepper's death wrong. Candace died much earlier, maybe six or seven in the evening, not nine o'clock, like she reported."

"Wow. Really? How did she mess that one up so bad?"

"It doesn't matter. What matters is Clark Hollingsworth no longer has an alibi. Plus Candace may have stumbled upon a secret he's been harboring—that he's not really Clark Hollingsworth. He's an impostor. A con man. And when he found out I was close to finding out the truth, he tried to run me down with a snowmobile."

"He did? You really should have reported that, Hayley."

"Again, Donnie, not the point. Just know that Clark's been gunning for me. And when he showed up at my house and I wasn't home, he scuffled with my brother, and now Randy's missing."

"How do you know he was at your house? Did you see him take your brother away?"

"No, but I saw signs of a struggle and tire tracks coming and going."

"How do you know it was Clark Hollingsworth? Or this pretend Clark Hollingsworth?"

"I just know, okay?"

"That's really not enough for me to put on my coat and trudge over to the judge's house to get him to sign a warrant and then hightail it all the way over to the Hollingsworth estate."

"Randy's life could depend on it, Donnie!"

"Should we call Sergio and get his take on this?"

Hayley couldn't control herself anymore. "No, you bonehead! Sergio's in Brazil, thousands of miles away! He can't do a damn thing! But if you don't do something soon, you're going to have to explain why you just stood by, doing nothing to save the love of his life, when you had the chance!"

Donnie pondered this. Then, after a long pause, he said, "Okay, okay. I'll head over to the judge's house. But you better be right about this, Hayley."

"I take full responsibility. Now call the judge and tell him you're on your way. Do it now, Donnie!"

Donnie hung up.

She knew in her gut she couldn't rely on him. He had been an unqualified disaster as acting chief. Randy was a dead man if it was up to Donnie to rescue him.

Hayley glanced down at Lex's prone body sprawled out on the floor, still snoring.

He wasn't going to be any help either.

Everyone else in town was holed up at home, waiting out the storm.

She was Randy's only chance.

Hayley lit another candle, picked it up, and raced over to the coat closet near the foyer. She swung open the door, dropped to her knees, and began rummaging around with one hand, while holding the candle up for light with the other.

She pushed aside a stack of cardboard boxes Randy used to store old clothes he was planning to donate in the spring. Behind them, Hayley found what she was looking for.

A pair of snowshoes.

She threw on her coat and carried the snowshoes outside, where she snapped them on her boots and began her arduous trek along the snowy shore path toward the Hollingsworth estate.

Hoping and praying that she wouldn't be too late.

Chapter 37

It took Hayley about twenty minutes to shuffle her way through the snow to the Hollingsworth estate. The lights were back on in the main house. But Hayley noticed the caretaker's house, where Lex lived, was still dark. This probably meant that Edgar could afford his own generator and didn't have to rely on the local power company. As she got closer, she noticed a black tarp hastily thrown over something next to the side of the house. She yanked off her snowshoes and carefully made her way over to the tarp, lifting it up to reveal a snowmobile. It looked similar to the one someone used to try and mow her down, but she couldn't be absolutely sure. Still, she was relatively confident it belonged to Clark and he was the one who came after her that day in the park.

Hayley quietly walked up the steps to the front door. She tried the knob. It was locked. She looked around for another way inside the house. She wasn't about to knock and announce her presence.

She crept around the house to the back and attempted to open a few windows. On her third try she found one that was unlocked. She used all her might to pry it open, as it was stuck. When it finally gave, it opened so fast that the pane banged noisily, and Hayley froze in her tracks, fearing Clark might hear her.

She waited a few moments to make sure no one was coming to investigate the loud noise, and then she hoisted herself up and crawled through the window.

She was in a small nook, just off the kitchen. She had only been in this house a few times over the years, so she wasn't that familiar with the layout. She was going to have to wing it.

Her adrenaline pumping, Hayley kicked off her boots and, in her stocking feet, soundlessly made her way forward into the main part of the house, acutely aware of the danger. But all she could think about was saving her brother.

There was no sign of Clark downstairs.

She kept close to the wall as she looked around, not wanting to move to the middle of the living room and risk exposing herself.

She stopped.

She heard a whirring sound and a pumping sound.

Like some kind of machine operating.

It was coming from upstairs.

She made her way over to the staircase, gripped the railing, and carefully ascended, taking great care to avoid any creaky steps.

The hallway light was off, but there was a glow coming from the master bedroom. She drew closer, until she was just outside the room. She poked her head around to look through the crack of the open door, and was surprised to discover Edgar Hollingsworth in his bed, hooked up to a variety of breathing machines, feeding tubes, and monitors, which were clicking and whirring and pumping and keeping his condition stable.

When did they send him home from the hospital?

Hayley stepped inside the room for a closer look.

Though rail thin and pale, Edgar looked as if he was just taking a nap.

So at peace. Completely unaware that an intruder had wormed his way into his house, claiming to be his nephew, and was now trying to take him for everything he was worth. And had even gone so far as to commit murder to keep his nefarious plot under wraps.

Hayley stepped forward, reaching out to touch Edgar's wrinkled, bony hand.

She closed her eyes, praying he would recover.

Edgar was a good man.

He deserved to make it through this.

The door behind her made a creaking sound.

As if someone was slowly closing it.

Hayley popped open her eyes and spun around.

Clark was standing in the room behind the door.

He had been here, watching her, the whole time.

"I've been expecting you," he said. There was a wicked smile on his face. "There was nothing more the doctors could do for poor Uncle Edgar, so I brought him home. Better to live out his final hours in the house he built, instead of some impersonal hospital room, don't you agree?"

"Where's my brother? What have you done with him?"

"He's fine. By the time they find him, I'll be long gone. I'm almost done here. Just a few more valuables to pack up and I'll be on my way."

"So I was right. You're a con man. You knew the real Clark was a recluse and very few people here in town had even seen him since he was a little boy. So you took advantage of that to come rob the place."

Clark inched closer to Hayley.

She backed away, until she was pressed up against Edgar's bed.

"Who are you, really?"

"The phantom. I come and I go. One month I may show up as a Hollingsworth cousin. Or maybe a Murdoch nephew. Or the adopted son of Sam Walton, and an heir to the Walmart fortune. When you throw rich names like that around, people tend to want to believe you. They think all that good fortune might rub off on them."

"You read about Edgar's illness and you knew his grandson was in prison."

"Easy score."

"Until Edgar's nurse, Candace, found out. She's lived in this town her whole life. Probably remembers the real Clark as a boy, just like I do. What happened? Did she catch you in a lie? Did she know something about Clark that you neglected to research and then confronted you with it? You couldn't have her blowing the whistle, not before you cleaned him out and got out of the state."

"You're playing a guessing game here."

"I know for a fact that Candace Culpepper had something on you. She must have somehow figured out your scheme."

"Well, if she did, she didn't tell me. You're the only one who has been a pain in my ass ever since I got here. I tried warning you with the snowmobile. But you just couldn't let it go. You had to keep sniffing around and asking questions. My only choice was to show up at your brother's house, where I knew you were staying, and put you on ice until I could get out of town. I had a rag soaked with chloroform and a garment bag to zip you up in so I could haul you back here. Unfortunately, you weren't there, but your brother was. He surprised me. He took one whiff of the chloroform and it quickly became clear to him I was up to no good. We wrestled around a bit before I managed to press the rag over his face and knock him out. I did capture a Powell—just not the one I went to find."

"So you're saying you didn't know Candace had

figured out your scheme? Does that mean you deny killing her?"

"No, I didn't kill her. My goal is never to harm anyone physically. I like things to go smoothly. No complications. Just in and out. Like the wind. And no one the wiser. But sometimes things don't go according to plan and you have to improvise."

He was almost on top of Hayley.

There was nowhere for her to go.

She was cornered.

"I need you to come down to the basement with me so I can reunite you with your brother. The two of you can enjoy each other's company while I finish up here and say my good-byes to dear old Uncle Edgar."

He reached out and grabbed Hayley by the arm.

She tried fighting him off, but his grip was strong.

"You're not tying me up in the basement!" Hayley said, struggling.

"I can't risk you calling the police. Not until I've had the chance to vanish again."

Suddenly the doorbell downstairs chimed and they both froze.

"Too late," Hayley said, a smile creeping across her face. "I already did."

Enraged, Clark wrapped his hands around Hayley's throat and began squeezing. She raised her arms, desperately trying to push him away.

She wrenched her head toward the door and tried to cry out for help. "Donnie!"

But she was all the way upstairs and the pressure on her windpipe from Clark's hands tightening made it come out as more of a tiny squeak.

They fell against the bed as they struggled, and Hayley feared they might endanger Edgar by knocking into vital tubes and machines that were keeping him alive. She tried to maneuver them away from the bed.

She was getting light-headed.

Clark's hands were like a vise.

Crushing her neck.

She was afraid she was about to pass out.

So she brought up her left knee and slammed it into his groin.

There was a grunt and a *whoosh* as air shot out of fake Clark's mouth.

He doubled over.

Hayley seized the opportunity to push him away and bolt out of the room, racing down the stairs to open the front door.

But Clark came up fast behind her, tackling her, and the two tumbled down the stairs, thumping hard against every step until they landed in a heap at the bottom.

Momentarily stunned, Hayley lifted her head to see Clark already springing to his feet and running over to grab an iron poker next to the fireplace. He raised it above his head and marched back over to beat Hayley with it.

She covered her eyes and screamed.

The front door burst open and Officers Donnie and Earl charged in, guns drawn.

"Put the poker down! Now!" Donnie yelled, impressively mustering up some authority for the first time.

And for that, Hayley was grateful.

Clark dropped the poker and it clattered to the floor.

He raised his hands above his head.

Earl was leaning down next to Hayley and rubbing her back.

"Are you all right?"

Hayley nodded. "Go down to the basement. He's got Randy down there. Make sure he's all right."

Earl's eyes widened with surprise. He couldn't believe such drama was actually happening on his shift. He took off running toward the door to the basement.

Donnie removed a pair of handcuffs from his belt with his free hand, ordered Clark to turn around so his back was to him, and then reholstered his gun and snapped the cuffs on Clark's wrists. He reached into his pants pocket and pulled out a slip of paper and started to read from it.

"'You have the right to remain silent. Anything you say can and will be used against you in a court of law. . . .'"

Donnie glanced up to see Hayley smiling at him, impressed that he came prepared. He gave her a wink and continued reading Clark his Miranda rights.

Hayley heard footsteps coming up from the basement. Earl was gently guiding Randy by the arm. He was a bit groggy from the chloroform, and his hair and clothes were disheveled, but otherwise he looked fine.

Hayley jumped to her feet and hugged her brother. "You had me so worried."

"I'm okay. . . . He said he wasn't going to hurt me. He was just going to hold me for a few days."

"Well, he's being arrested for kidnapping and murder. I think it's safe to say he's more dangerous than he claims he is," Hayley said.

Clark twisted his head around and barked, "I told you I didn't kill anybody!"

"Shut up!" Donnie warned as he led him outside. "Shit! I forgot. We didn't bring the squad car. That means we have to walk this guy all the way back to the station!"

Officer Earl turned to Hayley and Randy. "You guys coming?"

"No," Hayley said. "I'm going to call the hospital and have someone come over and check on Mr. Hollingsworth to make sure he's okay and all the life-support machines are still working properly."

Earl offered a quick wave good-bye and followed Donnie out the door.

"You did it, sis. You solved Candace Culpepper's murder. I'm so proud of you."

Hayley thought for a moment and shook her head.

"I'm starting to think I didn't."

"What do you mean?"

"I was so convinced the killer was Clark. I mean every piece of the puzzle fit perfectly into place. Except for one thing."

"What's that?"

"The killer used left-handed scissors to stab Candace. When Clark chased me down the stairs and picked up that poker he was going to swat at me with . . . he used his right hand," she said as she looked at Randy. "I think he may be telling the truth."

Chapter 38

Hayley stood as tall as she possibly could, a big smile plastered on her face, a bead of sweat trickling down her forehead from the intensity of the klieg lights set up all around her.

She was holding her breath.

Beep. Beep. Beep.

The cashier ran her coupons over the scanner, one at a time.

Slowly.

Meticulously.

This was taking forever.

Hayley looked around. The crew members of *Wild and Crazy Couponing* were spellbound.

This was it.

The final cash-out.

Who was going to win?

Drew Nickerson, wearing a Tom Ford suit and an insincere smile, gripped the microphone in his fist as he stared down Hayley.

She ignored his gaze. Instead, she glanced over to the next aisle, where Mona stood, arms folded, with a scowl.

Determined.

Focused.

Like a loyal soldier being debriefed by his commanding officer on how well he performed on the battlefield.

The show's director, a wiry, little guy with Coke bottle glasses, frantically waved at Mona from behind the camera. Pushing his cheeks upward with his two index fingers, he was miming and silently begging for her to smile.

But Mona was having none of it.

This was too much of a nail-biter.

She couldn't fake having a good time or pretend to be happy. Mona was here competing with her best friend for a giant cash prize.

Hayley could tell she was doing well.

The coupons kept lowering her total.

She was down to $26.43.

Whoever had to pay the lowest total won the show.

Hayley was racking up whopping savings, especially from her strategy of focusing on cleaning supplies.

Hayley took a step back so she could steal a glance at the next register, where Mona was being checked out.

Mona was still behind with a higher total.

$49.52.

Beep. Beep. Beep.

The suspense was killing Hayley.

She just wanted this whole ordeal finally to be over.

Mona finally flashed a quick smile.

Hayley craned her neck to get a look at the register again.

Mona was suddenly down to $18.36.

That's it.

Mona was done.

And Mona was now in the lead.

All eyes turned to Hayley as she pushed the rest of her coupons toward the cashier as if she were in Las Vegas placing all of her remaining chips on one last bet, and praying she didn't come up snake eyes.

Beep. Beep. Beep.

The cashier picked up the last of Hayley's coupons and slowly ran it over the scanner.

Beep.

Nobody was moving. Not the camera crew, the show's production staff, the director, Drew Nickerson, Mona, the other cashier, or the crowd of locals who had jammed into the store to watch the taping of the show and were standing elbow to elbow.

There wasn't a sound in the whole grocery store. Except the low hum of the glass case freezers in the frozen-food section nearby.

The cashier hit one last button.

Hayley's grand total was $11.68.

The audience watching burst into applause as

Hayley had to grip the black conveyor belt in the checkout lane to keep from fainting.

Drew Nickerson strutted over next to Hayley and shoved the microphone in her face with one hand as he firmly planted his other hand on Hayley's butt. "Congratulations, Hayley! You're our grand-prize winner! You're walking away with ten thousand dollars!"

Hayley surreptitiously reached around and grabbed Drew's fingers and twisted them back so hard that he actually squealed as he let go.

There was an awkward moment as the crew looked around at each other, wondering why their suave, macho host had just screamed like a little girl.

"Thank you, Drew. You don't know what this means to me!"

And Hayley meant it.

Ten grand.

Even after taxes, that meant she could afford a new furnace, repair her roof, and still have enough left over to put a modest down payment on a used car.

She was finally out of the woods.

"You're certainly now stocked up on groceries for the winter," Drew said, rubbing his still-throbbing fingers.

"Actually, I plan to donate all the groceries I bought today to Mrs. Imogen Tubbs. She just got home from the hospital, but she is still recovering from her car accident and is unable to do her weekly grocery shopping, so I figure this will help her out."

Mona was the first one to reach Hayley and envelop her in a bear hug.

"I'm so proud of you," Mona said, sniffling, unable to contain her emotions for once. "I'm not going to lie to you. I wanted to whup your ass. But if I had to lose to someone, I'm sure as hell glad it was you!"

"Thank you, Mona."

Out of the corner of her eye, Hayley spotted Lex hovering toward the back of the crowd in front of the sliding glass door at the entrance, looking on at all the hoopla surrounding her. He was trying to smile, but there was an inescapable sadness in his demeanor. He looked pale, tired, almost disoriented.

Hayley wriggled free of Mona's grip and whispered in her ear, "I'll call you later. Let's you, me, and Liddy go to Drinks Like A Fish and celebrate tonight."

"Sounds good to me," Mona said just as Drew Nickerson raced up to her, shoving the microphone in her face and putting his arm around her neck.

"You were a worthy adversary, Mona, but you came up short in the end. How do you feel?"

"Not half as bad as you will if you don't stop touching me," Mona said, twisting her head around as she narrowed her eyes to make her point. "I don't like to be touched. Unless you're

Alex Trebek. Every night I watch Alex Trebek. I'm a fan of Alex Trebek, and you, sir, are no Alex Trebek!"

Drew instantly dropped his arm and scurried away, tail between his legs.

Hayley worked her way through the crowd that surged forward to offer congratulations. It took her a few minutes to get to Lex. When she finally reached him, he leaned in and gave her a light kiss on the cheek.

"I knew you had it in you to win," Lex said.

"What happened, Lex? I can tell something's wrong."

"Edgar passed away a few hours ago, I didn't want to tell you before the competition, because I didn't want any sad news messing with your focus."

Hayley nodded solemnly. This was not unexpected. "I'm so sorry, Lex. If there's anything I can do . . ."

"There's more," Lex said. "The real Clark Hollingsworth is flying in tonight. He's the chief executor of his uncle's will. And there are some rumors flying around that he may sell the estate and donate the money to his charity work."

"What does that mean?"

"It means I might not get my job back," Lex said, before catching himself and putting on a brave face. "But why worry about something that hasn't happened yet? We should be celebrating your victory."

Officer Donnie interrupted them, slapping

Hayley a little too hard on the back. "I sure am happy for you, Hayley. You took Mona down! I was really rooting for you. I was totally on Team Hayley."

"I'm shocked, Donnie. Imagine you wanting Mona to lose!"

"Guess we're both winners this week."

"How do you mean?" Hayley asked.

"Well, you won big on this game show and I collared my first killer!"

"*You?* You collared the killer?"

"Yeah, Sergio had a hard time believing it, too, when I called him in Brazil and filled him in on all the details."

"Oh yes, I'm sure you gave him *all* the details," Hayley said.

Donnie chose to ignore the obvious sarcasm.

"Did you find out who he really is?" Lex asked.

"Oh yeah. Stuart Handley. He's singing like a bird now. Wants to cut some kind of deal. He's been all over the world posing as relatives of famous rich people, worming his way into people's lives and trying to bilk them out of money. It's been his MO for years now. Funny thing is, he's confessing to everything, but he's still claiming he didn't stab Candace. But don't you worry. I'll squeeze a full confession out of him. Earl and I are planning a little 'good cop/nice cop' number on the guy."

"You mean 'good cop/bad cop,'" Hayley said, shaking her head.

"Isn't that what I said?"

"Donnie, does it bother you at all that Candace was stabbed with a pair of scissors designed for a left-handed person and Clark was obviously right-handed?"

"Should it?" Donnie said, blinking, unable to comprehend the significance of that little detail.

"Never mind, Donnie," Hayley said. "Good luck with that confession."

Donnie saluted Hayley; and then seeing Mona wandering over in his direction, he skedaddled out the door back to his squad car, not wanting to risk another confrontation.

"So now you think Clark *didn't* kill Candace?" Lex asked.

"The murder weapon keeps bugging me. Cassidy Culpepper was left-handed, and the scissors did indeed belong to a left-handed person."

"So it's probably the sister," Lex said.

"Maybe. But Cassidy Culpepper isn't the only left-handed person in town. The killer could be anybody! I'm certain Sabrina got the time of death wrong but will never admit it! That means everyone who had an alibi for nine o'clock—all of them are suspects again."

Hayley was certain Candace Culpepper's killer was still out there, and probably feeling relieved that he or she had just gotten away with murder.

Chapter 39

Hayley's new furnace wasn't being delivered until the following morning, so she decided to stay one more night at her brother's house. She was planning to whip up a delicious dinner and spend some quality time with him before moving back home. It was obvious to her that he was still shaken up by his traumatic ordeal at the hands of the fake Clark Hollingsworth.

Stuff like that just didn't happen often in Bar Harbor.

Randy was ready more than ever for his police chief boyfriend to return home from Brazil. He was counting the days.

So was Hayley.

She wanted her kids home too.

Randy was lying on the couch, resting, watching *The Real Housewives of Boca Raton,* or some such thing, on TV, when Hayley walked in, carrying a bag of groceries full of ingredients she needed for tonight's menu.

"I still smell it," Randy said, lowering the volume on the TV with the remote in his hand.

"Still smell what?" Hayley asked, stopping and setting the bag down on the dining-room table before crossing into the living room closer to Randy.

"Blueberry."

"That's impossible. I scrubbed this place from top to bottom. I didn't miss one stain! You can't possibly still smell urine."

"It's here to stay. And if you think *my* sense of smell is good, just wait until Sergio comes home. His is like a superpower. He can smell what the Hoopers are having for dinner three houses down the shore path. I think we're going to have to sell the house. I can't live here under these conditions."

"Now you're just being overly dramatic," Hayley scoffed. "Here, I'll prove it to you."

Hayley marched into the kitchen and found the ultraviolet light Randy had bought to suss out Blueberry's messes. She walked back into the living room, shutting off all the lights in the house. It wasn't completely pitch-black outside yet, but it was dark enough to identify any lingering stains.

Randy sat up on the couch, shut off the TV, and watched Hayley, ready to prove his sister wrong.

Hayley flipped the light on and swept it across the room.

No stains.

"See? I told you," Hayley said.

"What's that?"

"What? Where?"

"Point the light back over there. I saw a stain."

Hayley turned the light toward the opposite side of the room. A stack of mail and some papers were on top of a small desk in the corner. There was a tiny white stain emanating from a small piece of paper.

"That? You can hardly see it."

"Well, what is it?" Randy asked, standing up and hustling over to the desk to examine it. He carefully picked up the tiny piece of paper.

"It's a coupon. For a can of beans. I found it in the drawer when I was doing some paperwork a little while ago and left it out on the desk, I guess."

The coupon Hayley found at the crime scene after the snow melted.

Suddenly a thought jolted her.

She knew who killed Candace Culpepper.

Hayley threw on her jacket, told Randy she would be back in a while to cook him dinner, and then trudged through the slushy snow straight over to Mrs. Tubbs's house. She knocked on the door, but she knew Mrs. Tubbs wouldn't answer.

Hayley turned the knob and the door opened.

"Mrs. Tubbs? It's me, Hayley."

"Come in, dear. I'm in the living room."

Hayley found Mrs. Tubbs sitting on the edge of her plush brown recliner, wearing a powder blue robe and matching slippers, clipping coupons from a newspaper flyer.

And she was using a brand-spanking-new pair of left-handed scissors.

"Hayley, you stocked me up with so much food, I won't have to go grocery shopping until at least Memorial Day, but I still can't resist hunting for bargains," Mrs. Tubbs said, giggling.

Hayley felt a presence behind her and then something tapped her leg. It was Blueberry's massive tail as he swished it from side to side, passing her with a look of disdain before hopping up in the chair with great effort, due to his bulk, and settling down in Mrs. Tubbs's lap.

He wasn't happy to see Hayley and never took his eyes off her.

"It was you, wasn't it?" Hayley said softly, almost under her breath, as if she still couldn't believe it.

"Excuse me, dear?"

"You killed Candace Culpepper."

"Good Lord, Hayley, what's gotten into you? They caught the awful man who did that horrible deed. The one posing as poor Edgar Hollingsworth's nephew."

"Yes. He was guilty of posing as Clark Hollingsworth. And Candace did believe he was a fake, but he never found out she knew because somebody else stabbed her to death before she had a chance to accuse him."

"I'm afraid I have no idea what you're talking

about. I was in the hospital when Candace was attacked."

"That's right. And Clark Hollingsworth was having dinner at the Porter House. But the thing is, Mrs. Tubbs, the coroner got the time of death wrong. Candace died a few hours earlier. So Clark Hollingsworth's alibi doesn't hold up anymore."

"Then you see, dear, case closed."

"And neither does yours. It's true you were in the hospital at nine o'clock when the original autopsy reported Candace died after the scissors punctured her lungs, but the new time of death is now sometime around six o'clock in the evening. And you were home then, weren't you? Right next door."

Mrs. Tubbs set the scissors down on an end table next to the chair and stroked Blueberry, who kept his eyes fixed on Hayley, a barely perceptible rumble coming out of his tense body. His tail was flapping up and down, ever more intensely.

Hayley pulled the coupon out of her coat pocket and held it up for Mrs. Tubbs to see. "I'm assuming this coupon for beans belongs to you. It certainly didn't belong to Candace. She hated beans of all kinds. But I found it right near where she was killed. You must have dropped it."

"As you can see, Hayley, I cut out dozens, even hundreds, of coupons. I can't remember every one," Mrs. Tubbs said, waving her hand over the current stack she was adding to from the flyer.

"But this particular coupon, this one is unique, because it has a urine stain on it. Blueberry peed on it!"

"Why are you trying to upset me like this, Hayley? I'm just home from the hospital after a serious car accident. I'm in a very fragile state."

"Oh, somehow I don't think you're as frail as you like people to believe. I think you've got a lot of life left in you. I wish Candace could say the same."

"Stop saying such terrible things. If you found that coupon next to Candace's body outside, any stray dog, any wild animal, could've been the one to pee on it. It wasn't Blueberry!"

"That's true. But Blueberry left quite a bit of his DNA behind at my brother Randy's house. So I had a kitty DNA test performed on *this* coupon."

"A kitty what?" Mrs. Tubbs said, a bit confused.

"That's right. And the results just came back. It's a match. Only Blueberry could've been the one to pee on this coupon."

This stopped Mrs. Tubbs cold.

Hayley watched as Mrs. Tubbs's mind raced, desperate to find some way out of this escalating mess.

"Well, if you found that coupon and had it in the house where you were staying, Blueberry could've soiled it there, while you were cat sitting him."

"Impossible. Blueberry never came in contact with the coupon after I found it. I kept it in a desk drawer. He couldn't have gotten near it. My brother only pulled it out today."

Checkmate.

"You want to tell me why you did it, Mrs. Tubbs?"

Mrs. Tubbs just stared at Hayley.

Almost a minute passed with neither of them saying a word.

Hayley was prepared to wait her out.

But finally Mrs. Tubbs sighed. "When she first moved into that house next door, we were friends. We'd have tea and scones in the afternoon before her shift at the hospital and watch *Judge Judy* together. But then it all went so terribly wrong. I have my newspaper delivered every morning. I'm old-fashioned. I hate reading about current events on the computer. Hurts my eyes. Anyway, one morning I caught Candace stealing the coupon flyer right out of my paper. She had the nerve to deny it. And things were never the same between us. And she kept doing it. I warned her to stop. But she just laughed and said I was a crazy old woman and dared me to prove it. So when I saw her doing it again a couple of weeks ago, I grabbed my scissors and ran outside and told her to give me my flyer back or else, and she just turned her back on me and started walking to her house."

"And that's when you stabbed her?"

"Yes. I didn't plan on it or anything. It just happened. She made me so mad! I stabbed her once in the back and she turned around, like she couldn't believe what I was doing. Then I stabbed her in the chest and she just gurgled and turned to run away, and I guess I stabbed her once more in the back before she fell to the ground. They won't send me to jail, will they? I mean it was justifiable. Just think of all the money I would've saved at the Shop 'n Save if she hadn't stolen my coupon flyers every day!"

"Are you serious? You killed someone over coupons?"

"It all happened so fast. The next thing I knew, Candace was facedown in the snow with my scissors sticking out of her back and I was standing over her in a state of shock. Once I got my bearings and realized what I had done, I just panicked."

"You got in your car to flee the scene of the crime and get as far away as possible, and that's when you lost control because of the icy roads and rear-ended the Garbers' car and wound up in the hospital," Hayley said.

Mrs. Tubbs nodded. "Yes."

Hayley fished out her cell phone and stopped the voice memo she was recording.

She had it all on tape.

Mrs. Tubbs leaned down and kissed Blueberry gently on the forehead. "It's a good thing I love you so much, Blueberry. Because you just made things very, very difficult for Mommy. I've never even heard of a kitty DNA test."

"Neither have I," Hayley said.

Mrs. Tubbs looked up, her head tilted to one side, bristling. "What?"

"I just made it up. I'm not sure if there is such a

thing. I just said I had the coupon tested to get you to confess."

"You—"

"Don't say it, Mrs. Tubbs. It's unbecoming for a woman your age to swear."

"Bitch!"

Mrs. Tubbs jumped up from her recliner and, with all her might, threw her fat cat, Blueberry, clear across the room at Hayley. Blueberry was stunned. With outstretched paws, sharpened claws, and wild eyes, he landed on Hayley's face like that slimy octopus-like creature that latched itself onto the scientist in the original *Alien* movie.

Hayley howled, grabbing Blueberry by the fur as she frantically tried pulling him off her. Blueberry hissed and growled and began biting her head as Hayley coughed up fur, fearing she might suffocate. She yanked as hard as she could, and Blueberry finally let go, slashing Hayley's cheek with a claw as he dropped to the floor on all fours and skittered away.

Mental note.

Rabies shot ASAP.

Hayley spun around to see Mrs. Tubbs halfway out the front door.

"Mrs. Tubbs, don't run! You'll slip and fall and break a hip!"

Hayley chased after her, but Mrs. Tubbs only made it a few feet across her lawn before the heel of her shoe sank into the mud and she lost her balance and fell forward, landing almost dead center in the exact same position where Hayley had found Candace Culpepper's body.

Mrs. Tubbs groaned.

But it was less from pain than from humiliation.

Hayley retrieved her phone from where she had dropped it when Blueberry landed on her face and called Donnie to break the news to him that he hadn't exactly solved the case.

Chapter 40

"How long will you be gone?" Hayley asked.

Lex shrugged. "I'm not sure. But there's not a lot of work in Bar Harbor during the winter, especially for a guy like me. I got a few leads on some construction jobs over in Burlington, which I'm going to go check out."

"Vermont?"

"It's still New England. I may be able to get back down here on weekends," Lex said, lowering his eyes, not truly believing what he was saying.

Hayley choked back tears. "So you're not here to break up with me?"

"Hell no. Not at all. I just have to go away for a while," Lex assured her, reaching out and lightly stroking her cheek.

But on some level they both knew this was the end.

It was just that neither could admit it.

A tear rolled down Hayley's cheek.

Lex wiped it away with his finger and then drew her into a hug, whispering in her ear, "This isn't the end. I promise."

"Don't make promises you can't keep," Hayley said, sniffing.

"I'll call you, once I'm settled," Lex said, stoic and solid to the end, practically devoid of emotion, but Hayley could tell this was incredibly hard for him.

They both had really wanted this to work.

And they had developed deep feelings for each other.

But sometimes life has other plans.

Lex stepped back and took a good, long look at her. "God, you're beautiful. Just like the day we first met."

"When I ran you over with my car." Hayley laughed, fondly remembering that day when she rushed him to the hospital to make sure he was okay. It had been quite a ride.

Maybe he was right.

Maybe this wasn't the end.

Or, at least, that's what she was going to keep telling herself so she wouldn't cry all night.

Lex kissed her gently on the lips, holding her tightly, not ready to let go. "I'm going to miss you."

Hayley nodded her head, unable to speak, choking back her tears, trying to hold it together.

Lex gently caressed her chin with his thumb for a moment and walked back to his truck.

He got in, slammed the door shut, and backed out of Hayley's driveway, never taking his eyes off her.

Finally the truck drove off and turned a corner, and Hayley couldn't see it anymore.

She just stood in the door, staring into space.

Lex Bansfield was gone.

"Hey, Mom, does the new car have satellite radio?" Dustin asked as he thumped up behind his mother.

"Uh, yeah," Hayley said, trying to disguise the fact that she was crying by wiping her face with the arm of her sweater. "We've got a free trial for a month before they start charging us, so enjoy it now."

"Sweet," Dustin said, smiling. "Let's take it for a spin and try it out."

"Can I drive?" Gemma screamed from upstairs. When she wasn't on her computer, tuned out to her surroundings, she had superhearing, just like her uncle Sergio had.

Hayley had picked up her kids yesterday. She had gone car shopping on Saturday morning and had surprised her kids when she picked them up at the airport later that afternoon, driving a new Kia Sedona SUV, with only ten thousand miles on it.

"Yes, you can drive!" Hayley yelled from the foot of the stairs to her daughter.

Dustin was already in his coat and pulling on his boots.

Gemma bounced down the stairs, excited,

wrapping a knitted scarf around her neck. "Driver gets to choose which station we listen to."

"That's not fair! I don't even have my permit!" Dustin wailed.

They argued and playfully shoved each other as they bolted out the door.

Hayley's family was finally home together again.

And despite a very painful good-bye just moments before, she couldn't remember being so happy.

Island Food & Spirits
by
Hayley Powell

Well, as you may have heard by now, I won the grand prize on *Wild and Crazy Couponing*! My brother and I decided to celebrate by blowing our food budget and having one of my favorite seafood recipes "Lobster Bar Harbor," since the two main ingredients, lobster and steak, never seem to be on sale! As we sipped our rum cocktails and began digging into our lobster-topped filets mignons (thanks to Mona for the lobster, because she keeps a tank running in her shop during the winter for special occasions), I remarked to Randy that I was surprised he was willing to eat lobster after the traumatic experience he suffered when we were kids. I was about twelve and he was ten (although he has since surpassed me in age because I like consistency and have decided to stay thirty, going on six years now).

Our uncle Ronnie had a lobster boat and invited us to join him one Saturday morning while he set and hauled a few traps. Our job was to help fill the bait bags for the traps to be set.

My mother, who always feared we wouldn't get enough food, packed us four sandwiches (peanut butter and grape jelly), one large bag of chips, one container of onion dip, an entire box of Twinkies, and two liters of Coca-Cola. It was a simpler time, before many people had even learned the word "nutrition."

As we motored out of the harbor, Randy quietly disappeared into the small cabin in the front of the boat, while I soaked up the sun on deck and kept an eye out for dolphins and seals, which were known to pop up from time to time, while we were heading out to sea.

Uncle Ronnie stopped the boat and began setting the traps with the bait bags I had prepared. Randy was still nowhere to be seen, so I headed to the cabin and found him on the floor, surrounded by a few stray potato chips, some crumpled Twinkie wrappers, and two empty Coke bottles. His face was smeared with peanut butter and jelly. I was so mad! I yelled at him to go up on deck and help Uncle Ronnie bait the bags while I cleaned up his mess!

When I finished cleaning, I joined Randy and Uncle Ronnie back on deck, where the smell of the stinky, slimy fish bait was wafting up Randy's nose. He began turning green and his eyes were watering, and then he dropped the bait bag and sprinted to the other side of the boat to heave his junk food lunch over the side. Uncle Ronnie was not about to cut his day short for one puking kid, when he could make a day's wage. So I got stuck baiting the rest of the bags, while Randy recovered (although I suspected he was just playing it up so he didn't have to do any of the work). Eventually Randy got bored and picked up two live lobsters and started doing funny cartoon voices, like he was putting on a puppet show and the two lobsters were having a conversation. Unfortunately, he failed to notice that one of the lobsters he grabbed was missing the black rubber band Uncle Ronnie had secured on its left claw to keep it closed and harmless. I didn't dare mention I had removed it earlier to tie my hair into a ponytail because the wind kept blowing my hair in my face—especially when the lobster's claw snapped onto Randy's right middle finger.

Randy jumped up and down, screaming, twirling in circles, trying to shake off the lobster. Uncle Ronnie had to hold a wailing Randy still with one hand, while trying to pry the lobster off with his other. I was no help whatsoever, because I was laughing hysterically.

After a stern lecture from

Uncle Ronnie about how lucky he was for not losing a finger from his fooling around, we headed back to the harbor with six lobsters to cook for dinner that night. Randy decided that day he didn't like lobsters anymore; so my mother had to order him a pizza, while we dined on fresh steamed lobsters, with hot melted butter.

Even when you're on a tight budget, there's nothing wrong with splurging every so often. Even if you don't have an uncle who has his own lobster boat, just go ahead and treat yourself. Nothing feeds the soul and the tummy more than a rich, decadent meal.

Rum Cocktail

<u>Ingredients</u>
1¾ ounce favorite rum
¾ ounce lemon juice
¾ ounce grenadine

Pour all the ingredients in a cocktail shaker filled with ice. Shake well and pour into chilled cocktail glasses.

Lobster Bar Harbor

Ingredients

4 eight-ounce beef tenderloin
   (filets mignons)
Kosher salt and fresh black
   ground pepper, to taste
½ teaspoon garlic powder
4 slices bacon
½ cup butter, divided
1 teaspoon Old Bay Seasoning
8 ounces steamed lobster tail
   and claws, chopped (Don't
   worry if you use more; you
   can never go wrong!)

Set your oven to broil, or heat
your grill, if you prefer grilling.

Sprinkle tenderloins all over
with kosher salt and fresh black
ground pepper and garlic
powder. Wrap each filet mignon
with bacon, and secure with a
toothpick. Place on a broiling
pan and broil to desired done-
ness, about 8 to 10 minutes per
side for medium rare.

While the tenderloins are cooking, melt ¼ cup of the butter over
medium heat with ½ teaspoon

of Old Bay Seasoning. Stir in chopped lobster meat until nicely heated through. Spoon the lobster meat over the tenderloins and return to broiler and cook until the lobster meat is just beginning to brown, and remove from oven and plate.

Meanwhile, heat the remaining butter in a small saucepan over medium-high heat and cook until it browns. Spoon the browned butter over the filets mignons topped with the lobster and sprinkle with remaining Old Bay Seasoning.

This is a mouthwatering and indulgent meal to serve to that special someone in your life.

Please turn the page for an exciting sneak peek of
the next Hayley Powell mystery

DEATH OF A CHOCOHOLIC

coming soon from Kensington Publishing!

Chapter 1

He was late.

Twenty-four minutes, to be precise.

Hayley knew this was a bad idea. How could she have allowed her friend Liddy to fix her up on a date? With Liddy's own cousin from Bucksport! He didn't even live in Bar Harbor. And how could she have agreed to meet him on Valentine's Day? Who goes on a blind date on Valentine's Day? That's reserved for moony newlyweds who coo and giggle and feed each other mushy, rich desserts with their fingers. Or for tired old married couples who feel forced to show the world the magic is still there by dining out at a romantic restaurant even though they would rather be eating in front of the TV watching *The X Factor* and not having to talk to each other.

She had tried to cancel, but Liddy wouldn't hear of it because she was convinced that what Hayley needed most right now was to get right back out there and date after her on-again, off-again boyfriend Lex Bansfield recently blew town for Vermont after losing his job.

Hayley checked her watch again.

This was torture.

Even though it was mid-February, there was no snow on the ground. The temperature was a brisk thirty-seven degrees. No ice on the roads. What possible excuse could he have for being this late? The trip from Bucksport to Bar Harbor was only a little over an hour if he took Route 3.

Hayley gulped down the last of her merlot and tried to signal Michelle, the bartender/waitress at her brother's bar Drinks Like a Fish, for her check.

Hayley was not going to wait longer than thirty minutes for a blind date to show up. And that was final. Michelle's back was turned, and then she scurried through the swinging doors into the kitchen and didn't see Hayley waving at her.

Hayley actually felt relieved. Now she could firmly tell Liddy that she had given the whole dating thing a try and it just didn't work out. She certainly wasn't too keen on starting a serious relationship. Especially so soon after Lex. Lex was a wonderful man, a real stand-up guy, but he was not without his issues, and Hayley just didn't have the energy right now to devote to a man. Her kids had been extremely demanding lately with their various teen dramas, and she wanted to focus more on them and her food and cocktails column at the *Island Times* newspaper.

Besides, dating was such a brutal endeavor. And she was never especially good at it. On her first date with Lex, she wound up arrested. But that was another story.

Michelle breezed out of the kitchen and Hayley finally caught her attention. Hayley quickly made a scribbling motion with her finger indicating she would like to pay for her wine and get the hell out of there, but then she suddenly felt a cold chill on her back as the front door to the bar swung open and a blast of winter air swept through the bar. She nearly jumped out of her chair as the door banged shut.

Hayley closed her eyes.

Please let this not be him.

Please let this not be him.

"Hayley?"

Hayley took a deep breath and swung her head around, hoping for the best.

"Yes. Ted?"

Ted nodded. He was taller than Hayley expected. Much taller. In fact, there was a quick pain in her neck as she cranked her head up to meet his face. The first thing she noticed was he had a beautiful head of dirty-blond hair. Wavy and thick and a bit shaggy. But then her eyes settled on his face. Nice features, but something was definitely off. Maybe it was the low lighting in the bar, but it looked almost as if his left cheek, no the whole left side of his face, was drooping or slightly deformed. This certainly didn't come across in the photos on his Facebook page that Hayley researched before agreeing to meet him.

He shed his winter coat and sat down across from Hayley. "I was hoping you wouldn't notice."

Hayley tried acting nonchalant. "Notice what?"

"My face. I had a small cosmetic procedure today, and the doctor warned me this might happen for a day or two until my face settles. My mother begged me to reschedule because with my nasty luck, she knew something like this might scare you off."

Cosmetic procedure?

Mother?

"Is it some kind of medical issue?"

"Oh no. Nothing that dramatic. Just a little facelift. We're not getting any younger, and you know what they say, if you want to sell the used car you need to keep it looking shiny and new."

Hayley had never heard anyone say that.

Facelift?

"So is it noticeable?" he asked, a mask of genuine concern on his face. Or at least half of it.

Hayley leaned forward slightly. "You can hardly tell."

That was a huge lie. He looked a bit like that Batman villain Two-Face. One side of the face normal. The other horribly disfigured.

Michelle stopped by the table. "What can I get you?"

Michelle's eyes nearly popped out of her head at the sight of Ted's misshapen face, but she instantly recovered and smiled, pretending not to be startled.

"Just some coffee. I have to drive back home to Bucksport. And do you have anything to eat? I have a raging sweet tooth."

"Yes, we do," Michelle said pointing to a plastic bar menu in a metal holder on the table. "I recommend the German chocolate cake."

Michelle winked at Hayley knowingly. Randy had recently decided to serve sandwiches and appetizers and a few desserts at his bar, and it had been a huge hit with the locals. Hayley helped out by baking a few of her signature desserts for him.

Ted ordered the German chocolate cake and Michelle scooted back into the kitchen, leaving Hayley with Droopy Face.

"So, Hayley, you're much prettier than your photo. Tell me a little bit about yourself," Ted said, trying to be seductive.

Hayley couldn't take her eyes off his sagging cheek. It was making her uncomfortable and she just wanted to bolt out of there, but she couldn't be rude and Liddy would never forgive her.

So she just rattled off a litany of bullet points about her life. Born and raised in Bar Harbor. Divorced. Two kids. Columnist for the paper. Then she quickly turned the conversation over to him, and he relished in talking about himself. How he had been a high school basketball star. How his dashing good looks drew women like flies but he had very high standards, which explained why he had yet to marry. He was engaged once but his mother didn't approve so the relationship was doomed.

There was that mother again.

Mentioned twice in five minutes.

Never a good sign.

His cell phone rang, interrupting his incredibly boring life story.

He fished it out of the back pocket of his khaki pants and glanced at it.

"It's my mother. I should take this."

Three times in five minutes.

Half his face lit up as he answered the call.

The other half sagged a bit more.

"Mother, you minx. You know I'm on a date," he said, winking at Hayley.

Hayley forced a smile.

"Yes, she's quite pretty. No, she says you can't notice it. I checked myself in the rearview mirror in the car before I came in and I thought it did look a bit slouchy so maybe she's just being polite. Oh. Okay."

Ted held out the phone. "She wants to talk to you."

"Excuse me?"

"Mother. She wants to speak with you."

Hayley just sat there, mouth agape for a few seconds before robotically holding out her hand for the phone and putting it to her ear. "Hello?"

"Hi, Hayley, this is Ted's mother, Mary Beth."

"Hello, Mary Beth."

Michelle delivered the cup of coffee and the German chocolate cake, and Hayley watched horrified as Ted scarfed it down, getting smears of the coconut pecan frosting lodged on the side of his sagging face while listening to his mother on the other side of the phone.

"I told Ted not to meet you so soon after his surgery. You need to put your best foot forward on a first date. Make a good impression. 'Why not give your face a couple of days to settle before meeting Hayley?' That's what I told him, but do you think he listened to me? Of course not! He insisted that from what Liddy told him, you would not be shallow enough to judge Teddy on a little temporary side effect from his procedure."

She was wrong.

Hayley was judging. She felt bad about it. But she just couldn't help herself.

Ted finished off the cake and was now slurping his coffee.

"He's normally quite handsome, Hayley. You're going to have to trust me on that," Mary Beth cooed. "All the women in Bucksport are after my Teddy, but they're just silly girls with no ambitions. I told Teddy he needed somebody of substance, someone with a career. Someone creative. I adore cooking. I'm somewhat of an amateur chef myself.

And when my niece Liddy mentioned you were a food writer, well, I just knew we had to meet you."

We? Did she just say we?

"Anyway, I would love for you to give him another chance. Try again in a couple of weeks once his face settles. I'm positive you won't be disappointed."

Hayley nodded, dumbfounded, before realizing Mary Beth couldn't see her through the phone. She cleared her throat. "Um, okay."

It was never going to happen.

"Thank you, Hayley. I cannot wait to meet you. I suspect we'll be fast friends."

"Bye," Hayely said flatly, handing the phone back to Ted, who pressed it to his ear and grinned.

"I hope you didn't embarrass me, Mother."

They chatted a few more seconds, and then Ted shut off his phone and stuffed it back into his pants pocket.

Michelle swung by the table. "How did you like the cake?"

"It was a little dry," Ted said huffily. "I think you need a new chef."

Michelle glanced at Hayley, who shook her head. Best not tell him she baked the cake.

Michelle turned back to Ted. "Can I get you anything else?"

"Just the check," Ted demanded.

Michelle tore it off her pad and slapped it down

on the table. As she walked away, Hayley noticed Ted checking out her ass.

Seriously?

Ted let the check sit there for a few seconds.

As if he was hoping Hayley was going to reach for it first.

So she did.

Ted raised the palm of his big bony hand to stop her. "No. No. Allow me."

Maybe chivalry wasn't dead in Bucksport.

"You can get it next time," he said.

Yes, it was quite dead.

He reached into the other back pocket of his khakis.

Half his face froze.

He then frantically searched the pockets of his winter coat, which was draped over the back of his chair, before giving Hayley a sheepish grin. "I must have left my wallet in the car. You wait here. I'll go get it."

"No!" Hayley almost screamed as she snatched the check out of his hand and slammed some money down on the table, perhaps a little too hard. She couldn't stand another minute with Droopy Dog. "You can get it next time."

"You really shouldn't have to pay. I mean, Liddy told me your brother owns this place. They should comp you. Kind of rude of him, don't you think?"

Hayley just stared at him. His sagging face actually fit his personality.

Liddy.

The mastermind behind this nightmare.

Hayley was going to have to resist the urge to murder her BFF for putting her through this.

Especially since she was about to have another dead body on her hands . . .